LIFE HACKS
FOR A LITTLE ALIEN

LIFE HACKS FOR A LITTLE ALIEN

Alice Franklin

LITTLE, BROWN AND COMPANY

New York Boston London

Hachette Book Group supports the right to free expression and the value of copyright. The purpose of copyright is to encourage writers and artists to produce the creative works that enrich our culture.

The scanning, uploading, and distribution of this book without permission is a theft of the author's intellectual property. If you would like permission to use material from the book (other than for review purposes), please contact permissions@hbgusa.com. Thank you for your support of the author's rights.

Little, Brown and Company
Hachette Book Group
1290 Avenue of the Americas, New York, NY 10104
littlebrown.com

First North American Edition: February 2025
Originally published in the United Kingdom by riverrun: February 2025

Little, Brown and Company is a division of Hachette Book Group, Inc. The Little, Brown name and logo are trademarks of Hachette Book Group, Inc.

The publisher is not responsible for websites (or their content) that are not owned by the publisher.

The Hachette Speakers Bureau provides a wide range of authors for speaking events. To find out more, go to hachettespeakersbureau.com or email hachettespeakers@hbgusa.com.

Little, Brown and Company books may be purchased in bulk for business, educational, or promotional use. For information, please contact your local bookseller or the Hachette Book Group Special Markets Department at special.markets@hbgusa.com.

ISBN 9780316576055 (hc) / 9780316594769 (Canadian pb)
LCCN 2024949561

Printing 1, 2024

LSC-C

Printed in the United States of America

LIFE HACKS
FOR A LITTLE ALIEN

PROLOGUE

YOU ARE SITTING ON the living room floor, spooning strawberry yoghurt onto the carpet. On the carpet, an insect crawls. Your mum asks what you're doing even though it's obvious what you're doing – you're spooning strawberry yoghurt onto the carpet where an insect crawls.

'What are you doing?' your mum asks. Her question is rhetorical but you don't know the meaning of rhetorical, let alone how to identify something rhetorical.

'I'm dying a spider,' you say.

You're three years old, and these are your first words. Your mum doesn't react. She doesn't look pleased or surprised. Instead, she gets up from the sofa and leaves the room, thinking about a book she has borrowed from the library – a book titled *So Your Child Is a Psychopath*. She is worried. Did you know you've worried your mum? Your first-ever sentence was a catastrophe. Did you know it was a catastrophe?

Let me explain. Firstly, that's not a spider; the tiny creature on the carpet is a beetle. Not all tiny creatures are spiders. Calling a beetle 'spider' is a silly mistake. However, I can probably let this go. After all, this kind of thing is common in the early stages of language acquisition. Children might call every insect 'spider', every female 'mum', and every spherical fruit 'orange'. This phenomenon is called overextending.* Overextending is just one of the reasons children are funny. And by funny, I mean strange and a little bit dim.

I don't know if I can forgive your verb choice, though. 'Dying' is an intransitive verb that cannot be followed by a direct object such as 'spider'. The verb you're looking for is 'kill'. You were supposed to say, 'I'm killing a spider that is actually a beetle.'

But is 'killing' even the right word here? This beetle won't necessarily be killed by the yoghurt globs. It will be maimed for sure, but killed? It might have been more apt to say: 'I am trying to kill this spider that is actually a beetle, but maybe I'll just maim it instead.'

That said, I imagine your mum isn't that worried about you overextending the odd noun or messing up the odd verb. I imagine she's just worried you are a psychopath. Like many parents, she places undue weight on her child's first words. She considers them a Very Significant Event. Your cousin's first word was 'moon'. This pleased your auntie. She thought it was a very significant event. She thought it meant he would become a well-paid astrophysicist.†

But now your mum is flicking through *So Your Child Is a Psychopath* and all she imagines for you is a short career as a vandal followed

---

* Under-extending happens too. Sometimes kids think the only orange in the world is the one they have just eaten and are baffled when there is more fruit by the same name.

† Your cousin's first word was not a very significant event. He won't be an astrophysicist or an astro-anything. He's not so bright, that kid.

by a long stretch behind bars. Don't worry too much. Parents are funny. And by funny, I mean strange and a little bit dim.

As it happens, I'm not dim. I'm a linguist,* and as a very smart linguist, I can say your mum is right to be worried. There is something wrong with you. I know this for certain. Something is wrong with you. Something is wrong with you right now as you sit on the carpet still holding the yoghurt pot. The yoghurt pot is empty and the beetle is still. You are contemplating the beetle, which is still. Stop contemplating the beetle. The beetle is so still, it is unlikely it will ever move again.

Look at me. I know you understand. Your vocabulary is enormous, or to be precise, your passive vocabulary is enormous and your active vocabulary is shite. I know having something wrong with you sounds scary, but don't worry. At least, not for the time being.

Hey, stop crying. Would it help if I told you a story? I have a really great one up my sleeve. It's all about you – everything you see and everything you do.

Sound good? Climb up here, Little Alien. Sit next to me. I will tell you about life on this planet. I will tell you how it goes.

Further reading:

So Your Child Is a Psychopath

---

* Linguists are language experts. They are people who know a lot about language. They are not necessarily people who know how to speak a lot of languages, or even people who know a lot about linguine, which is a type of pasta.

3

Part One

I

IT GOES LIKE THIS. You won't be normal. Aliens can't be normal. You'll be normal enough, though. And by this, I mean you'll have just enough normal to seem normal without actually being normal.

Let me explain. Like normal human children, you'll disregard every grammatical irregularity that comes your way. You'll say things like 'I goed to school with my mum', 'I eated the orange', and 'Colouring in is funner than skipping'.

If I were a prescriptivist, I would lambast you for these flagrant over-regularisations.* But as it happens, I am not a prescriptivist, I am a descriptivist.† And as a descriptivist, I applaud you. 'Goed' is more logical than 'went'. 'Eated' is more logical than 'ate'. 'Funner' is more logical than 'more fun' and it's a funner expression to boot.

---

* Prescriptivists are people who think there are right and wrong ways to use language. They wince at aspirated aitches and moan about unsightly neologisms. They can be a bit annoying.

† Descriptivists are people who study how language is actually used. They embrace the unrelenting sea of language change as neither a sign of progress nor a sign of decay. They can also be a bit annoying.

These assertions would chime with the internal grammars of many small humans. You're blending in. Well done.

But you're still wrong. 'Goed' and 'eated' and 'funner' aren't words. You won't find them in reputable dictionaries or even disreputable dictionaries. They're wrong. You're wrong. You're wrong all the time and you can't help it.

Let me explain. On your first day of school, you look cute in your tiny stripy tie. You go into the classroom, looking cute, holding your dad's hand – something that's also cute. When he lets go of your hand, you cling on to his elbow. When he shakes his elbow free, you wrap your entire body around his legs. When he wriggles you off him, he disappears out the door and you panic.

You are panicked. You don't know what to do. There are other children. The other children are busy. The other children are doing seemingly random activities. You wonder if you should join in with the seemingly random activities, but you don't know which activity to choose. Do you Play-Doh or colour in? Do you sandpit or clay? Do you Jenga or glockenspiel?

All these questions – or the absence of any answers to these questions – make your throat feel weird and your eyes well up. You're upset. This is what happens when you're upset. You don't know that yet, though. Your little body is still a mystery to you.

The teacher comes over, but only at a leisurely speed. For a human, she is not in very good condition. She is old and creaks when she walks. Slowly, she eases herself down to your level until her head is at your height. She asks if you're OK.

'Are you OK?' she asks.

You don't know if you're OK because you don't know what

'OK' means in this context. You don't currently have any unmet physiological needs. You don't need to eat or sleep or drink or pee. Does that mean you're OK?

'Do you want to play with Henry?' the teacher asks.

You wipe your nose on your sleeve. 'Henry' is just another word you do not understand.

'Let's go find Henry.'

The teacher prods you gently in the direction of outside. When you get outside, she prods you in the direction of the sandpit. When you get to the edge of the sandpit, she prods you until you step into the sandpit.

'Here's Henry,' the teacher says.

In the sandpit, there are three boys. One has red hair, one has brown hair, and one is blond. One of these boys must be Henry, but the teacher doesn't tell you which one. The three boys stare at you. You wonder if you have a Cheerio stuck on your forehead. You ate Cheerios that morning and it wouldn't be the first time one of them got stuck on your forehead, it would be the second. You rub your forehead. There is no Cheerio.

The teacher tells you she's going to leave you with Henry now.

'I'm going to leave you with Henry now,' the teacher says. 'Don't throw anything. If sand gets into anyone's eye, they'll have to go to hospital. Cheerio.'

When the teacher is gone, you stand with your arms at your sides while you sway, wondering if 'Henry' is the collective noun for a group of feral children.

At some point, the boy with red hair speaks.

'Why is she just standing there?' he asks.

Ten minutes later, you are covered in sand, standing in the creaky teacher's office. Your teacher is looking at you through her glasses. The glasses have a magnifying quality. They make her look like one of those animals with massive eyes.*

The teacher is talking to you about being nice. She is saying things like 'It's nice to be nice' and 'We don't attack each other with sand in this classroom'. You do not dignify these banalities with a nod, let alone a verbal response. In the end, the teacher tells you she is going to call your dad. She tells you this twice, and twice you do not care.

'I'm going to call your dad,' she says. 'I'm going to call your dad right now.' When your dad answers the phone, the teacher changes her tone. What was once a nasal drone is now a breathy singsong that makes her sound manically chipper, as if she's determined to have a really good time despite life being despicable. 'Your daughter is not saying anything . . . We didn't know she was . . . We really need to know . . . We need to know if children don't . . . No, she's not speaking at all . . . She's also just attacked several other children . . . Sand . . .'

You're pissed off when your dad arrives. You know this because you feel like frowning. You look at your dad, frowning. Your dad looks at you but he's not frowning. He doesn't say anything. He just starts walking you home. While he is walking you home, you want to ask him what on earth he was thinking, sending you to a school where they don't even teach you how to read. But then he asks you if you want pizza for tea.

'Do you want pizza for tea?' he asks.

---

* Bushbabies.

You nod. Even though you eated pizza yesterday, another pizza can't hurt.

'What do you say?'

In most families, when an adult asks a child what do you say, it means 'Don't be a little shit, say please' or 'Say thank you, you little shit'. In your family, however, it just means you are required to speak.

'Yes,' you say.

'What do you say?'

'Yes, please.'

Further reading:

Is Homeschooling Right for Your Child?
An Introduction to Literacy for Illiterate Kids
Bushbabies: Why the Massive Eyes?

2

You do not last very long at this particular school. And when I say this, I am employing a technique called 'litotes' – something that means you really don't last very long at all.

One Tuesday morning, your normal teacher is off sick. Another teacher is standing in. This teacher is not in control of you. She is not in control of anyone.

You are sitting next to a kid called Joe and a kid called Louis. The three of you are doing arts and crafts. You hold the safety scissors carefully, cut shapes out of the cardboard. The kid called Joe then sticks these shapes to another piece of cardboard. After this, the kid called Louis pours quantities of PVA glue over everything, and everyone heaps glitter everywhere. It's teamwork. It's dreamwork. It's art, but only kind of.

But lo! In the corner over there, a kid called Rebecca has just had an accident. By this, I mean she has just done a wee while still wearing her clothes. She is doing a lot of crying about this as she waddles around uncomfortably, her legs wide like a cowboy.

Even though such things go with the territory of teaching young children, the teacher seems alarmed by Rebecca's accident. She asks the assistant to take Rebecca out of the classroom and guide her somewhere – anywhere – else.

'Can you help her out the room?' she asks the assistant.

The assistant, an old, uncooperative woman, looks at the teacher for a few seconds. 'Where do you want me to take her?'

'The nurse's room, maybe?' the teacher says.

The assistant shakes her head. 'I don't know if this merits a trip to the nurse's room.'

'Wherever, then,' the teacher says. 'I don't know the protocol.'

'I think she just has to sit back down,' the assistant says. 'She'll dry out soon enough.'

The teacher's eyes go wide. 'I think someone needs to phone her mum or dad.'

The assistant crosses her arms. 'Excuse me,' she says. Then in a stage whisper everyone everywhere can hear: 'Don't you know Rebecca's parents are dead?'

At this, a still-damp Rebecca cries even harder, the teacher and the assistant go to comfort her, and Joe and Louis seize an opportunity.

To be specific, they ask you to go into the cupboard to grab some more supplies. They do this even though you are not allowed to go into the cupboard to grab some more supplies.

'That's not allowed,' you say.

'It's OK,' Joe says.

'Miss said you could,' Louis says.

'I'll come too,' Joe says.

'OK,' you say, now swayed.

There are a lot of cool things in the cupboard: paints, staplers, felt tips, whiteboard pens.

'Take those,' Joe says, lurking by the door to keep a lookout.

'Huh?' you ask.

'Those, there. We can cut them. Take them.'

You look to where he is pointing. You don't know what the books are, but they do have pretty pictures. Pictures of donkeys. Pictures of deserts. Pictures of mountains. Pictures of men.

You grab a few and plonk them back on your desk.

Joe and Louis start laughing when you begin cutting up the children's Bibles. Pleased, you smile along. When the teacher finally realises what you're doing, she sits down on the floor next to Rebecca and starts to wail.

Further reading:

For the Love of Art: Crafting for Kids
For the Love of God: The Bible for Kids

3

YOUR MIND IS SLUGGISH and your eyes heavy as you lounge in the living room, lying on your stomach under the rug but above the carpet.

Other more conventional seating options are available. For instance, you could be sitting on both the rug and the carpet, much like your cousin is currently doing. Or you could be lying on the sofa much like your dad normally does. Or perching on the pouffe much like your mum normally does. Or standing straight up on one leg, like flamingos do, even though they seem to have at least two legs at their disposal.

You don't do any of these things. Instead, you lie underneath the rug but above the carpet, watching *The Simpsons*. You are next to your cousin. Like a normal person, he is sitting cross-legged above both the rug and the carpet. Like an abnormal person, he is eating prawn cocktail crisps. You are not eating prawn cocktail crisps. You are eating salt and vinegar because salt and vinegar is a much better flavour than prawn cocktail. In your opinion, this isn't even an opinion. In your opinion, it is a fact.

But you are young, and due to the inclusion of words and phrases such as 'wang', 'crap factory', and 'homersexual', *The Simpsons* has an advisory viewing age of thirteen. Due to this advisory viewing age of thirteen, it is inadvisable that you, a four-and-a-half-year-old, watch it with your cousin, a six-and-a-half-year-old.

I imagine your mum isn't aware of this viewing advisory age, but if she were aware of this viewing advisory age, she probably wouldn't care. Why would she? Life throws age-inappropriate things at you all the time. What else are depressive episodes? What else are hangovers disproportionate to the quantity of alcohol imbibed? What else are unhelpful GP reception staff, polite requests for your child to find somewhere else to go to primary school, not-so-polite requests for your child to find somewhere else to go to primary school, and a relentless series of overdue library fines?

As it happens, you don't care about the viewing advisory age either. No one advises you on anything. Take this whole school situation. No one has spelt out what has been happening, and so you simply don't know. You don't know why your half-term holiday has been so long. Similarly, you don't know why tonight's dinner has so far just been salt and vinegar crisps when it has never before entailed even a single crisp.

The rug serves as a blanket; the carpet as your bed. On the telly, another alien exists.

'When I was a young boy,' the alien says, 'I wanted to be a baseball."

---

* 'Treehouse of Horror VII', *The Simpsons*, directed by Mike B. Anderson, season 8, episode 1, Gracie Films, 1996.

In the corridor, your mum and dad are talking. Your dad has just got home. They are talking about someone, but you don't know who. They are talking about someone but you don't think that it's you.

'But she's only been going there since September,' your dad is saying.

Your cousin turns up the volume. 'But tonight,' the alien says, 'we must move forward, not backward—'

'Hey,' your cousin interrupts, pointing at the green alien but looking at you. 'That one looks like you!'

You study the alien. After careful thought and consideration, you shake your head. 'No, he doesn't,' you say, calmly and accurately. This alien is not like you. He is green with tentacles and a balloon around his head. You do not have those things. Instead, you have arms, legs, a head, and a face.

'He so does,' your cousin says. 'You dribble like that too!'

You raise your hand to your mouth. There is no dribble. Not unless you reach right inside your mouth. Then there is dribble.

'I'm not an alien,' you say.

Your cousin lets out a scoff. 'You so are.'

You frown. You don't like your cousin saying you're an alien. You don't like it because it's not a nice thing to say. Also, you worry he might be right. You look at your arms and hands. Glowing in the light of the TV, they look alien to you.

In any case, your parents are still in the corridor. 'What did they say exactly? Let me read it.' Your dad's voice sounds different from how he normally sounds.

'I mean, how is this even allowed? Vandalism? She's not a vandal. She's a five-year-old girl—'

'She's four and a half.'

'Four and a half, whatever—'

'It's not just about the vandalism. They also have concerns about the class fish.'

'What class fish?'

'She tried to put it in the bin, apparently.'

'Jesus.'

You turn up the volume on the remote. You wonder if – technically speaking – you should look like the alien on TV. If you should be dribbling. If you should be green with tentacles and a balloon around your head.

'Oi, can you two turn that back down?'

You pretend not to have heard. Even though you are four and a half years old, and even though you are what human people commonly refer to as a girl, you don't want to think they are talking about you. How could they be talking about you? They are talking about someone who isn't going to school any more or might not be going to school any more, or at least not her usual school. But you go to school all the time – not recently, but all the time. Don't you?

Further reading:

So Homeschooling Is Right for Your Child

4

TIME PASSES GLOOPILY. THE Moon orbits the Earth which in turn orbits the Sun. A variety of flowers blossom. A variety of flowers die. Politicians resign. Farmers hoe. Buses arrive late and then all at once. Corporate strategists leverage synergy. Some people lose their jobs, others their wallets, others still their minds. Babies are born screaming. Old folks die silent, cold, and alone.

In other words, you are years into this so-called homeschooling – something that entails a lot of home but not a lot of schooling. Neither your mum nor your dad is teaching you much. You simply exist in your three-up, three-down suburban household in the south-east of England, UK. Your dad goes to work. Your mum stays at home. As far as you are concerned, every day is a weekend day. This is OK. You are still very young* and don't know any better.

Most mornings, you traipse around after your mum as she does her things – sometimes cleaning and sometimes laundry but mostly an awful lot of reading. Your mum loves her books,

---

* You are seven.

especially educational books, especially how-to books. Indeed, the more didactic the book is, the more she is bound to love it. One morning she'll be reading *How to Grow a Garden*. By the afternoon, she'll be reading *Metal Detecting: A Beginner's Guide*. By the evening, she'll be reading *How to Train Your Dog*. You don't have a dog. You just have a mum. You sit next to her, colouring in as she learns her lessons.

Occasionally, your mum doesn't read but watches the telly instead. Daytime TV shows are her favourites. She likes the ones set in hospitals, but also seems interested in the ones about traffic cops. During these shows, she likes to tell you things about the UK police force. Like this, you learn that UK police officers sometimes wear uniforms but sometimes just normal clothes. You also learn that you have a right to remain silent and that, if you ever see a police officer around the house, you must tell your mum.

When the mood seems to strike her, your mum chats to you as she would a friend. This is how you learn about the things she likes to eat and the things she likes to drink, the jobs she hopes to train for – when she feels ready, when she feels better, when she has time, when she finishes all the books she's been reading. Like a good girl, you don't say much in response. Like a good girl, you just sit and listen really nicely.

But today is a bit different. It's the first day summer has really kicked in. It's a Friday, twenty-something degrees, the Sun is blaring, and the sky is blue. In honour of this, today is a non-book day.

Your mum and your auntie are sitting in the garden, drinking white wine and basking in tranquillity and conversation as they brown off their pink skin. Inside, your cousin is in the living room, watching a

TV programme. You don't like the look of it, and so you join your mum and your auntie in the garden instead.

You lie yourself down on a lounger next to them. The lounger is plastic and white. Your mum and auntie have lounger cushions but you do not. This means your lounger is more uncomfortable. You try to make do, try to get comfy on an uncomfy thing.

Your mum and your auntie are having one of their conversations. You listen. Today, the conversation centres on someone who used to follow your mum wherever she went. In your opinion, this makes for a dull topic of conversation. What's more, the Sun is too bright, its rays are too warm, and you don't like toasting yourself like bread.

'Mum,' you say, trying to get your mum's attention.

Your mum, absorbed in the conversation, doesn't reply.

You try again. 'Mum, can I go over there and play with the hose?'

'So I left the supermarket this one time and he was right there,' your mum says.

'Uh-huh,' your auntie says back.

'Mum, can I go—'

'And when that happened I lost my temper completely—'

'Mum, can I go over there and—'

Your mum turns to you, chucks you under the chin and makes reassuring noises. 'Sounds good, petal,' she says. 'Have a great time.'

You locate the hose, which is attached to the side of the house on a green mount thing. Then you unwind it with a serious expression on your face. You have an activity in mind – an activity involving the hose.

Meanwhile, your dad is driving home from work. As I imagine it, his hands are at ten o'clock and two o'clock. He checks his blind spots when it's appropriate to do so. He mirrors, signals, and manoeuvres – also when it's appropriate to do so. When he gets bored of his thoughts, he turns on the radio, which then starts playing his station of choice as he goes around the roundabout then onto the A-road.

As I imagine it, the radio is playing a programme about the state of children today. According to the programme, the children of today are not in a very good state. Sometimes, they enter primary school without adequate toilet training. Often, they leave primary school without knowing how to read. They are wrapped up in cotton wool, sheltered from the harsh realities of the big, bad world. It takes ages for them to grow up, and when they do, things aren't much better. Weak and entitled, they expect to be handsomely rewarded for getting pregnant and binge drinking in abandoned playgrounds. Entitled and weak, they think they deserve to forgo hard work of any kind. According to the programme, the children of today are turning into adults without the skills necessary to survive in the modern workforce, let alone thrive.

Your dad does not use his critical thinking skills as he listens to the radio programme about the state of children today. He does not question whether what the people on the programme are saying is true, or whether he cares about what these people think. As a result, he is soon experiencing negative thoughts and feelings of doom and gloom. What if my child grows up to become a non-functional blob, he thinks. What if my child never leaves home, but instead depends on me financially and emotionally for the rest of her life, he also thinks. Unfortunately, your dad's feelings of doom and gloom are not alleviated when he gets home, largely because of what he finds when he gets there.

Upon entering the house, your dad sees your cousin lying on the couch, watching a medical drama. In your dad's opinion, the show is not age-appropriate, mainly because the character on screen currently has a bottle stuck up his bum hole. The character needs surgery. Your dad wonders if it's OK that your cousin, who has a toilet-based sense of humour and is accident-prone, is viewing this programme. It might give him ideas, your dad thinks.

'Oh, hi, Paul,' your dad says to your cousin, who is called Paul.

'Huh,' Cousin Paul says, because he did not hear your dad come in and is startled by the sudden sight of him.

Looking through the sliding doors, your dad spots you sitting in the middle of the garden. You aren't doing anything smart in the middle of the garden. Instead, you are digging a hole in the grass, which you have amply moistened with the hose. A concoction of soil and mud and grass is swimming in this hole.

I imagine that, while your dad thinks this is unfortunate behaviour, he knows it is not exactly unusual. In his opinion, children make magic mud potions when they are let loose in gardens, just as bees buzz and cars run on fuel. Granted, it is a shame that he will look at an unsightly lawn in the coming months, but he knows he will get over this. He likes his garden only a moderate amount. He can ignore unsightly patches of grass.

What he can't get over, however, is the fact that his wife and his wife's sister are sunning themselves on the lounger, apparently oblivious to the mess you are making, as well as to the risks of skin cancer.

To make matters worse, it has become apparent that you have not made a magic mud potion, at least not in your opinion. If you had, you would be stirring it with a stick like a normal child, perhaps chanting incantations while you did so. Instead, you have made a magic mud *soup*. You have a spoon, which you must have taken from the kitchen, with which your dad sees you take multiple sips. You don't grimace when the soup hits your tongue. From this, your dad deduces you might actively enjoy the taste of the mud soup.*

You are only vaguely aware of your dad emerging from the double doors and charging at you. Before you really know it, he is scooping you up into his arms – holding you aloft like a trophy. You neither register nor understand the look of horror on his face. You just grin at him, your pearly whites a muddy brown. 'Dad!' you say happily, for every time he comes home, you are filled with joy.

'Good god,' your dad says back. He is looking at your mouth. Only now does it occur to you that he isn't holding you aloft like a trophy, but instead like you're something smelly.

'Go ahh. Go ahh like you're at the dentist,' your dad says, his hands under your armpits, his eyes wide, and his brows furrowed.

'Ahhh,' you say, confused but happy to oblige.

Your dad plonks you back down, prises your mouth wider, and peeks inside to see your gums encased in mud. He reaches in, removes a leaf, looks at the leaf, then takes the Lord's name in vain once more.

'Jesus Christ,' he says.†

---

* As it happens, your dad is wrong. You don't enjoy the taste of the mud soup. You simply find it tolerable. Mud soup, you think, as you sip on the concoction. This tastes fine, you also think.

† Milder profanity often evokes religion (e.g. 'Jesus Christ', 'Goddamn'). Stronger profanity often evokes toileting (e.g. 'piss', 'arse'). Occasionally, profanity evokes both religion and toileting (e.g. 'holy shit', 'holy arse').

Your dad turns to your mum and your auntie, who have fallen silent. They look at your dad, at you, at the hole, at the mud soup and then at the hose.

Your dad throws them a dagger stare.

'What the hell?' he says.

Your mum and auntie regard your dad, then you, and then your dad again – much as if they are taking in the scene for the first time.

'Oh, wow,' your mum says, looking at you over her sunglasses. 'You've made a bit of a mess there, haven't you, darling?'

'Wow, chicken,' your auntie says. 'What have you been up to?'

'Gosh, that's a mess,' your mum says.

'You think?' your dad says. 'How did you let her do this?'

Your mum shakes her head. 'Were you eating that mess, darling? That's really not good, you know. There's all sorts in soil. Nasty things. Worms and that.'

'How – did – this – happen?' your dad says. If he had a towel or some other item, he would surely now throw it to the ground in a fit of rage – that's how annoyed he is.

Your auntie chips in. 'We thought Paul was looking after her.'

'Looking after her? He's lying on the sofa, thinking about what kind of bottle he wants to stick up his bum.'

Your auntie widens her eyes. 'Gosh, really?' She takes a thoughtful sip of her drink.

'And since when does he ever look after her?' your dad says.

Your dad curses under his breath – fucking this and Jesus that and fucking Jesus this and that. Meanwhile, he reaches for the hose. It is not clear what he wants to do with the hose, at least not to you, and you don't manage to ask him to explain his thoughts or feelings before he turns it on.

'What are you doing, babe?' your mum asks – as if reading your mind.

The hose splutters at first, then a powerful jet pours forth.

Your dad does not answer your mum's question. Instead, he turns to you – a half-apologetic, half-dead-to-the-world look on his face.

'I'm sorry, sweet pea,' he says to you, 'this is going to be a little bit cold and a little bit not nice.'

Later, you are sitting on the staircase, leaning against the bannister. Your mind is tired as you stare into space. You ruminate over the day's events. Replay the way you screamed as your dad chased you around the garden. Recall how your mum and auntie towelled you off as you stood naked and shivering in the hallway. Then you become aware of how sleepy you are. You think you should probably tip yourself into bed.

Your parents' conversation about your future floats up to you as you close your eyes and curl yourself up on the staircase. They always sit around and chat about you, like they're obsessed.

'She can barely speak.'

'They don't teach you to speak at school.'

'You know what I mean.'

'No, I don't.'

'Some days, I'm not sure she has a single thought.'

'That's not a nice thing to say.'

'It doesn't matter. She needs to speak. She needs to read. She needs to write.'

'In Finland, the kids don't learn to read till they're eight and in the end, they all turn out all right.'

'Where did you learn that?'

'In one of my books.'

'God.'

'*How the Finnish Learn to Read* or something like that.'

'That's interesting, because our daughter is never going to read any sort of book if she doesn't go to school.'

'She'll learn one day soon. When she feels ready.'

'And we're not in Finland. None of us are in Finland.'

'I'll teach her to read.'

'When?'

'I'll look it up tomorrow. I'll go to the library and find a book on how to read and then I'll teach her.'

'No.'

'What do you mean no?'

'I mean no. She's going back to school.'

'I don't want her going back there. I don't think they understood her.'

'No, no – not the same place. I don't think they'd be keen anyway. I have somewhere else in mind.'

'What do you mean, somewhere else? A school?'

'A school. A very good school.'

'Where did you hear about this school?'

'My colleague told me about it.'

'Which colleague?'

'Dave, the one with the kid with the—'

'The problems.'

'Yeah.'
'God.'
'Jesus.'
'Fuck.'

Further reading:

Metal Detecting: A Beginner's Guide
How to Train Your Dog
How the Finnish Learn to Read

5

YOU HAVE BEEN AT this school for, what, twelve months? And it feels like all you've done is run, run, run. Your little legs are sore and tired. Your little feet are blistered and tired. You are so tired that, every day, you long for the hour that it is acceptable to fall asleep.

You can't fall asleep. Not now. It is eight a.m. and you must do exactly what the PE teacher – a man with a face like a rat – says. The PE teacher tells you to do all manner of things. He tells you to squat, jump, scramble. He tells you to lie down, sit up, and rotate your body from side to side.

The exercise feels horrible. It makes you feel weirdly aware of your body, sinews, and muscles stretching and etching their way longwards and sidewards. It makes you feel exactly what you are: an alien consciousness trapped in the body of an over-evolved primate; a sack of blood, muscles, and veins attached to the soul of an extraterrestrial life form.

You can't sleep. Not right now. You have to run to one side, then to the other side, then to the other side, faster than the bleep, slower than the bleep, bleep, bleep, bleep—

'Focus! Fo-cus!'

You look around. Your heart does a little sink, swoosh, flutter. The other children have stopped running around and moved on to the next activity. Hurriedly, you throw yourself into what you fear will be a never-ending series of headstands, which come to a halt when you lose your balance and fall. When you hit your head on the blue mats that cover the floor, there is a sound that sounds like *thwack*. One classmate gasps.

'Whoa,' another classmate says.

You do not know if they are being empathetic or mocking or neither of the above.

No matter, the blue mats are there for this very eventuality – to protect the heads, limbs, and torsos of children who stumble and fall. And yet, you can confirm that they feel harder than the floor. For a full minute, your skull rings in a way that is wordlessly painful.

'Oi!' the teacher yells, looming over you.

You get up, half-heartedly throw your body upside down, and fall over again. Your stomach feels a little stirred up, then a lot stirred up, then really, really stirred up. You are throwing up. A partially digested version of your breakfast is releasing itself onto your sports uniform, feet, and floor. You sense that there is more vomit to come. With this in mind, you lurch towards the exit. But alas, you are sick again before you get there, and end up throwing up pretty much everywhere: on the balance beam, at the base of the scaffolding, at the bottom of the radiator, and on various classmates too.

You manage to reach the exit. But now you are on your knees again, the contents of your stomach leaving your mouth. This process repeats itself over and over again. It's incredible. You didn't know there could be so much in you to puke up. It just doesn't stop. You feel dizzy from the sheer exertion of it.

A stranger walks in, and you vomit once more, this time on their shoes. The stranger's shoes are pink. When you look up, you see they are a child of school age. The child of school age has dark curly hair, cut to the length of a bob. Much like the shoes, this haircut is feminine. And yet, the child is wearing masculine clothes: blue jeans and a navy T-shirt with a picture of a dinosaur on it. From your experience on Planet Earth, you know that this design indicates the stranger is a boy.

Next to the boy, there's a woman you assume is the boy's mum — such is the nature of her curly hair — the head teacher, and her deputy.

For a moment, all four of them look at the boy's vomit-covered shoes. Then they look at you lying on the ground, also covered in vomit. Then, the teachers carry on as if nothing is wrong. They don't acknowledge your presence. They do not acknowledge your vomit. They don't even acknowledge the looks of revulsion on the boy's face, the looks of bewilderment on your classmates' faces, or the look of apoplexy on the PE teacher's face. Instead, they engage in the polished prattle of salespeople, ignoring both the smell of sick and the growing cacophony as they gesture at the facilities.

'The light in this hall is excellent for healing troubled souls,' the head teacher is saying.

The boy and his mum look around, apparently confused by the sights they are seeing: a dilapidated sports hall propped up by antique scaffolding, children trying to wipe vomit from their clothes, and a PE teacher with anger issues getting redder and redder.

After a long pause, the mum speaks. 'And this thing,' she says, falteringly. 'What is this?'

'The scaffolding?' the deputy says. 'Oh, it's just a temporary structure.'

You try to get up. When you do so, you slip on your own sick and sit back down.

'How long has it been there?' the mum says.

The boy gesticulates animatedly. 'She was sick on me,' he says. 'It's gone all over my shoes!'

'Yes, indeed,' the deputy says.

'She was sick on me!' the boy repeats. 'Why does no one care she was sick on me?'

'Well, my Bobby boy,' the kid's mum says. 'It seems she was sick on everything. Don't worry. We'll wipe you down in a minute.'

The head teacher coughs. 'Shall we move on to the dining room? All this talk of exercise is making my stomach rumble.'

The deputy agrees. 'Mm,' he says. 'I agree.'

Exactly why the stench of vomit is making them hungry is beyond the scope of your comprehension. In any case, the four of them start to leave, the son leading the way with his mum behind him.

But before exiting the sports hall, the head teacher gives you a good looking at – brandishing one of her clipboards as she does.

'Pleased with yourself?' she asks.

You narrow your eyes. You don't like the head teacher. Since your arrival, you feel like she has been following you around. Sometimes, after watching you for an unspecified amount of time, she jots something down and smirks.

You look at her steadily — a chunk of vomit still visible on your chin. You don't know how to answer her question. You don't know what 'pleased with yourself' really means.

Behind you, the cacophony rages on. One kid has a splash of your sick on him, and is therefore crying. Another is running around in circles, emitting a high-pitched whine. Apparently, the PE teacher has placed a couple of yellow signs on the ground near your various sick patches. The yellow signs warn of wet floors and slip hazards.

He approaches you. 'You're it.'

'What?' you say.

'She's it!'

You are annoyed. You have just been violently ill. You want to lie down in the nurse's room for an hour or two. Perhaps someone could even phone your parents to let them know you need picking up early. Surely you cannot be expected to run around when you have no sustenance left in your little body, and are already so poor at all this sporting activity. Surely the other kids can't be expected to run away from you, not when half of them are covered with your spew.

But apparently, running is exactly what you are expected to do.

You can't keep up with the other kids. They are nimble. You are not. You have just thrown up. They have not. You are slow and weak and tired and in the throes of what could be a concussion. You try to catch up with one of them. You do not.

You aren't putting in any real effort. You are hating every second of this activity. You don't want to be chasing your classmates around the sports hall in your vest and pants. Chasing your classmates around the sports hall in your vest and pants will not earn you social currency. You need social currency, not exercise. You need clout. Not exercise. You need to mind that blue mat because you are going to trip and go flying—

'Get up!'

Later that day, you try to explain to your parents what happened. You are all sitting around the kitchen table, eating jacket potatoes. You still don't feel quite right. You also don't know how quite to explain how bad your experience was without coming across as overdramatic.

You prod the tuna, sweetcorn, and mayo topping.

'This new kid walked in,' you say. 'And I was sick on his shoes too.'

Your mum beams. 'That's great news.'

You frown at her. 'What?'

'You're not the new kid any more! And hey, maybe he can be your friend.'

You continue to frown. 'I was sick on him.'

Your mum does a dismissive wave of her hands. 'He won't remember.'

'No?'

'Next time he sees you, he'll just think, oh, who's this interesting girl?'

Somehow, you doubt what your mum is saying is true, though you think it wise not to probe further. You nod mildly, look at your potato, wondering why it seems particularly unappetising today.

'Dad,' you say, eventually, 'would you mind passing me the salt?'

Further reading:

Is Your Child Just Pretending to Be Ill?
10 Signs of Concussion
All in the Mind: How to Overcome Your Brain Injury

6

YOUR MUM IS RIGHT and your mum is wrong. The boy won't forget about the vomit, but he will become your friend.

He's not your friend yet, though. For now, you are just his shower-arounder – something that means it is your job to show him around, explain what newbies can't be expected to know.

For instance, you might tell him that you need to avoid the school dinner curries at all costs. This is not just because the last batch gave a number of people diarrhoea. It's also because it tastes bad.

Likewise, you could tell him everyone has to go boy-girl, boy-girl in queues – it's a school rule and a way of making sure no one is standing next to their friend. You could explain this with a bit of child psychology – say that, in the early years of education human children tend to naturally segregate themselves according to sex. You won't because you don't know anything about child psychology. But theoretically you could.

Similarly, you might tell him you need to walk and not run whenever travelling from A to B. You could mention that the no-running rule is strictly enforced everywhere outside physical education. This is despite the fact that running is faster than walking, and a running-allowed policy might even negate the need for so many physical education classes.

You could and would say all this, but the new kid is not here yet. He is late. You wait for him in the car park. You undo your school shoes, redo your school shoes, loosen your tie, tighten your tie. After a while, you lose all sense of decorum and rummage in the depths of your right nostril.

You are fidgeting. You are fussing. Why? You are anxious: the catch-all term for the feelings you are currently feeling. Right now, you can feel your heartbeat. Although your heart beats all the time, you are normally unaware of its pulsations. Now, though, you are very aware of the red thing in your chest as you loosen and unloosen your tie. Similarly, you are aware of your lungs (how tight they are), your hands (how shaky they are), and your feet (how tingly they are).

You are apprehensive. You are the new kid's shower-arounder: the most important, forward-facing job available to kids like you. It might even be something that you can put on your CV* – the very first thing. For such an important day, you have to be comfortable in your skin. For such an important day, you have to be smart in your clothes. For such an important day, you need him to arrive on time so that you can start on time.

After a few minutes – or maybe longer, gauging the passage of

---

* A CV is a written summary of someone's work experience, skills, and qualifications. It is an initialism – a string of initial letters pronounced separately – standing for curriculum vitae.

time is not your strong suit – the new kid arrives in a car that is tall and wide. The driver appears to be the same lady you saw before. You wonder if she is the new kid's sole caregiver. You wonder what happened to his dad.

The tall and wide car skids to a halt, and the new kid's mum looks at you. After this, she forehead-kisses the new kid. Then she says something you can't quite hear. Then the new kid says something you also can't hear. Then the new kid's mum raises her voice and pours forth what seems to be some animated encouragement. You can make out some words. To be specific, you can make out the words 'please', 'future', and 'education'.

The new kid remains unmoving. He doesn't budge, not after one, two, three warnings. After this, his mum leans over to unbuckle his seat belt, then opens the passenger door.

'Bobby, I'm sorry but this is it. I'm not driving you back home. Please, son. Get out of the car.'

Bobby does not exit the car normally. Instead, in an alarming turn of events, he keeps his body rigid and lets himself fall out of the car and onto the ground. As the ground is made up of concrete covered in gravel, his landing is not a soft one. Indeed, upon impact, he lets out a yelp. He then lies still for a while, looking up at the sky with mournful eyes.

'Oh my god,' Bobby's mum says, exiting the vehicle to go inspect her son. 'That's the silliest thing you've done all week!'

Bobby's mum crouches down next to her son. For a second, you wonder if he has departed this life and entered the next. Then he sits himself up and you see that his main injuries are two bloodied knees. Though the amount of blood is slight, you don't like it.

'I'm hurt, Mother,' Bobby says, clambering up to his feet. 'I can't go on. I must be returned home immediately.'

Your mind immediately goes to something you think is called 'septic tank'. You wonder if this kid has septic tank, or will have septic tank in the near future. You wonder if your showing-around duties will extend to the local hospital.*

Bobby's mum shakes her head. 'You're barely hurt.'

'I am.'

'You've grazed yourself. Intentionally too.' Bobby's mum gazes at the Victorian building towering above you, then rests her eyes on you. 'Maybe this person can take you to the nurse. I think she's here for you.' She nods your way, gives you a smile.

'Who?'

'This one over there.'

You wave. 'Hi,' you say in a voice that is suddenly and curiously American.

Bobby frowns at you but says nothing.

'All right,' Bobby's mum says, getting back in her car to drive away. 'Be good. Get those knees seen to. Please.'

Once the pair of you are alone, you point to the badge fastened

---

* Thanks to being raised by an anxious mother, a risk-aware father, and a TV diet of daytime medical documentaries, your knowledge of the medical lexicon is surprisingly extensive. However, in this instance, your choice of vocabulary is wrong. Septic tanks are large sewerage containers. If someone has a septic tank, they probably live in the countryside and don't have their waste connected to the mains. On the other hand, sepsis is blood poisoning. If someone has sepsis, then they might die. As it happens, the new kid has neither a septic tank nor sepsis. Like you, he lives in the suburbs. His plumbing is all tied up neatly to the mains. Neither sewerage nor sepsis can hurt him there.

to your acrylic navy-blue school jumper. 'Guide,' you say. Then, remembering to speak in full sentences, you speak in full sentences. 'I'm your guide. You're with me today. I can show you around.'

There is a pause. You can hear the bell sound out and the shuffling of two hundred trudging feet.

'You are supposed to be with me today,' you say again. 'You are supposed to follow me. I can take you to the nurse before our first class. Are you Robert?'

Bobby scowls. 'Don't call me that.'

You try to say pardon and sorry at the same time, but it comes out wrong. 'I'm pardon?' you say.

'Bobby. My name is Bobby,' the new kid says. 'I have a bob and my name is Bobby.'

'Oh, great news,' you say.

As you lead Bobby inside, you try to reassure yourself, tell yourself it's an ordinary Tuesday, that there is physical education then numeracy then physical education then break time then literacy time and lunchtime and some more physical education. You try to convince yourself that looking after this boy won't be difficult – that you'll take him to the nurse for two plasters, then everything will feel normal as he follows you around.

Except, on your way to the medical room, you realise that Bobby is nowhere to be seen.

'Bobby?' you say to an empty corridor. Panic courses through your veins. Bobby is meant to be with you at all times. This is really bad. On a scale of one to ten of badness, this is at least an eight.

Then you hear a flush of a toilet, and Bobby reappears. A wash of relief cascades over you. 'I was just going for a wee,' he says, shutting the door behind him. 'Chill out.' He wipes his hands dry on his trousers – something you know to be unhygienic.

'That's the staff toilet. You can't use the staff toilet. You're not staff.'

Bobby looks at you. From this look, you suspect that – fundamentally, at a profound, core level – he doesn't care about whether he is supposed to use the staff toilet.

'I don't care about staff toilets. I care about not wetting myself.' He pauses. 'I also care about not throwing up everywhere too.'

You continue heading towards the nurse's room. You pass the first physical education class – the one both of you are meant to be in. Here, your classmates are squatting and jumping and stepping and lunging and shuffling. Shortly, they will all go to maths and chant out the times tables one at a time.

You enter the nurse's room without knocking.

'Didn't think to knock?' she asks.

'No,' you say.

The nurse taps her red nails against her desk, sits back, and regards you suspiciously. You notice she's dressed very casually today. The only indication that she is at work is her lanyard, which says 'NURSE' and not 'STAFF' like every other member of staff. You have seen it before, but only now does this distinction interest you. A nurse is surely also classed as a member of staff, you think. 'STAFF' is a big word – its meaning roomy enough for 'NURSE' to fit inside. Why then does her lanyard not just say 'STAFF'?

'Well, who can I help?' the nurse asks, her eyes pausing on the gashes on Bobby's two knees.

You try to explain. 'So, I was, um, there was a car and he was in it and then his mum—'

'I'm injured,' Bobby interrupts, gesturing at his two bloodied knees. The injuries don't look so bad any more.

The nurse tuts. 'How were you injured?'

'I hurt my knees,' Bobby repeats, using both index fingers to indicate more pointedly.

The nurse shakes her head. 'No, how were you injured, as in how did it happen?'

'Oh.' Bobby frowns. 'I fell out of the car.'

'Hm.' The nurse purses her lips, then glances at you. 'You showing this one around?'

You nod.

'He's new?'

You nod.

'I thought as much. Not like you to have company.'

Your stomach does a swoosh.

'You going to speak?' the nurse asks you. 'You going to speak properly?'

You shrug, look at the floor. Her statement was true: it is not like you to have company. As a general rule, you arrive at school, learn at school, leave the others well alone, and are left by the others well alone. It doesn't occur to you to have it any other way. You are well alone. This is well OK.

The nurse provides Bobby with two plasters for his knees, a wad of wet paper towel to press against his forehead, and one grey sick bowl to clutch on to. Then she shoos the pair of you away.

You take Bobby outside, for it is now break time. Here, your classmates are making dens and shimmying up trees while screaming, wailing, and yelling. In the corner of the field, some familiar faces are acting out a funeral for a ladybird who sadly lost its life that morning.

'Are you going to . . .' Bobby starts. 'You know, join in?'

You look at Bobby, shake your head.

'Are you going to throw up on me again?' Bobby offers you the sick bowl. 'You can have this if you like.'

You shake your head once more, look away.

Bobby puts the sick bowl in the bin and scuttles off. You leave him to it – let him join in while you sway by the sidelines. He is a natural. You are not.

Like this, without fanfare, you abandon your role of shower-arounder. You don't tell Bobby that you mustn't touch the school dinner curry, that you have to go boy-girl, boy-girl in queues, or that you shouldn't run unless in a physical education class.

Why would you bother? It's not like you to have company, not like you to have friends.

Further reading:

Soil, Soilage and Septic Tanks
Septic Shock: A Sufferer's Guide

7

A WEEK LATER, YOU are in a reading class for children who cannot read. This is unfortunate, primarily because you are now able to read. In a short space of time, your comprehension of the written word has come on in leaps and bounds. For example, you can now read the sign on the door that says 'Remedial Reading Room', the badge on your teacher's breast that says 'Learning Difficulties', and even the sign on the door that says 'Remember Your Pleases and Thank Yous'. You can do this even though this particular sign is relatively far away from where you are sitting. Your eyesight and reading comprehension are that good.

All of this makes the lesson – with its cats that sit on mats and foxes that climb into boxes – mind-numbingly, soul-achingly dull.

Today, you have got away with selecting a vaguely interesting-looking book. Titled *Mike and Mark's Trip to the Moon*, it's about two characters called Mike and Mark who are very excited about a trip they are taking to the Moon. They don't look especially excited in the illustrations, however. Their faces are blank as sheets of paper – but you know they're excited because they say things like

'Wow!' and 'This is so exciting!' and 'I am so excited' – something that helps your emotional comprehension no end.

You are grateful for how explicitly Mike and Mark express their feelings. You would like it if everyone were like this. If you always knew when your dad was tetchy, you'd know to avoid him so he doesn't snap at you. If you always knew when your mum was worried, you'd know when you needed to soothe her. And if you knew someone was lonely – maybe one of these human children that you are surrounded by every weekday – then you'd approach them and begin the long and tiresome process of befriending them. You could hang out with them every day if need be. You'd be their best friend, their constant companion, their sidekick, their pal.

Or whatever.

You read your book. It's good. You wonder if Mike and Mark will find aliens when they get to the Moon. You wonder if the aliens will look like you, if they will be thick-fringed girls dressed in navy-blue school uniforms, or else if they will be sexless entities with green antennae and several ginormous eyes. You turn the pages. Mike and Mark strap themselves in. The rocket blasts off. Mike and Mark are really excited about this but they are also scared.

'I'm so excited,' says Mike.

'Me too,' says Mark.

'I'm scared as well, though,' says Mike.

'Yeah, me too,' says Mark.

There is a picture page of rocket fuel and flying stars, then Mike and Mark are hovering in space, their cartoon mouths wearing surprise in the shape of O's. You turn the page. Thoroughly engaged, you await the book's denouement with impatience.

Alas, when Mike and Mark land their rocket, the teacher finally clocks what you are reading. She puts her hand on her hip and wags her finger. Your heart sinks. Even before she says it, you know what she is going to say.

'Well, well, well,' she says. 'What have we here?'*

You don't dignify this question with an answer. As far as you're concerned, it's obvious what we have here. We have one teacher (her), three schoolchildren (you, another one, and another one), some books (not many), and some chairs (not comfy).

'Maybe we should try something a bit more nicer,' she says.†

Bereft, you watch as the teacher takes away *Mike and Mark's Trip to the Moon* and hands you a book for very small children. This book is printed on some sort of cardboard – a robust material for babies who are prone to randomly chewing, defecating, or vomiting – and is called *Why Do Rainbows Happen?* In another context, you might possibly be interested in finding out why rainbows happen. In this context, however, you find you don't want to know anything about the light spectrum at all.

'I'm not a baby,' you say, casting an eye on a stain on page two.

'Bless!' the teacher says, clasping a hand to her chest before doing

---

* It annoys you how she says this phrase so much. Someone is late to class and it's 'Well, well, well, what have we here?' Someone forgets to do their homework and it's 'Well, well, well, what have we here?' Someone actually remembers to do their homework and it's 'Well, well, what have we here?' Can she not just find another phrase?

† You will note she does not say 'nicer' but instead 'more nicer': a non-standard, over-regularised form of the qualitative comparative adjective 'nice'. This construction is common among children but not typically employed by adults.

a sort of squat to get down to your level. She is close now. You can smell her Herbal Essences shampoo.

'Don't worry, kid,' she says. 'Everyone learns at different speeds. That doesn't make anyone less special. It actually makes them more special, if you think about it.' She smiles a yellow smile. 'Why don't you think about it? Hm?'

You think about it for a second. After this second has passed, you decide that you are indeed very special but that her comment has nothing to do with the situation at hand.

'But I can read this book already,' you say.

'Why don't you read it out, then?'

You look at your two classmates. One of them is a girl whose pigtails are so high up they practically meet atop her head. Another is a boy whose hair is greasy and parted in the centre. The books lying on their respective laps look OK. The girl with the pigtails has a book about a mediaeval knight. The boy with the middle parting has a book about penguins. Unlike your book, these books have fewer pictures than words. Of this, you are envious.

The teacher raises her eyebrows at you. You hide your face in your book before shaking your head.

Further reading:

Mike and Mark's Trip to the Moon

47

8

WHEN YOU GET HOME that afternoon, you find your mum
with a number of cardboard boxes. The boxes are big and
strong – designed for people who want to pack up all their belongings
to move house. Your mum is putting stuff in them. To be specific,
she is putting books in them. Some of the books are books she
owns – *How to Overcome Low Self-Esteem*, *How to Sail*. Others are
library books – *How to Start Your Own Cleaning Business*, *The Lawful
Route: Is the Lawyering Life for You?* You don't think she should mix
library-owned and self-owned books, but she is doing just that as
she tips them all into a moving box.

After she's done with the books, she moves on to the dresser, with
its photo albums, crockery, fancy cups, and special cutlery. She packs
the things haphazardly. As a result, she breaks an ornamental spoon,
curses under her breath, then notices you standing there.

Her cheeks are red. You take this to mean she is stressed or worried or angry or confused. She looks at you. The look she is giving
you is vague, her eyes not quite focused.

You expect her to ask how you got home. Considering she didn't pick you up, it would be a good question. But your mum doesn't ask this. Instead, she tells you about the boxes.

'So these boxes are my stuff,' she says, 'and these boxes are items of shared ownership.'

'OK,' you say. You feel annoyed she is not asking how you got home. The journey was a nightmare. You had to walk the whole way by yourself even though you've never before walked the whole way by yourself. For the entirety of the twenty-four-minute journey, you felt vulnerable, afraid, confused, and concerned.

'You wouldn't believe how expensive boxes are, darling. This lot cost me a hundred quid.'

'All right,' you say. You feel annoyed your mum spent so much on boxes. She could have at least given you some bus money this morning, or maybe just picked you up herself.

In an attempt to communicate your annoyance, you force out a sigh and walk stompily to the kitchen. When you get there, you are startled: your mum has packed up everything in the kitchen too. There is no kettle or toaster, no mugs or cups. When you open the cupboard to look for the squash, there is no squash either.

This is terrible news. You're very thirsty after your long journey. You want a glass of squash. You can't have water. You don't like the taste. You need squash.

You go to the home phone in the hallway, then you hesitate. You don't like phoning people up. But you also don't like finding your own way home or being thirsty in a house with no squash.

'Hi, Dad,' you say, after he picks up.

'Angel, what's the matter?'

'There's no squash.'

'No squash?'

'None.'

'Are you sure?'

'No.'

'Well, why don't you have another look?'

'I think Mum's packed it away.'

'What do you mean?'

'She's packed the whole kitchen away. There's nothing in there.'

'Are you sure?'

'Yeah.'

'Good lord.'

Your dad tells you he's coming home. 'I'm coming home. I'll be ten minutes, OK?'

'OK.'

When you hang up, you go back to the living room. 'Dad's coming home,' you tell your mum. 'I just called him.'

Your mum doesn't respond to this comment. Instead, she starts packing another box. This time, she fills it with photograph albums.

Impatient, you wait for your dad in the driveway – pacing its length and breadth. Thirsty, you think about maybe drinking some water from the outside tap. Then you remember how bad plain water tastes and think better of it.*

When your dad pulls up in his car, he tells you that you haven't done anything wrong – but that it'd be best if you lie low in your bedroom this evening. He will bring your tea up later. He needs to

---

* Your tastes have developed since your mud-soup-drinking days.

help your mum unpack. He says this hurriedly, like he needs to get rid of you quickly.

'What does lilo mean?' you ask.*

'Lilo? Oh, lie low.' He opens the boot and removes his work bag. 'It just means you need to hide.'

Before your dad opens the front door, he asks you a seemingly random question. 'How was school?'

'School?'

'Yeah.'

You shake your head. 'They think I'm stupid.'

'Oh, I'm sure they don't.'

'They do.'

Upstairs in your room, you read about why rainbows happen in the book titled *Why Do Rainbows Happen?* The book doesn't explain anything about the light spectrum. Instead, it explains how God once killed almost everyone on Planet Earth.

Downstairs, your mum and dad are yelling at each other. Your mum is talking about the police. They are going to kill her at any moment, she says. Hence, she has to pack up her items to make it easier for the pair of you after her death.

Your dad is refuting these claims. The police are not going to kill her at any moment, and so there is no need for her to pack up so many belongings. At some point, he runs out of patience. 'You've lost it,' he tells her. 'You're gone in the head.'

You hide in your bedroom, lying low under the duvet. Later,

---

* A lilo is an inflatable in the shape of a bed. People lie on them while they float on water.

your dad brings you some dinner and some apple-and-blackcurrant squash. You know this because when you wake up the next morning, it's there, waiting for you — all of it cold, all of it delicious.

Further reading:

So Your Family Member Is Psychotic
Who's Out to Get You Today? A Short History of Paranoia
Why Do Rainbows Happen?

9

FOR QUITE SOME TIME, it has been clear that your school is falling apart in ways that are more serious than can be addressed by the odd bit of scaffolding.

For instance, in the girls' toilets, there are five cubicles. Only one of these cubicles contains a functioning lavatory, and even then, it's not a very nice one. Elsewhere, large patches of damp have started to travel around walls, turning the school's once-magnolia hue into a bruisy brown that is also blue and black. Weird fungal spores fill the air – the very same air you breathe. This is not good for your health, or indeed the health of anyone else.

Also, in the dining hall, parts of the ceiling have begun to crumble and fall. Sometimes a light dusting of ceiling dances like dandruff. Other times, larger pieces tumble downwards. The larger pieces are perilous. They go everywhere – people have to duck to avoid them. You are not sure, but you also suspect the ceiling is not good for your health or the health of anyone else.

It is lunchtime, and you are in the dining room – a cavernous space with echoey acoustics and too many children.

As per school procedure, all the students are sitting in their assigned places. At each table, there are three students plus one member of staff – the person whose job it is to ensure the students eat safely, not to mention behave. Your tablemates are Bobby and another boy called Nigel. Nigel has ginger hair and an unwashed look about him. According to your mum, Nigel is a perfectly ridiculous name for a small child because what is he, forty-five or something?

In any case, you are poking at your meal of Turkey Twizzlers and baked beans. You have already finished the accompanying mashed potato, even though it wasn't really mashed potato. Made from powder and water and kept in the fridge till it's needed, it's technically a potato substitute.

Opposite you, Bobby is banging on about paper. He is saying you can't eat paper. He is saying it is not good for people to eat it. Next to him, Nigel – who isn't the brightest – is telling Bobby he eats paper every day and he is fine. Bobby is saying he only thinks he's fine. Really, Bobby says, Nigel probably has a digestion issue he doesn't even know about. Nigel disagrees. He does a poo every week, he says, and wees all the time. There is no issue with his insides.

This conversation is not engaging, largely because they have these discussions every day. Nigel says he likes doing something. Bobby tells him he's dumb for liking to do something. The member of staff sits there like a lemon, telling them to shut up and eat their food.

On this day, however, Bobby and Nigel's conversation is rudely interrupted – not by the member of staff – but by the piece of ceiling that falls into your lunch. To be specific, the piece actually falls into your portion of baked beans. This causes tomato sauce to splatter over your shirt and tie.

'Oh dear,' the member of staff says.

You make a face at your food and the mess on your shirt. You try to clean the tomato sauce splatters with your palms but, in the end, you only succeed in smearing them around. Now you have bean sauce on your hands and your shirt. This is not ideal, so you try to wipe your hands on your skirt.

'Stop playing with your lunch,' the member of staff says. 'They spent a long time cooking that food. The least you can do is eat around the damage.'

You look at her in a way that you hope seems imploring. You don't know anything much about cooking. You haven't ever made anything more complicated than a glass of squash. That said, you just get the feeling that the dinner ladies didn't spend ages cooking this meal. You get the feeling they simply heated it up. Also, you really don't want to finish your meal now. Your meal has ceiling in it.

You know the piece of ceiling is small, at least as far as pieces of ceiling go. But it is a piece of ceiling nonetheless. The ceiling makes the meal look unappetising and you have a feeling that, much like paper, ceiling is not very easy to digest. Also, your dinner is now very cold.

You try to articulate these thoughts. But your thinking is sluggish. Indeed, every time you think a thought, another thought escapes you. It's like some wiring has gone wrong, some sort of fog has descended, like your tongue is far away from your brain.

'B-but . . .' you say. 'But . . .'

'But w-what?' the member of staff says, mocking your hesitation.

'But I c-can't—'

The member of staff throws her head back and laughs. 'Ah, ah, ah!' she says, wagging her finger right in your face. 'There is no such word as can't.'

Frustration bubbles within you like pasta water. You start to make something we shall from now on dub your noises.

Have I not mentioned your noises before? Your noises are sounds that you produce. They are somewhere between a hum, a moan, and a groan. They indicate that you are frustrated, annoyed, or overwhelmed. In this instance, the source of the frustration is relatively easy to locate – you are overwhelmed by the sheer idiocy of the member of staff assigned to your table. You know that 'can't' (and its longer form 'cannot') are perfectly real and useful words that most people employ at some point in their lives. Hearing an education professional telling you otherwise is, in your humble opinion, very strange.

But it's not just this. There are other things making you frustrated, annoyed, and overwhelmed too. For instance, it's really bright in the dining room, and the children are really loud – clattering their cutlery, scraping their plates, and speaking at an unnecessarily loud volume. Also, you are aware of Bobby staring at you. You start to sweat under his gaze. Your acrylic school jumper feels scratchy and not nice.

It must be said that your noises are not common. Not everyone makes these kinds of sounds. People tend to express their frustration in other ways. Sometimes they express their frustration via a conventional facial expression. Sometimes they utter a sentence such as, 'Oh Jesus, I've had enough of this.' With this in mind, when you make your noises, people tend to question what you are doing, or else give you a wide berth.

Today, it's Nigel's turn.

'Why is she making those sounds?' he says, leaning backwards in lieu of berthing you widely.

You try to muster up the strength to stop making your noises. You succeed – manage to lessen their volume, then stop doing them altogether. But you feel the need to do something else. The frustration can't just sit there. It has to go somewhere, be somewhere, manifest as something. And so, you do your body rocking – the other thing you do when you're frustrated. But alas, body rocking is another odd thing to do. Though not unheard of, it's largely uncommon – an easy target for ridicule.

'She was just making noises,' Nigel says, who seems frustrated now. 'Why was she making noises? Why's she moving like that?'

Behind you, a group of girls laugh. You don't know if they're laughing at what you are doing or what Nigel said. However, the thought they might be laughing at you distresses you, and so you resume your noises as you continue to rock.

'Stop that,' the member of staff tells you, pointlessly grabbing the sleeve of your jumper. 'Stop this silliness.'

You stop, put your hands on the back of your neck, massaging it weirdly.

Bobby pipes up. He puts down his knife and fork. His eyes dart from the Turkey Twizzlers to the member of staff to Nigel then back to the Turkey Twizzlers.

'She's not eating that,' he says, shaking his head, addressing the teacher but pointing at your meal. 'That's rank.'

'Excuse me,' the member of staff says, 'I think you'll find I'm in charge and she can eat that. She just has to eat around the mess.'

Bobby shakes his head again. 'No, she can't. It's rank. That's rank.'

The teacher shakes her head right back, eyes Bobby narrowly. 'Rank isn't a nice word,' she says.

Bobby shrugs. 'Rank might not be a nice word, but it's not a nice meal, is it?'

The member of staff clicks her tongue. 'What did you just say?'

'I didn't say anything.'

'Yes, you did.'

'Nah, I just did this and this.' Bobby re-enacts his shrug but not his comment. 'I shrugged.'

'I know you shrugged but you were also rude, weren't you?'

Bobby shakes his head. 'I don't care. She's not eating that.'

The member of staff and Bobby continue to quarrel. Out of the corner of your eye, you see a mouse darting from a corner of the dining room, stopping to pick up a random hunk of bread before darting out again. You do a little inside shiver. This school doesn't feel clean. Just the sight of the rodent makes you want to go home and scrub yourself in the bath.

The member of staff is now lecturing Bobby on social niceties. 'Talking back,' she says. 'Arguing, interrupting—'

'What's the matter with her?' Nigel interrupts, pointing at you. 'Why's she making those noises?'

Your noises have got even louder now. Now you are doing heavy and rapid rasping gasps. When you do this at home, either your mum dabs your forehead with a wet flannel and tells you to take deep breaths, or else tells you to snap out of it. You wonder if Bobby is going to do the same thing, but he does not.

Bobby looks at Nigel. He gestures at your plate of dinner, angry on your behalf. 'Well, Nigel,' he says. 'I think you'd make some noise too, if you were being asked to eat . . . to eat the ceiling!'

The member of staff stands up, folds her arms. 'All right. I'm going to have to ask you to leave, Bobby.'

Bobby stands up. For a second, it looks like he is going to accept her request. He doesn't even look that angry or annoyed any more. Not in his face, at least. As far as you can tell, Bobby doesn't look anything other than calm when he reaches over to your side of the table, picks up your plate, and lobs it right into the air.

If you could see in slow motion – if your vision had slo-mo capabilities – you'd now see individual beans splattering on white shirts, ceiling dust poofing into the air, and bits of Turkey Twizzlers flinging themselves far and wide. But of course, your vision lacks slo-mo capabilities, and so you simply see Bobby lob your plate of food, hear a smash, and feel some stray sauce spraying over your face. After this, Bobby gets up to vacate the room as per the member of staff's request.

It all happens very fast.

A few seconds of stunned silence ensue, followed by the sound of children making a great deal of noise. Their noises don't sound like your noises, but the sentiment behind them is much the same. The children are frustrated, annoyed, or overwhelmed. Some scream. Others yelp. Everyone does a lot of talking all at once – with many feeling the need to state the obvious.

'He threw her food,' they say. 'He threw her food. It went every-where and then he ran away.'

Some of the children nearer to your table are using their sleeves to wipe your lunch off their school uniforms. Your lobbed food achieved an impressive trajectory. Even kids by the wall are now splattered in tomato sauce. One girl has bean juice slicked over her white-blond hair.

The general hubbub turns into uproar and frustration. Nigel is whining in a high-pitched way. Somehow, the food on his crotch makes it look like he's soiled himself. Elsewhere, a previously laughing girl is crying. It is not until the deputy swoops in and yells 'Everyone get out of here now' that the noise subsides, and everyone gets on with their day.

Further reading:

The Art of Construction Management: Ceilings, Floors, and More

1 0

NORMALLY, THE CLASS AFTER lunch is a nice, sedentary way to end the day. The classroom is softly lit, and the lesson is about religion – a subject that doesn't demand too much of you.

In this class, you learn about the belief systems of Planet Earth. You learn that some say there was one god who created Planet Earth. You learn that some say there were many gods who created Planet Earth. You learn that some say everyone is born bad. You learn that some say you will be born over and over again. You learn so many things. Like a power shower, you let it wash over you.

'Thou shalt not lie with mankind, as with womankind: it is an abomination,' the chaplain is saying. 'Does anyone know what that means? Anyone at all?'

A deathly silence permeates the room. You don't know what it means. You know that lying – as in saying false things – is a sin, but you don't know what the word 'abomination' means. You might have heard it before, but you don't know.*

---

* You have not heard the word 'abomination' before. In any case, it means something disgusting or loathsome.

'Bobby, thou shalt not lie with mankind, as with womankind: it is an abomination. What does this passage mean, do you think? What's an abomination? Do you know?'

The silence continues. The teacher has evidently not registered that Bobby is not here. He gestures at the table Bobby usually sits at.

'Bobby? Pipe up, son. Can't hear you.'

'I don't think he's here, my lord,' a girl at your table says.

The teacher regards the girl weirdly. 'My lord?' he repeats, concernedly. 'There's no need to refer to me as "my lord".'

Titters ripple throughout the room.

'Where is he?' the chaplain asks. 'Gone to the toilet?'

The girl doesn't say anything. She shrugs, having evidently reached the end of her where-is-Bobby-based knowledge.

'Well, he must be having a poo because he's taking quite a while, isn't he?'

Titters re-ripple, louder this time. The children like this man and his use of the word 'poo'. You do too. You don't laugh, though. You are looking at your Bible. It has really thin pages and the text is really small. Usually, Bobby is the only one who understands it. If he were here, he would definitely know how to respond to the chaplain's question. You don't. Instead, you practise your signature over Leviticus 18:22.

'Do you know where Bobby is?' the chaplain asks you.

You emerge from your reverie. 'I haven't seen him since he threw my food everywhere at lunch.'

The chaplain raises his eyebrows. 'Say again?'

'I haven't seen him since he threw my food everywhere at lunch,' you say again.

'I didn't mean literally . . .' the chaplain says. 'Well, I guess that explains why some of you look so questionable today.'

There is a general murmur of agreement. The class does indeed look rather lunch-stricken. More than one student has a significant amount of tomato sauce on their shirt.

'I suppose I'll have to inform the powers that be . . .'

'God?' a boy asks.

The chaplain shakes his head. 'Not on this occasion,' he says seriously. 'On this occasion, it's just Sue.'

Twenty minutes later, you and the rest of the student population are outside sitting down on the ground, waiting for the emergency assembly to commence.

The playground is concrete and gravelled and not designed to be sat on sans chair. That said, it is common practice for this school's whole-school assemblies to be outside. In the dining hall – one of the two places that are big enough for everyone to sit down – there are mice and a variety of disgruntled dinner ladies mopping floors and wiping tables. In the sports hall – the other place that is big enough – the scaffolding propping up the ceiling gets in the way.

In any case, your schoolmates sit lined up in rows. They talk quietly among themselves. They are not raucous. They know better than to misbehave when an emergency assembly has been called.

You scan the crowd. Bobby is nowhere to be seen.

Eventually, the head teacher stands in front of the school and puts her hand up and says, 'Thank you, thank you.' The school silences itself.

The head teacher then speaks slowly and clearly. 'Now, I'm going to ask you something very important,' she says. 'And I want you lot to take what I am saying very seriously. Is that clear?'

'Yes, miss,' the school choruses.

'Does anyone know where Bobby is?'

Some individual children respond with individual responses of 'No, miss.' Others ask their neighbours if they know where Bobby is.

The head teacher raises her hand again. 'Thank you, thank you,' she says again.

Despite her 'Thank you, thank you', the hubbub continues. If anything, the children are louder than before.

'Excuse me!' she shouts. 'Pipe down!'

The school re-quietens itself. The head teacher lingers in the silence, then says, 'If you know where Bobby is, put your hand up.'

There is a long pause during which no one puts their hand up or even seems to breathe very much. In the distance, a wood pigeon coos.

The head teacher continues, 'If you don't know where Bobby is, put your hand up.'

All the pupils put their hands up.

Another teacher chips in. 'And if you don't know who Bobby is, put your hand up.'

No one puts their hands up, though you suspect that some people should.

The head teacher then says something to another teacher who says something to another teacher. They all appear to agree about something or other. There is a great deal of nodding.

She then points at you. 'Come to my office.'

Your stomach sinks. At first, you don't move. Then the kid next to you shoves you in the ribs.

'They mean you,' he says. 'Move it.'

You hesitate. Then, shaking, you get up. The whole school watches as you go.

'I DON'T KNOW IF he's my friend,' you say.

'He stood up for you at lunch.'

'He was sitting down.'

'Don't be deliberately obtuse.'

'I don't know what that means.'

The head teacher sighs. 'He stood up for you. That's what friends do for each other. I am pretty sure he's your friend.'

You open your mouth to speak. 'But—'

'Ah, ah, ah!' She raises her hand. 'Enough.'

You frown. You didn't know that sticking up for another person was a sign of friendship. You thought it was something that people did in films. But now you are reconsidering the past few weeks, you have to admit Bobby might be something like your friend. He has been nice to you in general, letting you copy his homework, sharing his Coca-Cola, even bringing you sweets from home one day. These are always what he calls old-man sweets. Werther's Originals. Parma Violets. Rhubarb and custard. Mint humbugs.

You sink back into your chair. You have been in this place once before. The room, not the chair. It's the head teacher's office, but it's more of a cupboard than an office. The head teacher is sitting behind her desk as she looks at you sternly. Her perfume smells sickly, like what you would imagine the colour pink would smell like.

'Do you know what I am going to ask you?'

You shake your head.

'I am going to ask you if you know where Bobby is.'

You wonder if this is her way of literally asking you where Bobby is or if she is simply informing you that she will imminently ask where Bobby is.

'Well?' she says.

You shake your head again. You don't know where Bobby is, though now that you are in this office you can rule this office out.

'Has the cat got your tongue?'

You think of cats (how stretchy they are), their tongues (how rough they are), and their tails (how mysterious they are). After many seconds spent trying to decipher the expression 'cat got your tongue', you accept that you have come up short.*

'Cat?' you ask.

The head teacher leans in. 'Are you going to speak? Are you going to tell me what you know? With words? By speaking to me using your words?'

You say nothing.

'What do you say?'

'Yes.'

'Yes, what?'

'I am going to speak to you using words.'

'What are you going to speak to me about using words?'

'About Bobby.'

---

* This is an idiom. Idioms are strings of words, divorced from their typical meanings. In this instance, 'Has the cat got your tongue?' just means 'I am annoyed you are not speaking.'

'So, you have seen Bobby?'

'Yes.'

'You have?'

'No.'

You can feel some of your noises brewing within you. This conversation is frustrating. The head teacher – it's like she's trying to not understand. Like she's being deliberately obtuse.

'I don't know where he is,' you say.

The head teacher drums her fingernails on her desk. 'I think you know where Bobby is. I think you're just not telling me. This is serious. Do you realise that?'

You sigh. You can tell that this conversation – as serious as it apparently is – is a lost cause. You open your mouth to speak, but nothing comes out. The head teacher continues to look at you. In your opinion, the expression on her face is unfriendly. You have survived unfriendlier stares before. But still, the unfriendliness bothers you.

'I'm going to leave you here,' she says. 'I'll come back later.'

'When?'

'Soon.'

'OK,' you say, though you don't like the idea of staying in this room for an unknown length of time. You are a little bit thirsty and this room is a little bit warm. Also, you don't know what you are allowed to do here, how you are supposed to pass the time. Being alone with your thoughts doesn't tickle your fancy. You would prefer almost anything else. Also, what does 'later' mean?*

---

* Depending on the context and the mood of the speaker, 'later' can mean in a few minutes, in half an hour, in an hour, in several hours, by tomorrow evening, or never.

The head teacher stands up to leave. You wonder if you can follow her. You do some rocking. You do some noises, then some breathing. Then the head teacher mutters something under her breath. The something sounds like 'Jesus Christ, not again'. Then the deputy bursts in.

'I found him!' the deputy says. 'In the sports hall. Up the scaffolding.'

The head teacher blinks at her colleague for a few seconds. Then her eyes flicker in your direction. 'Might I suggest you check your enthusiasm, seeing that we've got a guest.'

The deputy clearly wasn't expecting you to be here. Upon registering your presence, he takes a moment to collect his thoughts.

'Oh,' he says.

You relax. It seems that Bobby has been located and that you will no longer be locked in this suffocating cupboard. Perhaps it will be time for you to go back to your religion class. Or maybe it's even home time. You don't know. You've lost all sense of time. In any case, you find yourself wanting to do a little twirl. There is a lightness in your insides. Something like relief. Something like happiness.

'Well, we've located the missing boy.'

'OK.'

'We just need to get him down now.'

'OK.'

'He seems a bit reluctant to come down of his own accord.'

'Is that so?'

'What are you smiling at?' the deputy says.

You try to stifle your smile but find that you cannot. In fact, the more you try to suppress it, the more you feel it morph into a laugh. You shake your head. 'I don't know.'

'Well, I think I know who's going to get him back down,' the deputy says.

The head teacher raises her eyebrows. 'Should be worth a shot. Either that or the—'

'Fire service.'

'Yes.'

The deputy then points at you. 'All right. Follow me.'

IT TURNS OUT THE deputy is correct. Bobby is hiding in the sports hall, up the scaffolding. As far as hiding spots go, it's surprisingly good. After all, in a game of hide-and-seek, what normal person would think to look up?

'It's up to you now.'

'What?' you say. You are confused. As far as you are concerned, something being up to someone usually means that it is their choice whether they want to do whatever it is that is being proposed. However, there doesn't seem much room for choice here.

'Go get him down.'

'How?'

The deputy doesn't answer this directly. Instead, he says, 'Did you know that in Victorian times, they got little children to climb up chimneys to sweep them?'

'Yes,' you say, not seeing how this comment is relevant to the situation at hand.

'OK, then. He's your friend. Go up there. Coax him down.'

'How?'

'Speak to him. Talk him down. Use your powers of persuasion. Persuade him to see sense. Coax him back to safety. You can do it. I believe in you.'

You look at the rusty scaffolding. As the scaffolding is not a purpose-built climbing frame, there are significant gaps between the handholds and the footholds. And these really are only potential hand and footholds. The structure is really just a part-smooth, part-rusting monstrosity. It looks like it has been there for decades, holding up the crumbling ceiling, the creaking walls. You wonder how Bobby got so high.

You clear your throat. 'Bobby, can you come down?' you ask. Your voice is quiet, but you know it manages to travel. There is a short silence, then Bobby's tiny brown eyes look down at you, holding your gaze for what feels like a very long time. He gives you a little wink.

You continue: 'We will be really nice to you when you come down. We will do a nice thing together. Or separately. Whatever you want.'

'This isn't working,' the deputy says. 'Go up there and get him down.'

'But how will that help?'

'We have these mats everywhere, you see? They're there so that, if you guys fall, it won't hurt.'

You frown.

'Grab him and bring him down.' The deputy raises his eyebrows in a way that is clearly supposed to communicate something to you but doesn't.

'I'm not good at sport,' you say. 'If I climb up, I will probably fall and then die.'

'No, you won't,' he says. 'You won't fall. We're here, anyway. And the mats are here.'

You open your mouth to speak but then think better of it. You guess you might as well give it a go. You take your school shoes off, because you want to use the grippyness of your bare feet. After this, you do some stretching. Then you look up again, really crane your neck. The structure towers above you. Bobby is all the way up there. You can make out his dark curls. You grip two metal bars and hoick yourself up – one metre, two metres, higher, higher, higher, high. The rust is rough on your bare feet. The metal structure is cold. It's lucky you are a little tall for your age – if you were of average height, you wouldn't be able to reach the bars so easily.

Halfway up, you make the mistake of looking back down. The structure had looked tall to you previously – but not this tall. The teachers in the doorway below you look tiny like ants. You take a deep breath. The deep breath in question doesn't feel like it's deep enough. You try another one. Same problem. You are scared. Except for your brief experiences in planes, you have never been up so high.

You try to steady your shaking hand, decide to throw Bobby a loud whisper. He is now just a couple of metres upwards and side-wards from you.

'Bobby, why are you up here?' you say in a loud whisper.

Bobby doesn't look at you but you see that he has something wrong with his face. It is redder than normal and his eyes are puffy. As I imagine it, he doesn't know how to answer your question, how to say he did a stupid thing followed by an even stupider thing. He also doesn't know how to tell you he is feeling really bad – like he wants to sit at the top of this decaying school forever and a day, till he turns into a statue, till he expires in a puff of rust.

'Why are *you* up here?' he asks, deflecting the question back at you.

'To talk you down.'

Bobby frowns. 'I'm not a suicide.'

'What's that?'

'You don't know?'

You shake your head.

'Oh.'

There is a pause. Below you, the teachers are talking about something or other. You can't make out what the conversation is about — their voices are getting tangled in the cavernous acoustics. The reverberations are unpleasant, fill your head.

'I wouldn't stand there. It's wobbly,' he says.

'Where?'

'There.'

'Oof,' you say, regaining your footing. 'Thanks. We should get down. If I start climbing down, will you follow me?'

Bobby nods.

'Yeah?' you say.

'Yeah,' he says. 'Need a wee anyway.'

'OK,' you say, grinning.

On the way back down, you tread on the wobbly slat again, which causes you to slip. When Bobby sees you slip, he instinctively outstretches both hands to grab you — something that causes him to also slip. If you were nimbler or daintier, you could have recovered from this mistake, and the teaching staff wouldn't have watched as you and Bobby fell many metres onto the floor.

But here you are. The teachers are gathered around – all of them saying words to the effect of what were you thinking, what were you doing, that was way too fast. As you suspected, blue mats that were designed to cushion your fall do no such thing. You reel on the floor, the whole room spinning and spinning spin spin. Beside you, Bobby is lying strangely quiet. Moments later, he pipes up, starts to make a sound you've never before heard a person make.

Further reading:

Is Your Child Just Pretending to Be Ill?
10 Signs of a Broken Arm
All in the Arm: How to Overcome Your Arm Injury

YOU ARE STANDING OUTSIDE the head teacher's cupboard. You are supposed to be waiting there nicely, thinking benign thoughts while you gaze at the posters decorating the corridors. At least, that's what your dad told you to do.

You look at the posters. They show off the work of children you don't know. For example, there is a poster featuring a diagram of a tongue. According to the diagram, the tip can taste salty flavours, the back can taste bitter flavours, the sides can detect sour flavours, and the middle can detect both umami and sweet flavours.

You think about this for a second before becoming irretrievably bored. Once, just moments ago, the tongue diagram was interesting. Now, it's far less interesting than the conversation taking place inside the head teacher's cupboard. As the conversation concerns you – specifically your past, your present, and your future – you want to listen in. You want to know if you will be going to school tomorrow, the next day, the next day, and the next day, or else if you will be arranging to spend your time otherwise and elsewhere.

You press your ear to the door, then your nose to the glass. You can make out your dad (he is sitting in the chair in front of the desk), the head teacher (she is sitting in the chair behind the desk), and the deputy (he is standing cramped in the corner).

'We really can't manage her needs here,' the head teacher is saying. 'We just can't.'

There is a pause. You wonder if your dad is giving them one of his looks. Generally, these looks are reserved for workmen who are trying to rip him off, sneezers who don't cover their mouths, and civil enforcement officers who try to enforce civility.

'Which needs, specifically?' you hear him say.

'All of them, really,' the deputy says.

Your dad shakes his head, grabs his bag, stands up. 'And what is she supposed to do now? From now till September?'

For a while, the deputy doesn't say anything and neither does the head teacher.

'With the greatest respect,' the deputy says, 'that's not our problem.'

Ten minutes later, your dad is driving you home. I imagine that, during this drive, he replays the conversation with the head teachers in his head. From what they said, he understands you and this Bobby boy initiated a food fight. After this, you both put your health at risk by scaling the height of a temporary scaffolding structure.

According to the teachers, these two incidents amount to blatant disregard for the rules and a total absence of common sense – and are alone enough to merit a request to leave. But coupled with the fact you are struggling so much with your reading and writing, the request to leave is a firm one.

You are fidgeting in the passenger seat, undoing your tie, redoing your tie. You are aware of your dad glancing at you. You know that sometimes he doesn't like it when you fidget. You know that sometimes he doesn't like it when you move at all.

'Want this?' your dad asks suddenly, handing you a lollipop he had in his pocket. The lollipop's flavour is strawberry and cream. You know this because the label reads strawberry and cream. You wonder if strawberry and cream constitutes a salty, sweet, sour, bitter, or umami flavour. You unwrap it, stare at the light-pink lolly suspiciously.

'Is this bitter?' you ask.

Your dad frowns. 'Is it better?'

'Bitter. The lolly. Is it bitter? The flavour?'

'Um.' He indicates to turn left but then makes a right turn. 'Sweet, probably.'

You don't like this response. His use of 'probably' is no good. You don't want probably, you want certainty. 'Probably?' you say.

'Yes,' your dad says.

You can't remember which part of the tongue is supposed to accommodate sweetness, but through a process of elimination, it will be relatively easy to find out. With your tongue stuck out as far as it can go, you put the lolly on the front bit, the middle bit, the middle side, the other middle side, the back, and the very back – something that makes you splutter and gag and cough a little. As far as you can tell, all the parts of your tongue are registering the sweetness, meaning that either your tongue or the diagram is wrong or that there is some fault in the way you are conducting the experiment. Just to double-check, you opt to redo the experiment. This time, however, you lower the sun visor and angle it just so before sticking out your tongue. With the precision of mirror-based experimentation on your side, you again try the side bits, the middle bits, and the front bit. It is when you move on to the back bits that your dad decides that enough is enough.

Abruptly, he pulls into a lay-by, cuts the engine, undoes his seat belt, and turns to you. 'What are you doing?' he asks. Though he has never once hurt you, you recoil now, wondering if this will be the first time. You look at his cold, hard stare, countering it with one that is gormless.

'I'm checking to see, um . . .' You trail off. It's a complicated thing, to explain what you are doing. 'I don't know where the sweet bit is. This is sweet but I think all of it's sweet. The strawberry sides. The middle umami. But all of it's sweet. The diagram corridor.'

'Christ. You sound like you're having a stroke.'

You are taken aback. Normally, your dad speaks to you softly, with words that are gentle, in a tone that is kind. Right now, though, your dad is all jaws and unkindness. Hitting the steering wheel, he speaks himself into a small but frightening frenzy.

'What are you doing?' he says. 'What the fuck are you doing? What are you doing?'

Your dad hits the horn. The sound – sudden, loud, and horn-like – makes you jump and also startles a passer-by. The passer-by is on the pavement, wheeling one of those shopper things but also carrying a walking stick. When your dad presses the horn, she yelps, stops wheeling her groceries, and curses.

'Cunt!' she yells.

Your dad winds the window down, leans out. 'What did you just say?'

'I called you a cunt.'

Your dad looks a little surprised or confused, then maybe a little hostile or angry. You tense, brace yourself for whatever insult exchange is going to come. You wonder if he is good at exchanging insults.

It turns out he is not. 'Yeah? Well, you are an old, ugly bitch,' he says.

Despite your youth, you know that is an inadequate response, that being a cunt is far worse than being an old, ugly bitch.

The woman seems to agree with you. She wields her walking stick in his general direction and thwacks it thrice on the car bonnet. 'Well, it's better than being a cunt who threatens his son!'

Your dad turns the engine back on. 'She's a girl.'

'She looks like a boy!' The woman picks up her shopper. 'You've got a daughter that looks like a son!'

'She's a girl, she's a girl, she's a girl!'

Your dad puts his belt back on, cursing the lady under his breath as he pulls out. You don't like your dad like this. You don't like him whacking the steering wheel or threatening members of the public or speeding on the dual carriageway or telling strangers you're a girl, you're a girl, you're a girl.

You don't like it because he is being loud but also wrong. You are not a girl – you're an alien. You find this very sad – to be an alien – and so you cry. Your dad brakes too late at a roundabout, another car beeps at him, and for some reason this makes you cry harder – so hard your tears go silent before they are loud again.

In a mile and a half, you will be back home. You don't want to be back home. You don't want to be anywhere. You feel like you could cry for miles and miles more. You feel like you could cry for 25,000 miles – the circumference of the globe. You feel like you could cry for 240,000 miles – the distance to the Moon. You feel like you could cry for 140 million miles – the distance to Mars. You feel like you could cry for this much but also more, also a lot, lot more.

Further reading:

So Homeschooling Is Right for Your Child

Part Two

12

TIME PASSES GLOOPILY. THE Earth spins on its axis while it loops around the Sun. A variety of plants flourish. A variety of plants die. Gardeners dig. Leaders make tough decisions. Trains arrive late or not at all. Some people lose faith, others lose heart, still others lose hope. Babies are born furious. Old folks die with a sense of impending doom.

In other words, it's three in the morning, a few years later. You are older and wiser, sitting on the rug on the carpet in the living room. You can't sleep. Suffering as you do from a pesky ailment known as insomnia, you often can't.

It's funny you have insomnia. And by funny, I mean strange. Because what on earth keeps you awake at night? What have you got to worry about? You don't have enough experience to have regrets. You don't have a job or kids or a mortgage. You don't have a divorce or debt or a marriage. You're a child. After another stint of homeschooling, you're a student of mainstream education once more – attending your latest school Monday to Friday, mostly without issues. You have nothing to worry about. Because you have nothing to worry about, you are supposed to sleep – if not like a baby – then at least like someone who is still pretty young.

Or at least that's what your auntie says when your mum tells her over the phone that you have been up all night again, pacing the house, watching TV, eventually falling asleep in front of it. 'Not normal' is the phrase she uses. 'It's not normal that she's doing this.'

It's normal to you, though. From around nine p.m., you lie sleepy yet sleepless till, at midnight, you accept defeat – trudge downstairs to while away the night-time hours in front of the TV. Sometimes, you fall asleep in front of its blue and fuzzy glow. Tonight, however, you have remained decidedly awake.

On the TV, a documentary starts to play. Initially, you have no interest in the fuzzy grey people speaking on the fuzzy grey screen, and you scarcely pay attention as you skim the top of the rug with the palm of your right hand one way, then the other way, then the other. You do this over and over. The rug is fuzzy and nice, and repetitive movement helps you relax, think, focus, be at one with the world, or at least not rage against it.

In the documentary on the TV, a woman with crooked teeth is talking to someone the camera doesn't let you see. Perhaps, much like you, she doesn't much like making eye contact. Or perhaps she is lost in thought as she speaks about books but also the past. Behind this woman are books. She is also wearing glasses. This is how you know the woman is smart because, in TV land, only smart people sit in front of books while wearing glasses.

In the documentary on the TV, the woman is speaking about something called Beinecke MS 408. Beinecke MS 408 is something called a manuscript.* If you consult a dictionary, you will find that the word 'manuscript' has four or five meanings – one of which says something like 'a book or document written before printing was invented'. Beinecke MS 408 goes with this meaning. It is basically a book, and is more commonly known as the Voynich Manuscript.

The Voynich Manuscript was discovered by a man called Wilfrid Voynich in 1912, but it is not from 1912. The Voynich Manuscript is in fact very old; carbon dating has told us as much, and also it just looks old. It looks like someone's parent or guardian has dabbed homework with a cold teabag and then popped said homework in the oven – except it looks more convincing.

As it happens, it is kind of colourful too. There are pictures of green plants the shape of stars, of orange-brown roots the shape of snakes, of ghostly humans the shape of alchemists. But it's only *kind of* colourful. To you and me, it looks as though the author ran out of colouring pencils and just had to make do with what he had left. But, back in the day, they didn't really have colouring pencils. Back in the day, they didn't really have much at all – not even teabags and not even picture books. Instead, they had smallpox and serious books – sacred texts, lists of taxes collected and owed, lists of children born and later led astray, lists of marriages between people doomed never to divorce.

Anyway. You're sitting on the rug on the carpet, watching TV,

---

* The 'MS' stands for 'manuscript'. It is an abbreviation, created to save people the time and effort of writing the 'anu' to follow the 'm' and the 'cript' to follow the 's'.

and the woman on the TV is talking about her late husband and the Manuscript. Specifically, she is recounting the day her late husband said he had deciphered the Voynich Manuscript.

'Now my husband John came up to me one day,' the woman says, her voice a million cigarettes deep, 'he came up to me and he said to me, Margaret, I must tell you something, and I said, what is it, John, and then he said, the Voynich Manuscript, darling, I think it must be from another planet, it really doesn't make sense, I do believe it is an alien endeavour.'

It's after her alien comment that your interest is piqued. Piqued, you're now paying attention. You inch closer to the TV.

'And now of course I said, John, you must be working yourself too hard, you must be overtired. An alien endeavour? What rot. Of course, he was laughed right out of the room when he presented his findings to his university colleagues. Took to drink not long after and that was that, I'm afraid. Popped his clogs two weeks after his fortieth birthday. Most sad.'

The woman on the TV does not say 'most sad' convincingly. Instead, she says it in a way that makes her seem indifferent about the death of her husband.

The TV camera zooms into images of the Voynich Manuscript itself. It is a strange-looking thing. A picture-and-word book, it is full of alien plants, zodiac signs, and women, all accompanied by rows of text in an alien language. It looks lovely, brilliant, and also small – the hand of the person showing the camera the Manuscript is about as big as the Manuscript itself.

And then the shot of the Manuscript fizzles into a shot of the woman which then fizzles into the glass of whisky she is apparently holding. This is how the documentary maker tells the audience that this is a poignant moment. After this, the documentary maker presenter person appears in a quadrangle, wearing a long coat. He walks seriously towards the camera.

'Perhaps John was right,' the documentary maker presenter person says, his feet clipping against the paving stones. 'Perhaps aliens did write the Voynich Manuscript. Or perhaps John was mad as a hatter. We don't know. His knowledge was lost to ridicule, his mind to alcoholism, his notes to a fire. Whatever its history, the secrets of the Manuscript remain unknown.'

The screen goes dark and the credits roll. Over the credits, a man with a Scottish accent explains that the next programme will be about golf. You turn off the TV, the noise of the documentary's closing lines lingering. You are currently having many thoughts – in your brain, the cogs are whirring around – but you are mostly just having feelings. Until now, you didn't realise that aliens existed, at least not for real. Until now, you didn't realise they had their own language.

To you, it makes a lot of sense. It makes a lot of sense because sometimes you feel like your language isn't your language. Other people say things and you don't know what they mean. Other people do things and you don't know what they mean either. There is a disconnect, something profoundly wrong. You feel this strongly, feel it in your bones.

You go to the kitchen, get yourself a mug of milk, and trudge your bare feet up the carpeted stairs. You go to bed, tuck yourself in. Maybe you are not alone in the universe after all. Maybe you are just alone on Planet Earth. With this comforting thought, you fall into a deep, restorative sleep. The sleep is good for you. It helps you grow.

Further reading:

The Voynich Manuscript (Beinecke MS 408)

13

IT'S LIKE THERE WAS an on–off switch somewhere in you. Before learning about the Manuscript, you were off. Since learning about the Manuscript, you are on – alive, kicking, and awake. You find yourself thinking about what words are. About what it means to understand words. About how weird it all is. Words are just ink on a page, arranged in a fashion dictated by convention – and yet they mean things because people have decided that they do. That's weird.

Today, your mum is chopping up onions. Or perhaps 'hacking at' would be a more appropriate phrase, because your mum is chopping the onions not only at speed but also with carelessness. The pieces of onion are all different sizes. Your mum seems upset about this. She is crying about this. Or else, the onions are hurting her eyes. Or else, she is crying about something else. You can't tell. She is a complicated lady.*

---

* Your dad told you this once. He was crouching next to you as you lay there in bed. He apologised for your mum's earlier behaviour, even though it wasn't his fault. Then he said, 'She's a complicated lady, that one.'

In any case, you decide to make her feel better by approaching her silently and wrapping your arms around her big, soft belly without warning. Your mum doesn't appreciate this.

'Jesus!' she says. 'Why would you do that?'

You don't say anything. Instead, you squeeze harder, maintaining the hug.

'I'm holding a knife,' she says. An onlooker might interpret this sentence as a threat. You, however, know she just means that you should be careful around complicated people holding knives, that it's not a good idea to startle them.

Despite this, you keep yourself wrapped around her. Because who wouldn't want a hug from you? You are just so lovely. You look up at your mum. You can see the pores of her face skin and the hair up her nostrils. For reasons that escape both you and her, you sniff the knife.

'Get off,' your mum says, wriggling herself free. 'What do you want?'

You shrug, say nothing. She gets back to cooking. She is cooking soup but also toast. This seems to be a stressful activity. Red-faced, she is leaning over the bubbling saucepan.

'Mum,' you say eventually.

'Yes?'

'What's a manuscript?'

Your mum wipes her eyes and nose with the sleeve of her jumper. Behind her, you notice a dark spool of smoke rising from the toaster. You cannot be sure, but you think this means either the toast is on fire or will be shortly, or else the toaster is on fire or will be shortly.

'It's like a work in progress,' she says.

'And what's a work in progress?' you ask, your eyes now fixed on the toaster.

'It's like when something isn't finished. A book that isn't finished.'

The smoke alarm goes off. Your mum jumps, clocks the toaster, and curses. She unplugs it, shakes the black and smoking contents into the sink. The smoke alarm is loud, so much so you can barely hear your voice as you use it to ask another question.

'So, would it be a manuscript if I wrote a load of—'

'Urgh!' Your mum almost drops the saucepan on the floor.

'Would you – can you go find your dad, please?'

'Where's Da—'

'Garage! He's in the garage.'

Your dad is indeed in the garage. He is teaching your cousin how to put a new chain on an old bike.

'What's she doing here?' your cousin asks. From his manner, tone, and stance, you can tell he considers the garage to be a space in which you are not allowed.

'That's not a nice thing to say,' your dad says, before turning to you to ask the exact same thing. 'What are you doing here, sweet pea?'

You temporarily forget what you are doing here in the garage: the room of half-used paint cans, boxes, bikes, things that are dusty and old, things that are miscellaneous, things that only exist to be packed up when you all move to another house or die.

'What's a manuscript?' you say eventually.

Your dad blinks at you. 'Sorry?'

You repeat yourself. 'What's a manuscript?'

'Ah.' Your dad is still looking at you weirdly. You can't make his expression out, but it gives you a feeling in your chest you don't like.

'Like a book,' he says after a while. 'It's just another word for a type of book.'

You nod, stay quiet.

He pauses. 'Why do you ask?'

'No reason,' you say. You are out of the garage already. You are on your way upstairs already. You are already up and up and up and up.

Further reading:

The Dictionary

I 4

LITTLE ALIEN, DO YOU know about something called frequency bias? Also known as the Baader-Meinhof phenomenon,
frequency bias is a cognitive bias, which is in turn a fancy phrase
for a trick of the mind. It's that thing when, after learning about
something for the first time, you start to notice that this something
is everywhere.

For instance, a person might learn what a word means and then,
in the days and weeks that follow, this person might notice this
word everywhere. And it works with other things too. For instance,
a person might get a particular make of car, then start seeing this
particular make of car everywhere they go.

When you first learn about the word 'manuscript', you start
hearing people talk about manuscripts everywhere. In the school
corridor, you overhear a teacher saying the word 'manuscript'
to another teacher. Why? You have no idea. You didn't hear the
rest of their conversation. You just heard the word 'manuscript'.
Similarly, in the car on the way to a swimming lesson, you hear a
man on the radio speaking about another manuscript. And walking

through the town centre, you swear you hear a kid mention a manuscript too.

You perceive these instances as evidence of a sudden, generalised interest in manuscripts, and this strikes you as odd.

But you're not sure if people are talking about the same manuscript as you. You're not sure if they are referring to the one you learnt about on TV, the one whose language and script remain unknown, the one whose full name you can't remember. The Something Manuscript. It is known as the Something Manuscript. You think. You don't know. You can't remember.

You wonder if you'll ever get to see it. You want to see the Something Manuscript. You want to hold and feel it. It intrigues you. Intensely. Even if you don't remember what it's called. Even if you don't know where it is. How to find it. How to have it. How to hold it. What it means. Maybe, one day, you'll trip over and fall and you'll find it just lying there. Maybe, one day, you'll embrace criminality and steal it from an extra-secure bank vault buried underground.

You clear your throat.

The staff member at the front desk of the school library looks up. She has curly hair and so many freckles it is hard to see which part of her face is actually her face and which part of her face is freckle.

'Hello,' she says.

'Hello,' you say.

'Is there something you want?'

You nod. 'Do you have any manuscripts,' you say, forgetting to make your sentence go up at the end to indicate that what you're saying is a question.

'Manuscripts?' the woman says.

'Yeah, like old books except they're manuscripts.'

The woman cocks her head to one side, narrows her eyes. 'Nope,' she says with a curtness that borders on rudeness.

Your little chest deflates. 'None at all?'

The woman looks you up and down. 'This isn't a proper library,' she says. 'This is a school library. We don't have anything that interesting.'

You nod. 'OK,' you say. You try to hide your disappointment. You had to be brave to speak to this staff member at the front desk of the school library. Alas, it seems this bravery has not paid off.

The woman gets up from her chair, then goes to the nearest bookshelf. Here there are a large number of *Mike and Mark* books. You are very familiar with them. You read them all the time. Even though they're too young and too easy for you now, your teachers still insist you still need to read them, that you're not quite ready to spread your literary wings, that you're still finding them difficult.*

The woman returns to the front desk. 'So, we've got *Mike and Mark's Trip to the Moon*,' she says, placing the pile of books before you. 'And we've got *Mike and Mark's Trip to the Supermarket*, *Mike and Mark's Trip to America*. *Mike and Mark's Trip to France*. But nothing old. Nothing interesting. Nothing famous.'

'OK, then.'

'Why do you ask?'

'Why?'

---

* This is false. You read more advanced tomes at home. At home, you read proper books. Often, these are the books your mum also reads – that's how good you are at reading.

'Yeah, why are you interested in old books? I mean, what are you, like, eight?'

Hurt, you direct a scowl at the woman. You are most certainly not eight.* 'No reason,' you say.

The woman frowns. 'I feel that's not true.'

You look outside. A few of your schoolmates are running riot on the concrete but most are just milling around.

You try the truth. 'Well, I saw a documentary about a manuscript and a library and I wondered if every library had manuscripts or if it was just some libraries that had manuscripts.'

The woman nods. The truth may have worked. Her curiosity now seems sated.

'Do some libraries have fancy kinds of manuscripts and books,' you ask, again forgetting to make your voice go up at the end.

'Sure.'

'Which ones?'

The woman shrugs. 'I don't really know.'

'Like maybe the one in town?' you suggest, trying to be helpful.

The woman smiles. You don't notice that her smile is not a nice smile. You just notice it is a smile. For good measure, you smile back.

'The library in town?' the woman says, still smiling.

'Yeah.'

'Sure,' the woman says. 'Sure, the town centre has loads of that stuff. They'll sort you right out.'

At this moment, another staff librarian appears, basically from

---

* You are twelve. If you were eight, you would not be at this particular school as this particular school does not cater to eight-year-olds.

out of nowhere. She is a lot older than the woman with freckles. You have met her before. She always wears dangly earrings, has very few teeth, and speaks like she regularly reads the dictionary.

'Now that's a despicable attitude to have,' the older librarian says. 'This poor boy comes here to you with an enquiring mind and you tell him to go to town.'

The other woman blinks. 'I think this is a gi—'

'This is anathema to what we stand for,' the older librarian says. 'When we are presented with an enquiring mind, we attend to said enquiring mind with alacrity.'

The woman with freckles opens her mouth. 'I—'

'If a small boy or girl presents themselves to us with a mind enquiring about the nature and richness of our library, it is our job to elaborate, enlighten, engage,' the older librarian continues. 'These are the three e's. The three e's! Do they not teach you the three e's any more?'

'I just . . .' the woman with freckles says. 'But we don't have any old manuscripts here. We barely have anything.'

The older librarian narrows her eyes at the woman with freckles. 'We have four state-of-the-art computer machines.'

The older librarian allows her gaze to rest on you for a moment. A pause ensues. During this pause, you get the feeling she is trying to figure something out. Maybe she is trying to decide whether you are an alien or a human, or maybe just whether you are a girl or a boy. Your hair is short and, as you are still prepubescent, you have no childbearing hips or womanly curves. Your gender-based energy is also ambiguous. There is nothing rambunctiously boyish or carefully girly about you. You tread the line between nothing and neither.

97

After a moment of reflection, the older librarian comes over to you and wraps one arm around you. Unsure of what to do with your own arms, you leave them dangling, then sort of wrap them around her stomach. Her belly is big and soft.

'I will help you,' the older librarian tells you. 'You're interested in books?'

'Yes,' you say.

'Old books?'

'Yes.'

'Old books about what, darling?'

'Old books about words and languages that are old. And manuscripts.'

The older librarian nods solemnly, then snaps her fingers at the woman with freckles. 'Fetch this child an appropriate book.'

'Which one?' the woman asks. 'We literally have nothing here. That's my point.'

'Figuratively. You mean we figuratively have nothing here,' the older librarian says.* 'But actually, we do. I don't know how many times I have to explain this. We really, really do.'

The woman nods, then disappears. Many minutes later, she reappears to hand you a *Mike and Mark* book titled *Mike and Mark Visit a Group of Early Humans*.

The older librarian nods. 'See,' she says to the woman with freckles. 'What did I say?' The older librarian peers at *Mike and Mark Visit a Group of Early Humans*.

---

* If this older librarian had read the dictionary more carefully, she would have noticed that one of the definitions of 'literally' is 'in effect' or 'virtually'. Why? Dictionaries are descriptive, not prescriptive. They describe how words are actually used. They don't give out opinions on how words should be used.

'Do we get, like, proper books here?' you ask.

The older librarian frowns. 'What do you mean proper books?'

'Like, books that aren't *Mike and Mark* books. Like normal books.'

The older librarian looks profoundly confused. 'Why would you want to read anything other than a *Mike and Mark* book?'

You shrug. 'I don't know.'

'This is a special edition *Mike and Mark* book anyway. It's very advanced. You'll be engaged, I'm sure.'

You glance sceptically at *Mike and Mark Visit a Group of Early Humans*, before dutifully checking it out, and shoving it in your bag. Outside, the bell rings and masses of youths start to swarm their way back to class.

There is a pause. During this pause, you aren't sure if you should still be hanging around. Or if you have permission – nay, an obligation – to leave.

'Are you all right?' the older librarian asks you suddenly.

Startled, you say yes.

'Yes,' you say.

'Very good,' the older librarian says.

'Very good,' the woman with freckles also says.

'Very good,' you say.

Further reading:

Mike and Mark's Trip to the Supermarket
Mike and Mark's Trip to America
Mike and Mark's Trip to France

1 5

THAT NIGHT, YOUR MUM and dad tuck you into bed. You close your eyes. You wait for them to click the door shut. Then you wait for them to check on you five minutes later. Then you wait for them to go to bed themselves. Then you turn your light back on and prop yourself up.

Mike and Mark Visit a Group of Early Humans is, like every *Mike and Mark* book you have ever read, about two boys called Mike and Mark. One is blond and thin. The other is ginger and thin. Both have rosy cheeks and long arms. Despite the innumerable adventures they go on, Mike and Mark never seem to grow up.

In this particular book, Mike and Mark have travelled back in time to the era of early humans, who are developing an early language. These early humans are not babbling like children – they are not saying 'dadada', 'bababa', or 'tatata' – figuring out what noises they can make by simply making them. Instead, thanks to evolution, their oesophaguses and airways are separating, their tongues are becoming agile and strong, their vocal cords becoming capable of producing a variety of sounds.

In this *Mike and Mark* book, Mike and Mark actually only have minor roles. Mostly they stand there with their anachronistic clipboards – playing the role of anthropologists and making notes on the changes they are witnessing. To aid the pacing of the plot, time is sped up a gazillion-fold.

Mike and Mark hear the early humans making a variety of noises to one another. Over the course of years, they observe the early human community coming to a consensus about what sounds should denote what things. This keeps on happening. In the end, the early humans end up attaching sounds to everything in the whole wide world – not only concrete things such as spears and rocks, but also feelings such as anger, states such as death, and concepts such as hierarchy and the idea of language itself. As the sounds and shapes of their language get more complicated, so does the wiring that makes up the early humans' minds. For better or worse, with the development of language, the early humans get smarter.

Language spreads like a contagion. While Mike and Mark are witnessing just one early human community, words are sprouting up everywhere around Planet Earth. There is variation. Some communities have subcommunities, each with its own dialect. Other communities are more isolated, speaking incomprehensible languages whose resemblance to other tongues is, at most, passing.

At some point, Mike and Mark try to communicate with the early humans.

'You there!' Mark cries to a female early human. 'What are you doing with that stone? Are you writing down your language? Are you crafting yourself a tool?'

At this, the female early human smiles, but says nothing. She does not understand modern English. She is also not writing down her language. Written languages won't come about for ages.

A little later, the same human says some incomprehensible words to her son.

'This language sounds like Greek to me, Mark!'

'You're mistaken, Mike. Greek won't come about for millennia. Neither will the country of Greece. The tectonic plates have yet to form that land mass! That's how far in the past we have travelled!'

Our protagonists witness the rise and fall of oceans, the formation of volcanoes, and the erosion of whole mountain ranges. Meanwhile, thousands of languages grow, flourish, take flight on the back of sound waves, and then disappear. Most of these languages consist of sounds. Some of these languages consist of hand signs. All of them consist of gesture. All of them have rules. These rules need no real explanation; they are innate, implicit, even to small children. Indeed, children and adults know the rules without knowing that they know the rules. They acquire the ability to navigate these rules with dexterity.

After many, many thousands of years, some humans acquire the ability to write down their words.

These are no longer early humans. They are just humans. Mike and Mark get very excited when this happens. You know this because they say things like 'Ah, so this is writing!' and 'Wow, it's exciting they've developed their own writing system!' and 'That alphabet looks alien to me!'

That said, most of the humans don't write down their languages. This isn't because their languages are less interesting because, when it comes to language, there is no such thing as less interesting. Some societies simply get around to writing their words down, others don't, and that's it.

But the ones that are etched in stone – e.g. Sumerian, Hebrew, Greek, Latin, and Chinese – are destined to be remembered. The ones that exist just in time and space – most of the ones Mike and Mark witness – are destined to be forgotten.

Mike and Mark return to the present day. They try to remember what the early humans sounded like, but their memories are not great and they soon give up.

Further reading:

Mike and Mark Visit a Group of Early Humans

16

THE PROBLEM IS THAT the town centre and its library are full of people who can kidnap or kill you. They can hold you up at knifepoint, fill you up with nefarious ideas, or instil in you a distaste for authority. So, no, your mum doesn't want you to go into town by yourself. You're still too young.

'I just don't want you hanging around town,' your mum says, scrubbing the saucepan so hard it's like she wants to erode it. 'There are all sorts in town. I don't want you hanging with all sorts.'

You think of the phrase 'all sorts'. Then you think she could have just said no. She didn't have to dismiss your suggestion so thoroughly. As far as you're concerned, her refusal has been excessive and so unrelentingly negative that you half resolve to never ask her anything again.

Your dad comes downstairs, carrying the newspaper he was reading on the toilet.

'Hey, Dad,' you say forlornly, as you move the beans around your plate of breakfast.

He eyes the pair of you suspiciously. 'What's the matter? What's going on?'

'Apparently,' you say, 'I'm not old enough to go to the library in town by myself.'

'That's right,' your mum says, pouring more washing-up liquid.

Your dad frowns. 'I can take her,' he says. 'I'm going to work today anyway.'

'But it's Saturday,' your mum says.

'It's no problem,' your dad says, going about his leisurely I'm-leaving-the-house routine, patting his pocket to check his wallet is there, patting his other pocket to check his keys are there, then repeating these steps one more time.

'But it's Saturday,' your mum repeats, louder this time.

Your dad blinks at her.

'Why are you going to the office today?'

'Oh,' he says. 'Got to work. It's so busy. Hectic.'

'But why?'

'Work is mad these days.'

'Mad?'

'Yeah. Mad.'

'You've never been in on a Saturday before.'

'It's never been this mad before.'

'You've never used the word "mad" before either.'

'Sure I have.'

'Not like that, you haven't.'

There is a pause. During this pause, I imagine your mum is assessing what your dad is saying. She probably wonders if it's true that his work is busy these days, if that's actually the reason he's going to the office on a Saturday. She also wonders whether going to the library isn't a big deal after all. Compared to the possibility of an extramarital affair, your solo trip to town certainly seems less of a big deal.*

'But isn't she too young to go into town alone? Isn't the library full of troubled people who might—'

'She'll be fine.'

'I think she's too young.'

Your dad shrugs again. He doesn't want to rise (or stoop) to the role of reassurance provider. He just wants to focus on his work for the day. His work is currently mad. As it happens, he's an actuary. This means he assesses risk for a living. With regard to you and the library, he sees very little risk of harm.

'She'll be fine, she'll be fine. When I was a kid, my mum and dad kicked me out of the house at nine a.m. and didn't want me back till teatime.'

'What did you have for lunch?' you ask, startling your parents. Though they were literally just talking about you, you were being so quiet they had forgotten you were there.

'I ate jam sandwiches.'

'Where did you get them from? Did you have money?'

'My mum gave them to me.'

'She dropped them off?'

'She gave them to me before I left.'

'Ah, so she gave you, like, a packed lunch?'

'Yes.'

---

* Your dad is not having an affair or lying about where he is going. He really is going to the office to get some work done. His job is indeed currently hectic. The fact that the office is peaceful and quiet is simply an unintended perk.

You nod seriously. To you, it seems as though your dad has just divulged a crucial piece of information and, as such, you are satisfied. You file it away in your long-term memory. There it will stay, collecting metaphorical dust. Months or years or decades later, you can dust it off, air it out, and remember it fondly.

Further reading:

How to Leverage Your Library Card
100 Recipes for Jam
The Risky Route: Is the Actuarial Life for You?

THE FIRST THING YOU learn at the library is that you're not allowed to eat there. You learn this because, at the entrance, there is a sign with a picture of a sandwich, a burger, and some fries with a red cross crossing it out and the words 'Kindly do not eat, please'.

But whatever. It's eleven a.m. – not a classic eating time. You decide to put your jam sandwiches to one side (mentally speaking) and think about your principal task of the day.

Much like everyone else on Planet Earth, you don't know who or what wrote the Manuscript. This means you cannot narrow down your search based on the first letter of the author's last name, as people ordinarily would. Nor can you remember what, according to the documentary, the Manuscript is most commonly known as.

This leaves you in a fix. For a second, it seems you simply don't have enough information to proceed, and you wonder if it was silly of you to come.

You look around. Over there, a man is reading a book about horses. Over there, a woman is doing a crossword. By the far wall, there are small children sitting at computer machines – games of Solitaire, Pinball, and Minesweeper on their screens. It is oddly loud for a library. The people and the children and the computers are all making noises. The walls are also loud. Most are painted a headache-inducing pink.

You take some deep breaths, then decide to narrow your search by theme. You decide this because, in libraries, books are organised according to theme, as well as according to the first letter of the author's last name. You scan the books. There are rows and rows of them – all arranged on metal shelving, all wrapped in transparent plastic to protect them from the fingers of greasy strangers.

You pass gardening and horticulture.* You pass crime and punishment.† You pass angling, animals, local interest, and wildlife.‡ All of these books would interest your mum. You briefly wonder if you should borrow some for her. But then you get to the astronomy and space section and stop.

An alien endeavour, I do believe it is an alien endeavour . . .

Here, you peruse the shelves with more scrutiny. There is a book on the rings of Uranus.§ You skim it. It doesn't seem to mention anything about the literary pursuits of aliens. It is also not written in an unknown script or an unknown language, but instead the Roman script and the English language. The next book is more promising – *The Oort Cloud* – but you understand all the words except 'Oort'

---

* *How to Make Your Allotment a Success*; *The Lawn Owner's Manual.*
† *It's a Steal: A Looter's Guide to Thieving*; *Fanning the Flames: An Arsonist's Guide to Fire.*
‡ *Death to Badgers*; *How to Kill Carp.*
§ *The Rings of Uranus.*

and so you put it back down again also. *My Very Easy Method* and *How to Meet a Meteor* go much the same way.

You start to think that you'll never find the Manuscript or a book about the Manuscript. This makes you feel bad. You slump to the ground, suddenly depleted of energy and enthusiasm, resting against the shelving of the erotic and adult romance section. The day is not going well. You feel there is a distinct possibility the literature of your people will elude you forever and always.

It is not long before a member of staff spots you. You spot him spot you, then watch him approach. You imagine he is coming to berate you for sitting on the floor. You imagine this because, previously, humans have berated you for sitting on the floor.

Once he is nearer, you see that the member of staff is actually a woman. The woman looks great. If it wasn't for the lanyard, you'd think she was a super-famous photo model on her way to a fashion show.

'Are you OK, sweetheart?' the woman asks, looking at you through her glasses.

You do a small nod.

She smiles. 'Is that a yes?'

You nod again.

'Are you looking for something?'

You nod once more.

'A book?'

You shrug.

'Do you know what it's called?'

You shake your head.

'Do you know what colour it is? Sometimes people know the colour.'

You think about it for a second, then you shake your head again.

'Can you speak?'

'Yes,' you say.

'OK.' The woman is visibly relieved. 'That's OK. We like helping people find things here. Come over to the information desk and I'll do a search.'

The woman beckons for you to follow her to the information desk. You oblige. There is an older lady sitting at the information desk. She also seems nice. Her face, which is very large, seems like it's used to smiling a lot.

'Can you describe the book at all?' the woman asks.

You frown, try to recall the documentary. Fleetingly, you wonder if the documentary was a real thing that you saw and not just something that you thought you saw or dreamt.

'It's really old,' you say. 'Like really, really old.'

The woman blinks. 'Anything else?' she says.

'It hasn't been translated yet. So, like, it's in another language.'

'Ah, OK, and what language is it in—'

'Like it's impossible to translate. Like, they don't know who wrote it or why.'

The woman smiles, either amused or bemused by your interruption. 'Who are they?' she asks.

You blink. 'What?'

'Who're the people who don't know who wrote it or why?'

'I don't know. Someone thought it was written by aliens.'

'Who thought that?'

'I don't know. This man who was married to this lady.'

The woman looks at the computer keyboard her fingers are hovering above. She is frowning.

'We don't have much in other languages.'

'Oh, OK,' you say.

'We actually don't have *anything* in other languages. We are an English-language library here.'

'Oh, OK,' you say again.

Until this moment, you were liking this conversation. Now, you are not liking this conversation. Like a room without a clear exit, it has started to worry you.

'I think we have a book on Morse code, though. If that's of any interest?'

'Um.' You look at her blankly. You don't know if this book on Morse code is of any interest. You haven't read it yet, so you don't know if it's interesting. Also, you don't know what Morse code is.

'Or just a book on codes in general?' She frowns further. 'How old are you? Fifteen?'

You do a nod. The nod is a lie. The woman is able to tell this because you are grinning broadly. At no point has anyone else accused you of being so old and wise.

'Would you like to see it?'

You do another nod.

The woman raises her eyebrows. 'Yeah?'

'Yes, please.'

'I'll go fetch it, then.'

You sit down at a desk. The desk is OK. The space on it is plentiful, its chairs massive. The book, however, you know is not quite right. Morse code seems to have something to do with telegrams.

You don't think your Manuscript has much to do with telegrams. Opposite you is another library user. In defiance of the clear signage, he is eating fish and chips.

'The Voynich Manuscript,' the fish and chips man suddenly says, seemingly apropos of nothing.

You look up. The man is making intense eye contact with you. You don't like this.

'Sorry?' you say, as you didn't understand what he just said. It is possible, you think, that 'Voynich Manuscript' was an elaborate sneeze.

'You mean the Voynich Manuscript.' He nods towards the desk you were just at. 'That's what you were asking about.'

'I, um . . .' You compose yourself. Now he mentions it, Voynich does sound about right. 'OK. Thanks.'

The man waves a salty, greasy chip in your general direction. 'You don't believe me, do you?'

'No, I believe you.'

'You are thinking this is just a crazy homeless guy in the library eating chips, what does he know?'

'No.'

'Well, I know another thing too. You want to know what I know?'

'OK.'

'It's not here.'

'Oh, OK.'

He shakes his head. 'It's in the Beinecke, I think.'

You wonder if the man is sneezing again. 'What?'

'It's in the Beinecke Rare Book and Manuscript Library.'

'Oh. Where's that?'

'America.'

'Oh.'

The man smiles at you then, shows every single one of his pearly whites. Despite the fact he hasn't finished even half of his fish and chips, he then gets up, wipes his hands on his jeans, and starts to make his way out. He doesn't discard his leftovers. Instead, he leaves them there for someone else to deal with.

'Thanks, Tracy,' he says to the older woman at the computer desk.

'Thanks, Paul,' Tracy says.

'See you later, Maggie,' he says to the lovely woman at the computer desk.

'See you later, Paul,' Maggie says.

You stare after the man unblinkingly as he departs.

'You all right, kid?' Maggie says.

You don't think she's speaking to you, so you don't react.

'You all right, kid?' Maggie repeats.

'Oh, yeah,' you say, realising Maggie is addressing you.

Maggie raises her eyebrows. 'Did he bother you?'

'Who?'

'The guy who was just there.'

'The homeless man?' you ask.

Maggie smiles. 'He's not homeless.'

'Oh.'

'He's our boss.'

You feel silly. 'I didn't know that,' you say.

'That's OK, sweetie. Did he bother you?'

'No, he told me what I'm looking for.'

'Ah!' Maggie seems pleased. 'And what are you looking for?'

You shake your head. 'I can't remember.'

Maggie seems displeased. 'You can't remember.'

'No.'

'That's a shame, isn't it—'

'The Voynich Manuscript,' you interrupt because you suddenly just remembered.

Maggie beckons you over. 'I thought you said you couldn't remember.'

You shrug. 'I suddenly just remembered.'

Maggie nods slowly, types the words 'Voynich Manuscript' into her search bar. A list of book titles then appears. There are codes next to the book titles. These explain to her where each book is. If she hovers over the title of the book, she can find out what it's about more generally.

'All right, we have some stuff.'

'Yeah?'

'Yeah. Not much, but we can order some more stuff. Don't you worry. Don't you worry at all.'

Further reading:

The Voynich Manuscript: A Theory
Wilfrid and Me: A Memoir
The Voynich Manuscript: An Explanation
The Voynich Manuscript: History or Hoax?

18

THAT NIGHT, YOU WAIT until your parents go to sleep. A few minutes after they switch off the lights, you turn on yours and start to read *The Man Behind the Manuscript: A Slightly Fictionalised Life of Wilfrid Voynich.*

According to the book, a long time ago, all the way back in 1912, a man called Wilfrid Voynich was travelling through Italy when he stumbled across a curious codex* nestled in the library of a Jesuit residence. Though the library was overflowing with a dizzying array of fabulous tomes, this was the only book that caught Wilfrid's eye.

Indeed, as soon as he laid eyes on it, Wilfrid's heart started beating a little faster and a little harder. He felt like someone somewhere was telling him something. With shaking hands, he turned the pages as gently as he could. The script, tiny and impenetrable, resisted his cursory attempts at understanding, just as the images of naked women and alien plants resisted his comprehension.

---

* An early kind of book. The plural of 'codex' is 'codices'. The Voynich Manuscript was and is a codex.

Attempting to compose himself, Wilfrid approached a loitering librarian. Although Wilfrid was a charming man who could ordinarily strike up a rapport with anyone, the librarian remained curiously uncharmed.

'Brother,' Wilfrid said in Italian – for Italian is the language of Italy – 'this one looks interesting. What is this book? Who is its author?'

The librarian looked at Wilfrid with a steady gaze – one that suggested to Wilfrid that the librarian neither respected nor cared for rare book dealers. 'I don't know,' he said eventually. 'I've never read it.'

Something about the librarian unnerved Wilfrid. Nevertheless, he persisted. 'But for how long has it been here? From where did you get it?'

The librarian shrugged. 'It has always been here.'

'I would . . . May I, I mean, I—?'

'Take it?' the librarian interrupted. 'Certainly. But are you sure you want it?'

'Yes, I am sure.'

'Then away with you,' the librarian said. 'Go take your book and leave.'

'You don't want pay—' Wilfrid almost stopped himself. 'Payment?'

The librarian raised his eyebrows. Wilfrid patted his pockets as if searching for his wallet. He didn't want a man of God to accuse him of being a thief.

'Just leave,' the librarian said.

Wilfrid lingered a moment longer, before turning on his heels.

Once he was outside, he started to run. As he did so, he could feel the slight movement of the codex in his satchel, wrapped up snugly in a woolly jumper the day was too hot for. The villagers he passed regarded him with interest. Though he knew they were interested in nothing more than the sight of a strange man running, Wilfrid wished they would look elsewhere. He imagined their minds could beam their way into his, understand the significance of the codex nestled in his bag.

Wilfrid took the train to Rome. From Rome, he headed north, barely stopping for breath till he reached the Swiss border. Once there, he booked himself into a hotel. With his silver hair, cadaverous skin, and pale eyes, the hotel proprietor managed to seem entirely grey.

As bad luck would have it, almost as soon as he crossed the threshold of his new lodgings, Wilfrid came down with an inexplicable illness whose symptoms were as vague as they were debilitating.* For weeks, our book dealer was in the throes of nausea, fatigue, dissociation, heartburn, and persistent, wide-ranging stabbing pains. For weeks, he stayed inside his room, sleeping himself into feverish dreams of alchemists' recipes and botanical cures.

Whenever he awoke, instead of drinking water, nourishing himself, or engaging in personal hygiene, he pored over the 120 vellum leaves. The pictures he could just about understand – surely the plants were just plants, the women just women, the stars just stars – but

---

* Little did Wilfrid know that, by the time he had reached the Swiss border, the librarian was breathing the first of his last breaths, his body growing weaker and sleepier and slower and colder, his body halfway to hell or heaven or somewhere in between.

the script was incomprehensible. His command of Polish, Russian, French, was of no use, nor was his command of Italian, Spanish, or Ukrainian. After weeks of study, he had no conception of even this language's most basic elements. He did not know if the script was supposed to be read left to right or right to left or up and down. He did not even know if it was an alphabet or a syllabary.* To make matters worse, in his delirium, he saw no letters or shapes, but instead disconnected blobs of ancient ink and the deity who must have created it all.

Alas, Wilfrid was not a man accustomed to the feeling of not understanding things. As a result, the codex both enraged and fascinated him. Hunched over in his room, his fever waxing and waning like the Moon, he wrote furious and nonsensical notes – mind and body refusing to accept the mystery, and his focus refusing to notice the proprietor's frantic knocks at the door.

He woke up in a hospital bed some days later, a nurse propping him up so he could take a drink.

On realising where he was – or rather, where he wasn't – Wilfrid spun into a fury. 'Where is it?' he cried. 'My notes? The Manuscript?'

'Hush,' the nurse said, tipping water down his throat.

'But what have you done with it? You have to tell me.' Wilfrid grabbed her lapels. 'What have you done with it? Tell me!'

At this, the nurse gave him a short, sharp slap on the cheek, before casting him a glare that was just as striking. 'We'll have none of that here,' she said. 'You were brought here by the hotel

---

* An alphabet is a writing system in which each symbol represents a sound. A syllabary is a writing system in which each symbol represents a syllable.

proprietor who found you unresponsive on his first floor. If you want to rant and rave, you are more than welcome to go to the asylum. I can take you there myself, it would be no trouble. In fact, it's just next door.'

In the end, he did not go to the asylum (though perhaps his life would have been easier if he had). Instead, he did what the nurse told him to do. For several days, he drank, ate, washed, and slept. After this, he returned to the hotel to find the blessed codex still intact.

The proprietor watched Wilfrid pack up his things without speaking. When our book dealer appeared to be ready, he made his request. He said to Wilfrid in French – for French is one of the four languages of Switzerland – 'Monsieur, please do not darken my doorstep ever again.'

'*Pardon?*' Wilfrid said, for he had not heard or even noticed the phantom proprietor hovering around.

'My door,' the proprietor said again. 'Please do not darken it, not ever again.'

Wilfrid squinted at this pale specimen of a man, then grunted in acquiescence. He had no qualms about heeding this request, and so heed it he did.

After his stint of sickness in Switzerland, he sailed to New York, where he opened a bookshop similar to one he had previously been famed for in London. For the rest of his life, a steady stream of intellectuals came in, scanning the tomes crammed on his shelves.

But though the New York bookshop was just like his London bookshop, it was not nearly as successful. The reason? Wilfrid was not the salesperson he used to be. Whenever patrons enquired about a book, he did not even try to disguise his boredom.

'Is this a first edition?' a patron might ask, gesturing at a tattered copy of the Bible.

'Probably,' Wilfrid would say, his voice hazy and lazy and brusque.

'What can you tell me about it?'

'Oh, I don't know. It's not very interesting. Quite old. I think.'

Occasionally, Wilfrid would show a patron the codex in the back room. He would tell them about it. He would explain what he knew for certain – that the book was old and mysterious – and what he thought about it – that it was a treasure map, that it was evidence of an elite but now extinct civilisation, that it was a recipe for alchemical pursuits. In response, either the patron would listen politely, become intrigued or uninterested. If Wilfrid were to thrust the text upon them, they would not be able to understand the text either. The meaning behind the text of the codex remained unyielding.

'Do you understand this text?' Wilfrid would prompt. 'Do you have an inkling what, say, this page might be about?'

The patron would hesitate. 'Um, I think—'

'So, you don't.'

'I mean, it's, um—'

'You suspect it's written in a very ancient, very complicated language that's hitherto unknown?'

'I mean—'

'Ancient Hebrew? Mycenaean Greek? Ugaritic? Akkadian?'

'Um.'

'The pictures point to some kind of rudimentary plant science, surely. And these pages are certainly to do with the study of the stars.'

The patron's eyes would dart to the door. 'That sounds right,' they might say.

Relieved, Wilfrid would nod. Of course, he was right. He knew he was right. He knew he was right, right up until he was dead.

One night, Wilfrid was arguing with his wife, who had been berating him for obsessive focus on that blasted book. They were having it out on the roof – shouting stuff, screaming stuff, throwing stuff. Midway through ranting and raving about the phonology of Proto-Indo-European, his wife removed a handgun from her handbag and shot him straight through the heart. She had simply had enough.

Days later, the codex was dubbed the Voynich Manuscript by the journalist writing Wilfrid's obituary. Months later, the text began circulating among the great and the good of North America. Boring old farts fingered its fragile pages. Scholars waxed academic about its meaning or lack thereof. Decades passed. Glaciers melted. Oil spilt and so did milk. You were born and the Voynich Manuscript wound up at the Beinecke Library – where it became the 408th manuscript of its collection. This is where it currently resides. Beinecke MS 408, otherwise known as the Voynich Manuscript.

No one has ever come to understand what the Voynich Manuscript means. The language it's written in is unknown. The Manuscript is the only example of it.

Of course, there has been ample speculation. Some have dubbed it a monk's fever dream, a child's secret language, a madman's lonely ramblings, a simple shopping list. Others have dubbed it a women's health manual, a dream diary, the musings of a scribe with too much time on his hands, an ancient Yellow Pages.

If it is a language, it is a language isolate – one that bears no resemblance to any known tongue. If it is not a language isolate, then it's some sort of code. If it is not some sort of code, it's an elaborate idiolect, an over-the-top joke.

It could be a book of nonsense, of course. If the Manuscript hasn't been understood yet, this could be because there's nothing to understand. But this is unlikely. The distribution of letters corresponds to that of a natural language. And it feels real. Every single human who has held the Voynich Manuscript in their hands has felt and wanted it to be real. They have felt the hum of history in their palms, the buzz of knowledge unknown. And so, it is real. We are sure that it is real.

Further reading:

The Man Behind the Manuscript: A Slightly Fictionalised Life of Wilfrid Voynich

19

L ITTLE ALIEN, HOW DO I describe how it feels to learn about the Manuscript? It's like a taste, a flavour, like the feeling has a flavour and the flavour is tasty. By this, I mean the process of imbibing new information about the Manuscript, understanding the new information about the Manuscript is enjoyable. Indeed, it is so enjoyable, it is almost as though it has its own flavour, as though everything about it is so satisfactory that the feeling pours into your other senses too – in this instance, gustatorily.

Hunched over the library desk, you glug away at whatever information is to hand. Maggie has been generous with her book ordering. The county's interlibrary exchange programme means that there is plenty for you to read.

You deepen and widen your knowledge of the Manuscript. You learn how old it is[*] and what people think it is about.[†] You learn the best human brains of Planet Earth have tried to unpick the text for

---

[*] It's from the 1400s.
[†] Women's health, alchemy, astronomy, astrology.

years on end, but that the symbols and ink splotches have never yielded anything sensical to anyone. You also learn there are six sections of the Manuscript,* that they — the people who know things about the Manuscript — know this because of the pictures, not the language, because both the language and script are unknown.

But not even all the pictures make that much sense. For instance, some of the plants depicted in the herbal section don't match up to known plants. And some of the stars depicted in the cosmological section don't match up with known constellations. Also, the naked ladies might look like naked ladies — they have faces and hips and boobies — but many of them appear to be carrying their ovaries in the pictures. In other pictures, monochrome rainbows are pouring out of their heads. These are not things that happen in real life. Not on this planet, at least. In your opinion, this raises questions about an alien library or community building colliding with Planet Earth via an asteroid.

You also learn about things related to the Manuscript. For instance, you learn about Wilfrid. You learn he lived a colourful life. You learn he was exiled to Siberia, albeit before finding the Manuscript. You learn that he played fast and loose with the truth — that his accounts of where and when and how he acquired the Manuscript varied over time.

Perhaps more importantly, you learn that — despite all the books about the Voynich Manuscript — there is simply too much that you don't understand. Sometimes, after hour five or six or seven at the

---

* A herbal section, an astronomical section, a cosmological section, a biological section, a pharmaceutical section, and a recipe section.

library, you feel overwhelmed by the weight of what you don't know. Sometimes, your chest feels tight as you pick up a new book and for a few moments, you find that you have to do your noises.

This is happening right now. You are opening a new book – *The Voynich Manuscript: The What, the Where, and the Why*, loaned all the way from Portsmouth. Around you, a number of mums are chivvying their children in different directions. In the corner, there is a kids' entertainer with a guitar and a rabbit. He is tuning the guitar. You don't like the prospect of reading *The Voynich Manuscript: The What, the Where, and the Why*. It's too advanced. It's maddening to look up the definitions of the words such as 'cypher', 'codex', 'phonology', 'morphology', and 'syntax'. It's even more maddening to look up the definitions of the words found in definitions.

And so, you make your noises under the desk – a place no book can hurt you.

It is Maggie who finds you. 'Darling,' she says. 'Are you making your noises again?'

You throw a noise at her in return. The noise sounds like 'huurgh'. Much like the Voynich Manuscript, the meaning of 'huurgh' is as of yet unknown.

'Come on out, please.'

You fall silent but don't move. Suddenly, you feel too embarrassed to move.

'Come on out, now please. Other people are trying to work.' As if she knows you need some help, Maggie offers you her hand, which you take.

Still holding your hand, Maggie walks you to the information desk where she hands you a glass of squash and tells you to take a pew. The man with the guitar starts his first song. Absent-mindedly, you pick up a book lying on the information desk. The book bears a picture of a woman swooning in the arms of a dashing man. Like all the books you have ever come across, you think it looks interesting.

Seeing what you're doing, Maggie bats at your hand. 'No,' she says, snatching the book away and shoving it in a drawer. 'No more reading for you.'

'What?' you ask. 'Why?'

'Shh,' Maggie says.

At the other end of the desk is Tracy. Tracy shakes her head at you. 'You need what the Americans call a time out, darling. Do you know that phrase, Mags? Americans have a thing called a time out.'

Maggie shakes her head. 'It's horrible.'

Tracy frowns questioningly. 'What is?'

'Time out. Doesn't bear thinking about.'

Tracy evidently finds this funny. 'Ha!' she barks, before resuming her typing.

You rest your head against the desk – its wood an uncomfortable pillow. Moments later, the man with the guitar starts singing a song about freedom, and your dad bursts in, apologising for being late, saying he had to take your mum to the hospital.

Further reading:

The Voynich Manuscript: The What, the Where, and the Why
Kumbaya and Other Songs for Children

20

YOUR MUM IS GOING a bit loopy again. At least, that's what your dad says as he makes you dinner. She had to make a quick trip to the emergency department. It's nothing serious though, you needn't worry, needn't think about it very much at all. He's just telling you this so you are in the loop, so to speak, but please do excuse the pun.

'Do you know what that means?' he asks.

You nod because, yes, you know what 'loopy' means, and you can guess that 'in the loop' means 'in the know' but maybe also 'loopy'.

'What do you say?' your dad says, scooping the beans onto your toast and plonking the egg atop the lot.

'Yes,' you say.

'Very good. So, we've got to be kind to her, OK?'

'OK.'

'When she comes back, don't make a massive fuss. Just be kind.'

'OK.'

'Just be normal.'

'OK.'

The next morning, your mum comes home in a taxi cab, walks in through the front door. When she does, she kisses your dad on the lips and you on the cheek. She then accepts your dad's offer of a cup of tea, sits down on the sofa, turns the TV on. She lets you sit next to her. You watch the TV but also her.

You wonder what happened to her specifically, what provoked the quick trip to the emergency department. Not much, you suppose. It wasn't a very long stay – not even twenty-four hours. You wonder if she even got to sleep there. She seems very tired, can barely keep her eyes open.

The TV show is a documentary set in a hospital. In the hospital, there is a small child with a high fever. Next to the child is an old lady. The old lady is the boy's grandma. She looks after the kid because his parents died. You wonder if it's appropriate viewing. You wonder if a cop show might be better. Your mum doesn't seem disturbed. She doesn't seem anything other than blank.

After a while, she rests her head on the cushion and sleeps. You fetch a blanket, put it on her lap so she doesn't get cold. When you do this, she startles back awake. You are worried she is going to admonish you, but she doesn't. Instead, she emits a grunt of thanks, curls up more formally, and falls back asleep.

You don't know what to do now, how to be kind and normal when she is asleep. Eventually, you absent yourself to the garden. The sky is slate grey but the air temperature is warm. You can hear more than one neighbour mowing their lawn, and more than one kid shouting and making noise. It's not an angry kind of shouting. It's the kind of shouting kids do when they get carried away.

You peer through the double doors into the living room. Your mum is still asleep. You wonder if your mum's fatigue is down to her loopiness, or the fact that she didn't sleep. Maybe it's the weather. It really is a sleepy day. Even the bees seem heavy.

Further reading:

Loopy Loops: A History of Cursive
Loop the Loop: A History of Roller Coasters

THE NEXT WEEKEND, YOUR dad is driving you to the library. It feels like ages since you've been there, but it's just been a week – no time at all really.

Your dad is trying to make small talk with you.

'Lovely day today.'

'Yes.'

'I wonder if it'll be busy in town.'

'Mm.'

When he merges onto the dual carriageway, your dad cuts to the chase. He says you've been such a good girl looking after yourself in the town centre library, would it be all right if you spent some more time there?

'Maybe instead of just Saturday, it could be Saturday and Sunday, you know?' he says.

'Right.'

'How does that sound?' your dad asks, as he swerves to avoid some litter dropped onto the road.

'Yeah, OK,' you say.

The dual carriageway turns itself into a roundabout. 'You don't mind?' your dad asks.

'No.'

You pass a car with a dog in it. The dog is sticking its head out the window, its pink tongue and long ears flopping in the wind. You briefly consider winding down the window to find out how it feels to stick your head out like that, but know your dad wouldn't like it.

'At least until your mum feels more normal again.'

'Right.'

'You're a good girl,' your dad repeats, saying this phrase in the same way someone might say to a dog, perhaps even the dog you just passed. He pulls into the drop-off lay-by, gives you a kiss on the forehead, then says he will see you in a few hours.

You hesitate – your hand hovering over the door handle. You don't know whether to tell him he forgot the jam sandwiches. You don't feel hungry now, but you know you will later, so maybe you should. Then again, perhaps good girls are expected to fend for themselves on a Saturday. Perhaps good girls don't care if they are hungry when mid-afternoon hits.

And so, you get out and go to the library. When you get there, you wave at Maggie and Tracy, who wave right back, then get settled in. At your table, you take a deep breath. Another day, another dollar, you think. Another day, another book. Another concept, another understanding, another word, another word, another word.

You begin devouring all the information all at once. When the author of your book writes the phrases 'substitution cypher' and 'polyalphabetic cypher', you look up the words 'substitution', 'polyalphabetic', and 'cypher' in the dictionary. Then you try to understand these words in their context and think about what they mean. When you come across these phrases again, mere paragraphs later, you try to remember what you just learnt. This is all very tricky.

It's only eleven a.m. and already you are starting to make your noises. They are gentle and light versions of your noises. But they are noises all the same. You get a feeling this is going to be a bad day.

Maggie looks over at you with narrowed eyes, but it's Homeless Paul who approaches.

'You are going about this wrong,' he says, munching on crisps. 'You have to start at the start. At the beginning, not the middle, not the end.' He sits himself down, looks around. You are currently sitting in the English as a Foreign Language section. 'Not a bad place to start,' he says.

Mere minutes later, you have a pile of books before you. *How to Master Phrasal Verbs. The History of the English Language. Prepositions and What to Do with Them. Commas: What Are They? How to Teach English as A Foreign Language.*

'Look,' Homeless Paul says, pointing at a page of *An Introduction to Late-Onset Bilingualism.* 'Here is a quote for you. "If you want to know how other languages work, you have to know how your own works." Isn't that good? Isn't that exactly what I was saying about starting at the start?'

He looks at you expectantly. You nod, impatient for him to leave so you can read alone for the rest of the afternoon, but also wondering if he might share some of his crisps.

'Here,' he says, passing you his crisps. 'You can finish these, if you like.'

*

THE NEXT TIME YOU come to the library – the next day – you learn some interesting things. For instance, you learn that healthy languages are always in a process of change. Words shift, shape, and twist. Parents pronounce words differently from their children who pronounce words differently from their grandchildren. Quotidian words become rarefied words. Hip and happening terminology morphs into cringe terminology. And written language changes too. Spellings simplify or complexify or morph to more accurately mirror speech. A correct way to spell a word becomes an antiquated way to spell a word.

You learn that unrelenting change is a sign that languages are living. They don't respire or reproduce but, still, they are living. They are alive in that they are changing every day in the mouths and the minds of everyone who speaks them. The only languages that don't change are dead languages – stuck in the inertia of ancient books and lost to the sound waves of time.

And you learn that languages cannot be protected from change. There is no dictionary or panel or academy that can police a language's parameters, at least not effectively.

And you learn that there are thousands of languages. You learn that you speak one of the most widely spoken languages but that this doesn't mean it's the best one. You learn all languages are interesting, even if some don't ever exist in the written form, even if many won't live for that much longer.

And naturally, while all the things you learn tickle you, it is the facts about living languages versus dead and dying languages that tickle you the most. Because, in your opinion, the language that appears in the Voynich Manuscript is a dead language. You think that this is the most obvious reason people can't understand the text. Also, you've seen pictures of the Voynich Manuscript. You've seen the pictures in books but also online. It looked dead to you.

But the facts about spoken languages versus written languages also tickle you. If things were up to you, if you were the ruler of the world, languages would be unspoken. Instead of speaking, people would carefully consider the thoughts they want to express and then write them down. That way, there would be no misunderstandings based on unintended tonal shifts, unintended emphasis, unintended facial expressions.

'Maggie, did you know that languages are not written down sometimes?' you say, sitting at the information desk with Maggie.

'Hm?' Maggie is typing at the massive computer.

'Yeah,' you continue. 'People just speak it. If they want to read or write they have to do so in another language.'

'That's interesting.'

'So, like, they don't do books or anything. They just use their voices.'

'Whoa.'

'Maggie, do you think that there's a language that's not spoken, it's just written?'

Maggie seems more interested in typing her things on the massive computer. 'Um, I don't know,' she says eventually. 'Maybe Latin.'

'Latin,' you repeat. You don't want to tell her you're not a hundred percent sure what Latin is. You are an autodidact. This means the gaps in your knowledge are significant.

'I didn't know, um, I didn't know Latin wasn't spoken,' you say eventually, trying to speak generally so as not to be caught out.

'Well,' Maggie says, 'it was spoken. Just not the way it's taught in schools. You don't know Latin?'

'No.'

'They don't teach it to you in your school?'

'No.'

'Well, it's not very useful, to be honest. What do they teach you?'

You think about this for a minute. 'We do English.'

'You already speak English, though.'

'And maths.'

'Pftt.'

Maggie stops typing, turns to face you properly. 'Well,' she says. 'I don't know why only-written-down languages would exist. I don't know if anyone would want a language that's just written down and not spoken. It wouldn't be very useful. And as much as I like reading, I don't want to read everyone's crappy handwriting every day.'

Tracy, who is sitting at the other end of the information desk, chips in. 'Yeah, and sometimes people wouldn't have a pen and pad to hand.'

Maggie nods. 'And some people just can't learn to read or write. Not many people. But some.'

You think about it for a moment, then pipe up again. 'What if there are people who don't want to speak? What if there are people who just want to write? Shouldn't they get their own language, like, just for them?'

Maggie shakes her head. 'I don't think there would be enough people. And besides, you wouldn't need a new language for that scenario. You could just use the existing languages.'

'You might want to be a nun, darling,' Tracy says. 'Take a vow of silence and hide away with some other ladies in a mountain somewhere.'

'I never said I wanted that,' you say, defensive now.

Homeless Paul appears from the back office. He is rubbing his belly but not eating anything. 'Did you know that biro is an eponym?' he asks you suddenly.

You shake your head. 'No,' you say. You find it mildly annoying when he bandies words you don't know. On this occasion, however, your annoyance diminishes when he passes you a book. The book he passes you is called *Words for Words* – a book-length glossary of words that refer to other words. A quick skim reveals that it includes the word 'eponym',* the word 'andronym'†, and the word 'synonym'.‡

'And did you know your dad's here?'

'No,' you say again, looking up to see your dad, who is indeed coming down the corridor.

When your dad looks at you, he does not smile a smile of greeting. Instead, he raises his eyebrows and says, 'Ready to go?'

'OK,' you say.

Homeless Paul gives your dad a look. 'Just so you know,' he says, eventually. 'We don't usually provide childcare services.'

'I see,' your dad says.

---

* A word named after a person. A man called László Biró invented ballpoint pens, which are also known as biros.

† A man's name.

‡ A word that has the same meaning as another word.

'We usually encourage children to be accompanied by a parent or guardian.'

Your dad nods. 'Of course. Sounds sensible.'

'So will we be seeing your daughter again soon?'

Your dad shrugs. 'Quite possibly,' he says.

'Will we be seeing her next weekend?'

'It may be the case, yes. It may well be the case.'

'Does that mean yes?'

'Sure.'

'Yes?'

'Yes. I think that would be likely.'

Further reading:

How to Master Phrasal Verbs

The History of the English Language

Prepositions and What to Do with Them

Commas: What Are They?

How to Teach English as a Foreign Language

An Introduction to Late-Onset Bilingualism

Words for Words

22

THAT NIGHT, YOU LIE in bed, staring at the ceiling. There are stars on the ceiling – your dad put them there when you were younger. The stars are glow-in-the-dark. You don't know how they work, exactly. You just know that when everything is pitch-black, you can still see them on the ceiling. You count them. There are a hundred and five.

Even though it is very late, you don't feel tired. For this reason, when you hear your mum pottering around downstairs, you decide to join her.

Your mum is in the living room, packing a suitcase. The suitcase is lying open on the carpet. It already contains clothes, shoes, and toiletries. She now seems to be in the process of choosing which books to pack.

'Moving out, Mum?'

Your mum looks at you, presses a finger to her lips, and beckons you over to the window. Out the window, the lamp posts are bathing everything from your front garden to the wheelie bins of the house opposite in a warm orange light.

'You see that car?' she says to you, pointing to a van parked outside your house.

'Yeah,' you say.

'It's the police.'

'Oh.' You don't think the van looks like a police van. In your opinion, it just looks like a normal van. You suppose it could be an unmarked police vehicle. Maybe your mum saw some police officers enter or exit the vehicle earlier. Or maybe she is mistaken and the van is just a van. 'How do you know?' you ask her.

Your mum looks at you and taps her right index finger against her right temple – a gesture that means she does not want to explain how she knows.

She walks back over to the bookcase, removes *Psychopharmacology: A Short Guide* and *So You're a Paranoid Person*.

'Which one should I pack, do you think?'

'Um.' You don't know which one she should pack, largely because you don't know where she's going. *Psychopharmacology: A Short Guide* looks very long and complicated. If your mum is going to be away for a long time, then maybe this is a good option, as it will last her a while. That said, you think *So You're a Paranoid Person* might be more relevant to her current state of mind.

'I don't know. I think it depends where you're going.'

'Oh, I'll just lie low in a hotel for a few weeks.'

'Right, OK.' You make a small noise. 'Why, though?'

'Police,' your mum says, as if this explains anything. 'Did you not see them?'

'The van?'

'Yes, the police.'

'Yes.'

'Well, then.'

You think about waking your dad up. He might be annoyed, you think, but then again maybe he would stop your mum from leaving. Then you think about distracting her. Maybe you could tell her some fun facts about the Voynich Manuscript. Tell her that it was passed around Europe for centuries – tell her that, before Wilfrid Voynich owned it, a Holy Roman Emperor owned it, a mathematician owned it, and a pharmacist owned it.

'Mum.'

'Yeah?'

'I don't think you should leave tonight. I think we should go to bed.'

'OK, sweetie.'

'Also, that van isn't a police van. It's just a van. I think it belongs to next door. The man that works there is a plumber, remember?'

'Next door?'

'Yeah.'

'Well, I'll be damned. I thought it was the police.'

'It's not.'

'I feel a bit silly.'

'Don't worry, Mum.'

In the end, neither of you goes to bed. Instead, you watch one film, then another. The first film is about a fish that goes missing. The second film is about a lion whose dad dies. They are pretty good films. They take you all the way to morning time. At seven a.m., your dad comes down and makes you both a cup of tea. At eight a.m., the neighbour opens up his van, gets in his van, and drives away.

Further reading:

Psychopharmacology: A Short Guide
So You're a Paranoid Person

2 3

YOUR TEACHER WANTS YOU all to write an essay on a hobby
or interest. The hobby or interest can be anything, he says. If
you like swimming, it can be on swimming. If you like football, it can
be on football. He says the essay needs to be roughly one thousand
words. This is a long essay, longer than you are used to. He advises
that you choose your hobby or interest carefully. This is because, if
you opt for something that you really like, it will be easier for you to
write. The essay is important, the teacher says, because it will help
him place you in the appropriate set for the next two years.

The teacher is a shrinking man with white hair coming out of
his nostrils. He speaks slowly. A chronic over-explainer, he always
assumes his requests are unusual and difficult to comprehend, and that
his students are slow. He enunciates his words carefully – sending
every one of his students off to sleep in no time at all.

'Any questions?' the teacher asks.

All around you, slack jaws and glassy eyes abound. Above you,
a slightly broken fluorescent light emits a gentle hum and buzz – a
fly is repeatedly ramming itself into it.

As soon as he explains the task, you know you want to write your essay on the Manuscript. If the teacher were to shut up for a second, you could get on and write it. By evening, you would be finished. You have dozens of paragraphs in you already. It wouldn't take very long to write them. You suspect you'd get a good mark, knowing as much as you do on the subject. If you manage to write nice sentences, you will surely do quite well.

'Do we have to write about a sport?' one classmate with a squeaky voice asks.

The teacher shakes his head, evidently realising he has to explain the essay further, or maybe even all over again.

'One thousand words,' he says. 'And you can write about a hobby or interest of your choice. Any hobby. Any interest. If you like knitting, you can write about knitting. If you like, um . . .' he struggles to come up with another non-sport example '. . . metalwork, you can write about metalwork.'

Another child puts their hand up. 'Does it have to be related to making stuff?'

The teacher winces. 'Ah, no.'

'Can it be on frogs?' the same child asks.

'Frogs?' The teacher widens his eyes. It is only now that you see he looks like a frog. 'If that is your hobby or interest, then yes, by all means, please do tell me about frogs. But make sure it's an essay. Make sure you have a beginning, a middle, and an end. Make sure you have a thousand words and something to say.'

You are grateful when the school bell rings to signal the end of the day. You pack your bag quickly, get up, and leave without even a cursory farewell to anyone.

Even though the teacher said you have a few weeks to complete the essay, you decide you'll get started on it tomorrow. You're scheduled to be at the library then because it's Saturday. But you'll also be at the library the day after, because the day after is Sunday. You can get to work on the essay then. You can sit in the corner, in the quietest spot. You should be able to write it all out – your thoughts about the Manuscript, the product of your months upon months of research. You wonder how the teacher will react. You wonder if he will be cowed by the sudden emergence of your linguistic genius. You wonder if he will demand that you be sent up several years or else enrolled in university right away. You'll have to make sure it's well written, of course. But mostly, you'll have to make sure it's brilliant, insightful, perspicuous.

Further reading:

Who Let the Frogs Out?
Knit Happens: A Yarn About Life, Love, and Laughter

2 4

THE NEXT MORNING, YOU go downstairs to ask your mum for a lift into town. You have your backpack all ready. In it, you have some Voynich-related tomes, a pad of paper, and an unnecessarily large number of pens.

Your mum is brushing her hair while looking in the hallway mirror. Her hair seems to be thinning. Clumps of it are coming out as she brushes it. She doesn't seem to care. She just brushes it again and again – her manner serene. You think maybe she's turning into an old man or something. Briefly, you think having an old man for a mum might be nice.

'Can you drop me off today?' you say, after hovering for a while.

Your mum looks at you in the mirror. 'Where?' she asks, as she brushes and brushes and brushes. 'You want me to take you to Bobby's house?'

You frown. 'Who's Bobby?'

Your mum also frowns. 'What do you mean, who's Bobby? He's your friend. He's your friend from school.'

'Oh, that was years ago. That was my old school. I don't know him any more.'

Your mum gazes at you in the mirror, stops brushing her hair. 'He's not your friend any more? Did you have a falling-out?'

You backtrack. 'Maybe he's my friend. I just haven't seen him in a while.'

'Then why don't you want to go to his house?'

'I just meant I wanted to go to the library. I usually go to the library these days. I have an essay to work on.'

'An essay?'

'Yes.'

'Gosh. How time flies.' Your mum inspects the hairbrush. 'I thought Bobby was your friend.'

'He was.'

You think about your friends. There's a girl who smiles at you in the chemistry lab, the same one who asks to copy your homework sometimes. Maybe she is your friend. Or maybe Maggie and Tracy are your friends. You are not sure. You think friends might have to be the same age as you. Also, it's kind of their job to speak to you, or at least be cordial, so you aren't sure they count as anything much.

'He *was* my friend,' you clarify. 'But he's not my friend any more. We don't go to the same school so we don't get to hang out as much.'

Your mum resumes brushing. 'I see,' she says, dragging the comb from the top to the bottom of her hair.

'So, can you drop me off today?'

'Where?'

'Town. I want to go to the library in town.'

'The library?'

147

'Yeah.'

'Ah, no, no can do. Not today.'

You despair internally. 'No? Why not?'

'You're not going there today.'

You despair some more. 'Why not?'

'You know those people I see? The people I see about my mental health?'

'Yeah,' you say, because you do. Once or twice, they have come inside the house, brandishing their clipboards. Mostly, though, you think your mum goes to them. Your dad drives her.

'Well, they suggested we hang out more. Go on day trips. Make memories together.'

'OK.'

'And my sister agreed. Though she can't actually come. It'll just be me, you, Dad, and Cousin Paul.'

'Why's Cousin Paul coming?'

'Your auntie's working. He can't be by himself all day.'

'Right. And what memories are we making?'

'We're making the memory of going to a museum. In London.'

'OK.'

'Does that sound fun?'

'Sure.'

You have no idea if a museum in London sounds like fun. You can't remember ever going to one.

At your thoughtful face, your mum puts the hairbrush down, looks at you concernedly in the mirror. Her eyes are round and sad again. 'You don't think it sounds fun? You think we should go somewhere else?'

You look at her reflection. 'Oh, no,' you say, 'I think it sounds really fun. I'll really like it. I'm sure.'

'It's a museum about the universe and space. I remember you used to have a thing about aliens. Maybe they will have an exhibit on aliens and the universe and you will really like it.'

Your dad appears from the kitchen. 'It's not just about the universe,' he says. 'It's fun for all the family.'

'All the family?'

'Yes.'

'Well, that sounds good, then.'

YOU THINK YOU FEEL excited about the trip to the London museum. You think that's what your belly is telling you. Or maybe it's telling you you're hungry. It's certainly telling you something.

You watch the rain come down as your dad zips down the M3. Your cousin is sitting next to you. You try to ignore him, let yourself sink into a daydream. In your daydream, an old woman lets you into the museum with a crooked key. In your daydream, the museum turns out not to be a museum but instead a kind of library – as big as an aircraft hangar, with rows upon rows of ancient and dusty texts in temperature-controlled cabinets.

'She's talking to herself again,' Cousin Paul says.

Your dad is frowning at the car in front of him. Your mum appears to be asleep.

'So she is,' your dad says, uninterested, braking to join a queue of traffic.

In the end, the museum is nothing like a library the size of an aircraft hangar. Instead, it is simply a museum designed for human children, in which there are indeed many human children. Some of the human children run around, pointing at the various bits of the exhibits. Others sit on benches or loll on the floor. There are parents, guardians, and accompanying adults too, many wandering around with blank expressions on their faces.

You are also wearing a blank expression. In your opinion, the fun for all the family is not that fun.

Here you are – squishing your nose against the glass panel behind which a skull of a Neanderthal is displayed. Though the skull is very near to you – and though this is the closest to a Neanderthal skull you'll ever get – the skull feels about as real as a pixelated image on a TV screen. You wish you could be more interested in it – this skull of this early human. But to be more interested in it, you'd need to be closer. You'd need to hold the skull aloft to feel how much it weighs. You'd need to peer inside and see its hollowed-out insides. You'd need to give it a little sniff.

Your mum jabs you sharply in the ribs. 'What did you just do?' she asks, her voice stern.

You turn to your mum. It's not like your mum to jab you. You look at her fearfully, wondering what possessed her as you nurse your ribs.

'Did you just lick that?' she asks.

You hesitate. If you recall correctly, you did indeed just lick the glass. But you didn't mean to. You were daydreaming, not quite aware of what you were doing.

Your mum shakes her head. 'Jesus Christ,' she says.

Your cousin appears. 'Did she just lick what?'

'She licked the glass,' your mum says.

Your cousin grins. 'Cannibal!' he says, skipping around. 'Cannibal, cannibal, cannibal!'

Your dad – who was only moments ago conversing with a volunteer – now comes marching over.

'She just licked the glass,' your cousin says to him.

'She just licked the glass,' your mum repeats.

Your dad seems uninterested in this fact. He doesn't ask you if you just licked the glass. Instead, he asks your mum if she just jabbed you.

'Did you seriously just poke her like that?'

Your mum falters. 'She, um . . .'

'Are you OK?' your dad says to you.

You nod. 'Yeah,' you say.

'Are you sure?'

'Yeah,' you say again.

'Come here,' your dad says.

You don't come there. Instead, your dad comes to you and proceeds to give you a big squeeze. Otherwise known as a hug, this big squeeze slightly stresses you out. However, you know that your dad is doing it out of kindness – and so you give him a squeeze right back. He seems to appreciate this. After what feels like far too long, he backs off, puts his hands on your face to cradle your Neanderthal skull.

'I love you, sweet pea,' he says. 'Let's have a nice day.'

You nod. 'OK, Dad,' you say. 'I love you too.'

Next, he turns to your cousin. 'Let's have a nice day, OK?' he says to your cousin, his tone more threatening than loving.

Your cousin shrugs. 'OK.'

Finally, he turns to your mum. 'Let's have a nice day, OK?' he says to her, his tone now closer to loving again.

'OK,' she says.

And so, you move on to the other things in this museum. These things are more interesting. According to a sign, they are 'interactive'. You mull over the word. You aren't sure what it means. Does 'inter' mean between, just like 'international' means 'between nations'? Does 'active' mean 'exercise'? What would 'between-exercise' mean? You look around for a passing academic to discuss your linguistic conundrum, but all you see are parents with tension headaches and children running amok.

In any case, over there is a massive model of an ear. As several other children are demonstrating, it is possible to walk through its ear canal. This intrigues you. You start to wander towards the ear canal, but your dad beckons you to another room. It is time to move on again. You wonder if – in his attempt to have a nice day – he is trying to speed through it.

You are now in a room for those drawn to goriness. In this room, there is a body of a human being that you are welcome to dissect. The human body in question is not a real human body. It is simply a model human body made of bits of plastic – *the revolutionary material of the twentieth century! see PLASTIC FANTASTIC next door* – that you are welcome to pull apart and put back together again under the supervision of several members of staff.

Your mum apparently finds this a bit too much, and so you move on to the extensive exhibit on electricity. Here, you can pedal on a static bike to see it light up a bulb and also touch a globe-like thing.

When you place your hand against the globe, tiny lightning bolts are drawn towards you as if by magic and not by science.

This is when your mum approaches you. 'What do you want to do, sweet pea?' she asks. 'Do you not like it here?'

'No, I do.'

'You want to stay? You want to look at the things?'

'Yeah, yeah I do.'

You finger the leaflet in your pocket. According to the leaflet – which you read earlier – there is a section on aliens and space stuff. It is in the basement, next to a space called a 'planetarium'. Also according to the leaflet, the planetarium is the perfect place for your kids to see horizons stretch out and feel inspired. You don't have any kids, but perhaps you would like to see horizons stretch out and feel inspired.

'Can we . . .' you say, trailing off a little. 'Um, you know you said that, um . . .'

'What is it, angel?'

'You said space stuff? You said there was space stuff?'

Your mum nods enthusiastically. 'You want to see the space stuff? I thought you'd like that.'

'Yeah.'

'Oh, I'm so glad. I'll grab the boys.'

Your mum fetches your dad and cousin, and then off you go.

As it turns out, the planetarium is a kind of cinema. In this cinema, there are seats that tilt backwards. This is because the screen is on the ceiling, so you need a tilted seat to see it. Also, the cinema only shows one film on repeat – a thirty-minute thing called *The Solar System*.

You sit down. On your left is your cousin. On your left-left is your dad. On your left-left-left is your mum. On your right is a boy. He is not part of your family. However, he looks oddly familiar.

Various members of the public gasp when the room darkens abruptly. Others let out a yelp when the chairs tilt backwards and the hitherto unremarkable ceiling comes alive.

On the ceiling-screen, flaming spheres and icy winds and the infinite void appear. A beat later, the sound of a man's voice surrounds you via the cinema's state-of-the-art surround-sound speakers. He is the narrator. Within the first two minutes, he says the words 'billion' and 'trillion' and 'quadrillion' a million times. You don't exactly know what 'billion' and 'trillion' and 'quadrillion' mean – at least not in the same way you know what 'three' and 'twelve' and 'fourteen' mean. As far as you are concerned, these words just mean 'really big' or 'really lots'.

You are enjoying the show, but are soon brought back to earth by your cousin's voice berating your dad.

'Oi,' your cousin says. 'Oi, wake up.'

You glance to your left, see that your dad has fallen asleep, so much so that he is actually snoring. Your cousin – apparently as annoyed as you are by this – shakes him awake.

'Sorry,' your dad says, before falling back asleep again almost immediately.

'Hello,' the familiar boy says on your right.

You examine the familiar boy. You definitely recognise him. Curly hair. There are only so many people you know in the world and even fewer of these people have curly hair.

Your mum leans over to grab your wrist gently. 'Sweet pea, please stop talking. We're meant to be quiet when the film is on.'

You bat her away. 'Go away,' you say, batting her away.

You focus on the familiar boy. You recognise the familiar boy, then you remember the familiar boy – who he is and why he is familiar. He looks the same, you think. A bit taller, you think – though of course he is sitting down. A bit goofier, maybe. He has adult teeth now. They are slightly too big for his mouth. You can tell this because he is grinning at you and the grin takes up half his face.

'You came back,' Bobby says warmly and brightly and nicely and kindly.

Your cousin pokes you in the ribs. 'Who is this? Who are you talking to?'

You bat your cousin away. 'Go away,' you say, batting him away.

In but a moment, the narrator will explain how small you are compared to the infinite sprawl of the expanding universe. Planets, asteroids, celestial bodies not otherwise specified will whoosh by you in super-fun HD. You will feel dizzy with the bigness.

'Welcome to the universe,' the narrator will say. 'We hope you'll feel at home.'

Further reading:

The Solar System: A Short Guide
101 Super Fun Family Days Out
Really Big Numbers: A Bazillion Indefinite Hyperbolic Numerals

2 5

THE ENSUING MEAL IS totally spontaneous. Bobby's mum keeps on saying this. She keeps on saying 'This is totally spontaneous' and your mum keeps on agreeing with her. Your dad presses the button at the pedestrian crossing. The six of you then wait for the red man to turn green, standing on the bobbly patch of the pavement.

All the while, Bobby speaks to you. He says the bobbly patch is there so blind and partially sighted people know there's danger ahead – the danger in this instance being the road. He says people in the UK drive on the left but actually in most countries they drive on the right. He says he read there's a planet that's been discovered recently. He says his neck hurts because he slept funny and that he didn't know he was wearing odd socks till just now.

Bobby runs out of fun facts and three red tall buses pass by you very close, all of them breathing out a grime that fills your nostrils and then your lungs.

'See?' he says, as if this proves his previous point about road traffic safety.

'Wow,' you say.

'This is totally spontaneous!' Bobby's mum says again.

'It really is,' your mum agrees.

You wonder if your mum wants to ask you about Bobby. You wonder if she wants to ask you about what you said earlier, about him not being your friend any more. You wonder if – like you – she is bowled over by the coincidence. Or if she suspects that you misled her.

'I know there are few restaurants over here,' Bobby's mum is saying. 'Oh! Cross now, guys, it's green, it's green, it's green . . .'

There are indeed a few restaurants over there: Pizza Express, Pizza Hut, Pizza Palace. Pizza is a thing you know how to order and how to eat. You are grateful this street doesn't want to gastronomically stretch anyone who doesn't want to be gastronomically stretched. Indeed, the only non-pizza-based eatery seems to be a Spanish restaurant. You know this because one of the front windows says 'SPANISH RESTAURANT'. The Spanish restaurant has a mustard-yellow awning, on which is a picture of an octopus followed by the words '*el pulpo*'. You wonder if '*el pulpo*' means 'pulp' because it's kind of a similar word. At the same time, you wonder if '*el pulpo*' instead means 'octopus' because of the picture.

'Shall we try this one?' Bobby's mum says, already making to open the door.

'Um,' your mum says, frowning at the awning.

'It looks interesting,' your dad says.

Bobby looks at you. '*¿Te gustan las tapas?*'

You blink at him blankly.

'*¿Te gustan las tapas?*' he says, louder this time.

You blink some more. 'What?' you say.

'Do you not speak Spanish?'

You furrow your brow. 'What? No.'

'Do you not know what tapas are, then?'

'No.'

Bobby's mum opens the door and you go in. You see a chalkboard with the word 'tapas' on it. Now this word only reminds you of the word taps – something that makes you wonder if this is a liquid-only restaurant where everything is pulped and turned into soup. But then you think of tap-dancing – an activity you have never personally attempted but have seen from afar. This makes you wonder if the waiters are dancers, perhaps dancers who struggle to get by on dancing alone. Then you wonder if the 's' simply means that it's a plural word. You wonder if this means tapas are many small things instead of one big thing, the plural of another word called 'tapa'.

The six of you sit at a central table. All around you, sound abounds. A waiter drops something made of glass. A champagne bottle pops open. A woman laughs shriekingly. You grimace.

Bobby points to all the words he knows on the menu. He doesn't seem to know many of the words. Instead, he just seems to know 'patata' (which he says means 'potato'), and 'patatas' (which he says means potatoes). This confirms your previous suspicion about 'tapa' being singular and 'tapas' being plural.

You shuffle around in your seat. You wish the museum had been a library.

Your mum asks Bobby's mum a question. 'So, what is it you do, again, um?' your mum asks, apparently having forgotten Bobby's mum's name.

'I'm a speech and language therapist,' Bobby's mum says. 'What about yourself?'

Your mum takes a large gulp of water. 'Um, I'm in between contracts right now.'

You wonder what contracts your mum is talking about. You wonder why she didn't just say 'I'm a stay-at-home mum' or 'I don't work because I'm mentally unwell' or 'I don't work, instead I read instruction manuals and how-to guides'.

However, Bobby's mum seems unfazed by your mum's answer. Perhaps she is deeply familiar with the contracts your mum is talking about. 'And you? What do you do?' Bobby's mum says to your dad.

'Actuary,' your dad says, in a voice so loud Bobby's mum seems genuinely taken aback.

'Gosh,' Bobby's mum says. 'That sounds important.'

A man arrives. He is wearing a sombrero and carrying a notepad. 'You guys ready? What can I get you?' he asks.

'Um,' your dad says.

Bobby's mum pipes up. 'Pulpo, please,' she says.

The sombrero man raises his eyebrows. 'Just pulpo. Nothing else?'

'And patatas,' Bobby says. 'Pulpo and patatas for everyone too.'

Your mum and dad exchange a look. You wonder if they are unsure what pulpo and patatas are. Before they have time to protest, the man takes away the menus and Bobby's mum's interrogations resume.

'And why did you come here today? Just a day out?'

Your mum nods. 'Well, this one,' she nods towards you, 'is really quite good at learning and we wanted to encourage that.'

'Oh really?' Bobby's mum says. 'What do you like learning about?'

'She likes all sorts of things but she's really good at words and books,' your mum says.

Bobby's mum raises her eyebrows. 'Ah yes?'

'She's a bit into this one book, actually.'

Bobby's mum leans in, as if she wants to make sure she's hearing this right. 'She likes a book?'

'Yes, this really old one,' your dad says. 'What is it, darling?'

'The Voynich Manuscript,' you say quietly.

'The what?' Bobby's mum says.

'The Voynich Manuscript,' you say again.

'Never heard of it,' Bobby's mum says, pouring a glass of water from a bottle of water situated on the table. 'Not so many books in the Science Museum, though. That must have been a disappointment.'

Your mum's cheeks flush a little. 'Right. Well, she likes all sorts, don't you, sweetie? Like the planets and space, which was actually what, um, what prompted our visit today.'

You nod enthusiastically. You want your mum to feel nice. You want her to feel like she is saying the right things at the right times.

'Space, the planets, aliens, all that stuff, she really likes it,' your dad adds.

'Wow,' Bobby's mum says.

'She's really smart,' your mum says.

'Sounds it.'

'Yes,' you agree.

There is a pause. During this pause, your dad lets out a massive sneeze.

'Gosh,' Bobby's mum says again. 'And this one?' She points at your cousin, apparently not finished with her interview. 'Is this your son? What's your name?'

Your cousin looks glassily at Bobby's mum. It doesn't take a genius to figure out he's not feeling OK. From the nature of his slack jaw and blank face, the most likely options seem boredom or a stroke.

'Oh, don't worry about him,' your dad says. 'This is just Paul.'

'My sister's kid,' your mum adds, patting Paul on the head a little.

'We look after him sometimes.'

'My sister's a single mum.'

'Shift work, you know how it is.'

'Gotcha,' Bobby's mum says.

There is another pause.

'Well, I'd be happy if you two' – Bobby's mum's eyes dart from you to Bobby – 'or maybe you guys' – Bobby's mum gestures at you and Bobby and Paul – 'got together and maybe, well you're a bit too old for play dates now, aren't you?'

'Yes,' Bobby says, frowning.

'But maybe I can take your number, um' – it is clear Bobby's mum doesn't know your mum's name either – 'and we can arrange something.'

Your mum beams. 'That would be great.'

'He's really good at learning too, aren't you, Bobster?'

Bobster nods. 'Sure.'

'It would be great if he had a friend on his level.'

Your mum also nods. 'Sure,' she also says.

'Oh!' Bobby's mum interrupts. 'The food's here. That's quick. I hope they cooked it properly.'

The waiter places a tray laden with pulpo and patatas on the table. Bobby tucks a serviette into the collar of his T-shirt and rolls up his sleeves.

'Enjoy, kids,' Bobby's mum says. 'Enjoy.'

'Oh, yes,' your mum adds, regarding the tentacled lunch. 'Please do eat as much as you want.'

Further reading:

The Pluralisation of Spanish Nouns
101 Super Fun Potato Recipes

2 6

I N THE DAYS THAT follow the London museum trip, Bobby calls
you every evening. During these calls, he speaks to you at a rate
of knots. What does he speak to you about? Whatever he wants.
You are a good listener. He is a good talker. And both of you are
children with nowhere to be.

One evening, he speaks to you about his Spanish class and reels
off reams of Spanish vocabulary. *Huevos. Ojos. Chicos.* Another day,
he speaks to you about his French class and reels off reams of French
vocabulary. *Table. Moustache. Ordinateur.*

On still another day, he changes tack.

'What was that book your mum said you're interested in?'

'Huh?'

'At the lunch. Your parents said you really like this one book.'

'Oh. The Voynich Manuscript.'

'Say again?'

'The Voynich Manuscript.'

'Can you spell that?'

'V-o-y-n-i-c-h. M-a-n-u-s-c-r-i-p-t.'

'OK. And why do you like it?'

'Oh, it's very cool,' you say, unsure if 'cool' is the right word.

'Really?'

'Well, maybe not cool. But it's interesting and fun. That's why I like it.'

A few days later, Bobby calls you at his usual hour.

'So, the Voynich Manuscript is in America,' Bobby is saying, as if you didn't already know this. 'It's in a library in America.'

'OK,' you say, as if you didn't already know this.

'And it's in this library in this university, this super-weird library and it has lots of books that are all super rare . . .'

In the space of days, Bobby has decided to become an expert on all things to do with the Voynich Manuscript. You have three main feelings about this. First, you are alarmed. Where did Bobby get the time to swot up so much? Did he do extensive reading under the desk at school? Second, you are pleased. You like the idea you'll have someone to talk to about your interest or hobby and maybe he will want to read your essay when you're done with it. Third, you are annoyed. Bobby is smart enough to grasp everything you know and more. He will overtake you in no time.

'. . . and apparently this man travelled all the way to Italy to see the Manuscript. He didn't even want to look at anything else. He just went straight to the Manuscript even though—'

You swap phone hands but keep the same phone ear. You are lying on your bed.

'. . . so we can't go there because it's far away and I don't think they'd let us on planes alone, or at least not without a really, really good excuse. Like maybe if we said our American relative was in hospital and . . .'

You look at the big light. It's far too bright. Its white light beams at you aggressively, hurting your eyes but also your mind.

'But we could go to London.'

It takes you a while to register Bobby has stopped speaking. But even when you do register this, you still don't quite understand what he's saying about London.

'Sorry, what did you say?'

'So, we could go to London to see it.'

'But why would we want to go to London if it's America?'

'Because it's on loan. Weren't you listening? You know about library loans?'

You are mildly insulted by this question. 'I know about them very well,' you say. 'I get things out on loan all the time.'

'All right, then.'

'When is it there?'

'Like, now.'

'Now?'

'Yeah, till February, apparently.'

You can hear Bobby type something on his keyboard. You wonder if this is how he's been learning about the Voynich Manuscript – if he's been using his computer to access information on the internet.

'It's not a copy or a fake or anything?'

'It's the real thing. What would we want to see a copy for anyway? We can probably see a copy anywhere.' He types something else, then corrects himself. 'Well, I dunno about anywhere. I mean, have you actually ever seen a copy?'

You think about the times you have seen the Manuscript – or rather, pictures of the Manuscript.

'I've seen pictures of it,' you say, eventually. The phone is warm against your left ear, so you switch to your right.

'It's kind of weird that you like this thing so much but you've not seen it yet. You should've seen it by now, I mean—'

'Maggie found pictures of it online and she showed me them and printed them off for me.'

'Oh yeah?'

'Yeah.'

'Well, I'm just suggesting we actually see it. The real thing. Cos seeing a printed-out copy isn't seeing the real thing. And you can write about it for your essay. It'll make your essay so much better.'

You think about it. 'I don't know if my parents will be up for going to London again. We've just been there, if you remember. And my mum's gone a bit, you know, a bit weirder this past week actually so I don't know.'

'No, we can go ourselves. We don't have to ask anyone to take us.'

'We can't go to London by ourselves. We wouldn't know how to get there. It's miles and miles away. We'll get lost.'

You get up from where you were lying on your bed, pick up a tennis ball and then proceed to throw it up and down.

'Yeah, we can,' Bobby says.

'How?'

Another pause ensues. You can hear Bobby typing again in the background.

'Do you get any pocket money?' he asks eventually.

'Only sometimes.'

'Birthday money?'

'Yeah, I get birthday money.'

'Do you have fifteen pounds, then?'

'Probably.'

'Then we can probably take the train.'

Even though you're on the phone and Bobby can't see you, you shake your head and pull a face. You find the idea of making your way into the world without adult supervision frightening. Things might go wrong. It's new and uncharted territory. As a general rule, you don't mind new territory. But you tend to prefer when it's charted.

'But why do we even need to go there?'

'So we can present our ideas to the custodian.'

'Custodian?' You wonder if Bobby knows what that word means.

'Yeah, like there are probably loads of, like, people who guard the Manuscript. We can speak to them. They can help us publish our paper maybe. Or let us touch it.'

'Paper? Do you mean my essay?'

'Yeah.'

'But I haven't written it yet. And *we* haven't written anything. So there is no *our essay*.'

'Not yet, but we will.'

'We will?'

'Sure, we will.'

'What will it be about?'

'It'll put forward our translation and our ideas and stuff. We can co-author it after you finish your first solo one.'

You let out a sigh, flop yourself back onto your bed, lying on your back. 'I guess it might be cool to see it at last.'

'It'll be so cool,' Bobby says. 'We will be basking in the light of, you know, the thing we're really interested in.'

'It was the thing I was interested in first, though.'

'I know,' Bobby says, typing something again. 'But sharing is caring.'

Even though you are speaking on the phone and Bobby cannot see you, you nod. Sharing *is* caring. How you could have forgotten this is unclear.

'All right,' you say, nodding. 'So, what do I have to do? What do you want me to do?'

'You just meet me at the train station tomorrow. Tell your parents you're going to mine, I'll tell my mum I'm going to yours, then we'll take the train to London instead.'

'How do I get to the station?'

'The train station? You can walk. You know the way?'

'Yeah.'

'Good. It's literally by your house, so I was hoping you'd know the way there.'

As if on cue, a train whooshes past your house, its speed rattling the windows. You can tell from the time of the day and the intensity and length of the noise that it's a freight train.

'And I'll meet you there? At the station? You'll be there?'

'Yeah,' Bobby says. 'Don't forget to bring your money, though. We'll need to buy the tickets when we get there.'

'OK.'

Sensing your continued doubt and lingering unwillingness, Bobby offers you some reassurance. 'Don't worry,' he says. 'I go to London all the time on my own. I know what I'm doing. It'll be fine.'

Further reading:

London A–Z Street Atlas

2 7

I**T TURNS OUT BOBBY** only sort of knows what he's doing. He knows how to work the ticket machines at your local train station, check the board for the platform number, walk to the platform, and wait for the train. But when he gets on board the train, he seems to get a bit stressed – incessantly checking if the train has reached its final destination even when it's clear it can't have reached its final destination.

'Not here yet,' he says, after checking out the window after the train has slowed for a moment. 'This isn't it, this isn't it.'

'OK,' you say. You check your watch. You are not expected to reach London for another forty minutes.

You are also worried – albeit not about missing your final destination. You wonder if this day out is a good idea. You wonder if the Voynich Manuscript will be as you hoped. Maybe it will be like the museum-library aircraft hangar you daydreamt of. You wonder if there will be scholars walking around the Manuscript in a carefully ordered circle, exchanging ideas and theories while regarding its incomprehensible script.

The ticket inspector appears at the other end of the carriage.

'Tickets, please,' she says.

Your stomach does a sink, swoosh, flutter. Even though you know neither of you is doing anything illegal, suddenly you feel as though you are. The ticket inspector will surely sense this, you think. She might call the British Transport Police. She might call your mum.

'Oh my god,' Bobby says, presumably feeling similarly.

'It's OK,' you say, before trying to reassure him that you are in receipt of an appropriate ticket, and can therefore go anywhere the ticket says you can go. 'We've got the tickets. We bought the tickets and so we can go where the ticket says, no problem.'

Meanwhile, the ticket inspector moves nearer and nearer. You ramble on. 'Back in the day, my nan gave my dad some jam sandwiches at nine a.m. and didn't want to see him again till tea time. He didn't even have water sometimes, he just got thirsty and stayed that way. But it's OK because we've got water—'

Bobby hits the flat of his hand down on the train table between you. 'What are you talking about? I'm looking for my ticket. Have you seen it? Did I give it to you?'

You blink at him, trying to quash a feeling of hurt. Then you remember that yes, you have seen his train ticket – it is in your pocket for safekeeping.

'Yes,' you say, proffering his ticket from your pocket, where it was for safekeeping.

Bobby takes it.

The ticket inspector looms over you. 'Tickets, please,' she says.

You hand the ticket inspector your ticket. She takes out a marker, marks the ticket, and then returns it to you. After this, Bobby passes his ticket over; she does the same thing before moving on.

Both you and Bobby sink back into your seats. Bobby seems relaxed now he has his ticket. Now he has his ticket, he seems to feel OK.

Further reading:

Fares and Fairness: Train Tickets Throughout the Ages

2 8

THE WOMAN AT THE front desk looks at you very carefully. You are wearing a fixed smile, which you direct at her. You are doing this because you are trying to look nice and polite and not like a street urchin. You feel like a street urchin. You feel like the trip on the London Underground has covered you in a layer of dirt that'll take years to come off. Also, you are spending all your birthday money today. This means you feel poor – much like a street urchin.

'I'm sorry,' the woman at the front desk says. 'I still don't understand. Are you someone's kids?'

You nod because, yes, you are both indeed someone's kids. But at the same time, Bobby shakes his head emphatically and says no.

'No,' he says, shaking his head emphatically, prompting you to change your nod to a shake. When you realise this is a weird sequence of gestures for you to do, you try to style it out by pretending you're bopping your head to some non-existent music.

'We are not anyone's kids,' Bobby continues. 'We're just here because we have learnt all about the Voynich Manuscript and we want to see it. It's for our research.'

The woman continues to regard you with evident curiosity. You can tell this place is very different from your local library. Everything about it is very smart. No one is eating chips or shouting.

'I see,' she says, narrowing her eyes suspiciously. 'And is this research a school thing?'

Bobby shakes his head once more. 'It's not a school thing. We're independent researchers doing independent research.' As if to seem impressive, he adds: 'We came here on the train then the Tube by ourselves. We would like to view the Manuscript for our research. By ourselves.'

The woman smiles. You can't tell if the smile is a smiling-at-you smile or a smiling-with-you smile. In any case, you suspect she is not impressed by people doing things by themselves. She is an older lady. Maybe even twenty-five. In your opinion, it's likely she does everything by herself.

'The thing is,' the woman at the front desk says, 'this is a university library. We're not open to the general public. People can only come in if they're part of the university.'

'But we won't be very long,' Bobby says. 'And we might actually end up studying here anyway. After we leave school, we will want to study somewhere to further our research.'

The woman at the front desk shakes her head, still smiling. 'It doesn't matter. If you're not a member of the university now, you can't come in now. I'm sorry.'

Starting to feel impatient, you roll on the balls of your feet. Bobby exhales, turns his head to look towards the turnstiles. Beyond the turnstiles, the library apparently starts properly. You can see its ground-floor printers and the edges of its infinity of bookshelves. At the moment, you are just in the entrance hall, which is cavernous but devoid of books. London is so big, you think, that it doesn't need to put things everywhere. It can have whole cathedral-sized areas filled with just empty space.

You follow Bobby's gaze. You wonder if he is imagining making a break for it, jumping the turnstiles, and heading to hide in the stacks. Bobby does not do this. Instead, he bows deeply. 'Thank you for your time, Chantelle,' he says, using the name displayed on the woman's name badge. 'We won't bother you any further.'

The woman at the front desk – Chantelle, apparently – appears startled by Bobby's brazen use of her name. You offer her a half-bow of apology, which she doesn't acknowledge or maybe even see. Then, you follow Bobby out the door, trotting to keep up with his brisk pace.

You get to the other side of the entrance. The entrance is huge. Through it, pint-sized students and staff come and go, wearing head-phones and backpacks and frowns of concentration. They whoosh by you, wearing clothes you wouldn't see in your town centre library. After a small amount of consideration, you decide that not only would you not see their clothes but you wouldn't see the people wearing the clothes. These people, you decide, could only exist here.

'Oh boy, oh boy, oh boy,' Bobby says, shuffling from one foot to the other.

The pair of you hover outside. It's really cold and windy. Dead leaves skirt the floor. Your jumper is not coat-like enough to keep you warm. You regret not bringing a more coat-like jumper, or perhaps just a coat-like coat.

'We'll just have to go home,' you say, rubbing your hands together while Bobby does his thinking.

Bobby shakes his head. 'We've come all this way.'

You also shake your head. 'They won't let us in. And it's getting dark. And cold. And I'm hungry. And my parents'll think I've been killed or something. They'll probably be phoning the police soon.'

Bobby puts a finger up to your lips – a gesture borrowed from the scene of a film. 'I have an idea.'

'Oh, great,' you say. 'What is it, then?'

Bobby looks at you. 'We just have to wait for Chantelle to go on a break.'

'Oh, god.'

'Then we try again with her replacement. But we will have to have a different story this time. A better story. Like, maybe we should actually say we're someone's kids.'

'How would that even work?'

Bobby looks as though he can't understand why you don't get the significance of being someone's kids. Then he presses his face against the door. His breath fogs up the glass and the glass squooshes his nose. You do the same. It doesn't take long for Chantelle to spot you. Clasping her hand to her forehead, she then picks up a phone to have an animated-looking conversation.

A few minutes later, you see her marching in your direction. She is accompanied by a security guard. You know he is a security guard because on the front of his jacket is the word 'SECURITY' and on the back of his jacket is also the word 'SECURITY'.

'Hi, guys,' Chantelle says to you, the security man lurking behind her.

You open your mouth to say 'Hi, Chantelle' back, then think better of it. In any case, she proceeds to ignore you and addresses the security guard. 'These two need to leave, please,' she says, pointing at you both without looking at either of you. 'They don't have permission to be here. They're not part of the university and they're not anyone's kids.'

The security guard regards you, then Bobby, then you, then Bobby. He has a babyish face. Even though you are bad at telling how old people are, you can tell this man is young. This is confirmed by the fact that, when he speaks, he does so in a high voice. 'They're kids, though. I can't manhandle kids.'

She frowns at him. 'Then don't manhandle them. But whatever you do, they need to leave.' At this, Chantelle makes her way back inside, leaving the small security guard to deal with the situation at hand. The security guard clicks his tongue.

'Hi, guys,' the security guard says to you both, as if you hadn't both overheard the conversation he was just having. 'Would you mind not standing here?'

Bobby frowns. 'We're technically on a public pavement.'

The security guard nods. 'I know,' he says. 'But they want you to leave so would you mind leaving? Maybe you could hang out over there.' He points at what you assume is the far distance but could also just be the park opposite.

Bobby pauses, then nods. 'OK,' he says. 'We'll be back, though. We have business here. Things to do. Things to see.' He touches his temple with his index finger. 'Research.'

YOU SIT ON A bench in the park. The Sun is starting to go down but it's not that late – it's just December. When you look at your hands, you notice they have taken on a blueish tinge. When you look at the air in front of you, you notice it is making clouds. It doesn't take too long to get past the feeling of cold and arrive at a feeling of death. Your feet feel especially cold. Unlike the rest of you, they feel so cold you imagine they might drop off at some point.

'Can we just go home?' you say to Bobby, who has buried his face in the hood of his hoodie.

'Yeah, I suppose so,' he says. 'I guess it didn't work out.'

You nod. 'How do we get home? Do you know?'

'I only really looked up how to get here.'

'Oh.'

'I guess we'll just try to do the same journey as before but backwards.'

'OK.'

But you don't move. Instead, you sit there – struck by the feeling you really don't want to return home. Indeed, if there were an option for you to stay in this park forever, you might take it, start a new life with Bobby and the squirrels. In this new life, you would occasionally write letters to your mum and dad, saying things like, 'All is well in my new life, I hope you are also well.'

As for Bobby, he's not moving either. I imagine he isn't struck by a feeling that he doesn't want to go home. At some point, he will want to go home because home is where all his stuff is. Instead, he isn't moving because he is still thinking about the Manuscript. He is wondering if he cares about it any more.

And so, both of you sit on the bench in a mutual sort of silence, your bodies becoming as cold as the roots of the winter trees. If you stayed there forever, you'd get hypothermia and die, you think. If you stayed there forever, you would disintegrate into the earth.

At the other end of the park, someone rings a bell. After this, out of the falling darkness, a man approaches you. His hair is long and greasy and his clothes curiously formal.

'Hey, kids,' the man says, 'they lock up the park when it gets dark. Didn't you know?'

You look at Bobby. You don't know if this man is an OK person to talk to. Bobby doesn't seem to be fazed. Instead, he just responds in an ordinary fashion, as if this stranger is no danger at all.

'Oh, we'll just have to leave, then,' Bobby says, mildly, adding to you: 'Come on.'

You stand up and the pair of you make your way to the exit. You walk briskly, and your feet come back alive. But you can still feel the stranger's eyes boring into the back of your neck.

He does a jog to catch up with you again. 'Hey, kids,' he says again. 'Were you two outside the library just before? Trying to get in?'

You both stop, turn to face the stranger.

'Yeah, that was us,' Bobby says.

'You wanted to get in?'

'Yeah.'

'Did you say you were someone's kids?'

'No.'

'What did you say you wanted to see?'

'The Voynich Manuscript.'

The man nods. 'I thought that's what you said. You know, I actually have something to do with that.'

You perk up. 'You work on the Voynich Manuscript?'

The man looks you up and down and side to side, as though trying to suss you out. 'That's what I said,' he says eventually, before returning his focus to Bobby.

'I can let you in, if you want. Then you can see it.'

Bobby eyes the man narrowly. 'I'm not sure Chantelle will be keen. She doesn't like us much.'

'Chantelle?'

'The lady on the front desk.'

'Oh. She'll get over it. We'll just have to tell her you're my kids.'

As if this suggestion makes sense, Bobby says OK.

'OK,' he says.

The man addresses you now. 'OK?'

'OK,' you say, though you are less sure.

The three of you make your way to the park gate. But by the time you reach it, it's closed. Each of you tries to open the gate to no avail.

'What do we do?' you say.

For a few moments, you panic. You start to think that you might actually have to start a new life in this central London park. It doesn't seem so appealing now. You wonder what you will do for food. You wonder if you will have to steal nuts from the squirrels. You wonder if your parents will be sad without you. You wonder if they will come to visit you sometimes – look on at you mournfully as you sit in your tree. You wonder if you will miss them, then you are sure that you will.

'What do we do?' you say again, louder, and more frantically.

'Don't worry,' the man says. 'I'll give you a leg-up.'

You don't know what a 'leg-up' is, but it soon transpires it means helping someone climb over something. The man turns his hands into a kind of makeshift step and kneels down. Bobby goes first, stepping on the man's hands with confidence, scrambling up the fence nimbly, before landing on the ground.

Then it's your turn. You bluster forward, step on the man's hands with one foot, and grab the railing. After this, the man pushes you upwards. But becoming suddenly taller and hauling your body over the slightly pointy top of the fence alarms you. In the end, you sort of just fall over the top, landing splat on your belly on the ground. When you get up, you swear you can feel bruises already forming on your knees and torso.

'Steady!' the man says, pointlessly.

'You OK?' Bobby asks, also pointlessly.

You dust off your hands, which you used to break your fall. You are not OK. Not only are you cold, hungry, and tired but you are also now hurting and hurt.

'Yeah, I'm OK,' you say.

Bobby nods, apparently reassured.

The man launches himself over with more elegance than you but less elegance than Bobby. Then the three of you make your way back to the library, enter through the massive doors.

'They're my kids,' the man says, to a confused-looking Chantelle.

'For god's sake,' she says, shaking her head.

The man ignores her, uses a blank card to beep you all through the turnstiles. When he does so, you are in the library proper. It's that simple.

The library is really nice and really handsome. Its dark wooden bookshelves house rows upon rows of lovely-looking books. The books are not bound in protective plastic jackets like they are in your local library. Instead, they are bound in fabric. The mere sight of them makes you want to twirl around in a marvelling manner, like people do in films.

But you don't do this. Instead, you crane your neck upwards. All around are windows of stained glass. Street lamps beam through them, casting a Technicolor light upon the people sitting at their desks. The ceiling is really high. There are some stairs leading up to something called a mezzanine. Here, the books seem to be arranged according to the colour of their spines. Intentionally or not, the spines spell out the colours of the rainbow. The library is huge. Like a museum-library aircraft hangar.

The man takes you down some handsome stairs to a basement.

'Wow,' you say again, grinning involuntarily.

'Wow,' Bobby says also.

The man starts talking. He comes here every day, he says, to work on his research on undeciphered and untranslated codices. He has been working on the Manuscript for over seven years now. He has many theories but, as of yet, no breakthrough.

'This place is open twenty-four hours a day, you know?' the man says. 'So, if you didn't ever want to leave, you wouldn't ever have to.'

You like the idea of a twenty-four-hour library. In fact, you feel you'd like a twenty-four-hour library so much that you try and fail to emit a low whistle of appreciation.

The man whisks you down some more stairs, up some more stairs, and through some more doors. He really does walk like he owns the place. His confidence reassures you. It seems that he is allowed to be here – that he didn't lie to you about being a researcher who researches things in this place.

Still, you wonder why he is being so nice.

Eventually, he shows you to a room that appears to be your final destination. It looks like somewhere between an office and a panic room. Much like an office, there is a large desk and ample book-casing. Much like a panic room, there are no windows. If he wanted to murder you, this would be the perfect place.

As if reading your mind, Bobby asks the man if this is his office. 'Um, is this really your office?' he asks.

'No, it's not anyone's office. More of a shared space.'

'Where is everyone?'

The man looks at Bobby, says nothing.

You scan the books. One is titled *Deciphering Cyphers*. Another is titled *The History of Zodiac Signs*. Still another is called *Who Was Roger Bacon?* You know some people think the Voynich Manuscript isn't written in a language but a cypher. You also know that zodiac signs are some of the recognisable pictures in the text. You also know that, once upon a time, people thought a scholarly man called Roger Bacon was responsible for writing the Voynich Manuscript.

'So, I have to leave you here for a minute to fetch it, all right?' he says.

'OK,' Bobby says.

'It's in a safe just next door. Won't be long.'

'Right,' Bobby says again.

'Don't steal anything while I'm gone. If you do steal something, I'll probably catch you red-handed.'

'We won't.'

The man leaves through the door you all came through. As soon as he does, you turn to Bobby. 'Do you think this was a bad idea?' you say, in a voice only just louder than a whisper.

Bobby looks serious. 'He's a bit odd, isn't he?'

'Do you think he's going to kill us?'

Bobby scratches his nose. 'Maybe.'

'Do you think he'll strangle us?' you ask. 'Or shoot us?'

'I don't know how people usually get killed.' Bobby pauses. 'Maybe he just wants to help us with our research.'

'Why would he want to do that? Why would he want to help us with anything?'

'I don't know.'

'It seems more likely he wants to kill us.'

Bobby purses his lips. 'Maybe he wants to nurture the minds of tomorrow with the resources of today.'

You regard him suspiciously. 'Where did you read that?'

'What?'

'That phrase you just said.'

Bobby looks sheepish. 'I think it's my school motto.'

'You think?'

'I know it's my school motto.'

'It's your school motto?'

'Yes, it's my school motto.'

'Well, I don't think he goes to your school, Bobster.'

Bobby does a half-smile, and your conversation lulls into quiet.

You are aware of time passing. It has been more than a minute. You wonder if something has happened to the man. You wonder if he has been killed – if a rival researcher has struck him down. Perhaps the secrets of the Manuscript were too terrible to let out and he needed to be taken out of the equation, metaphorically speaking.

'This room is so weird,' Bobby says.

You look around. It is. Not only are there no windows, but the walls appear to have padding on them – noise insulation, maybe. You wonder if the man is already killing you. Perhaps he is using some newfangled device to suck all the air out of the room to suffocate you.

'Maybe this is the only room you're allowed to observe the Manuscript in?' Bobby says. 'Maybe that's why it's such a weird room.'

You frown. This may be the case. After all, there is no possibility of sunlight damage in a room without windows. Also, the air is dry in here – like an aeroplane – the gentle hum in the background indicative of climate control. In the centre, there is a long dining-room-type table, over which lamps hover. The only thing that doesn't look quite right is the noise insulation. You're not sure what that's for. Perhaps, you think, it's simply there to stifle your screams.

A woman arrives through the same door the man left through. She has a lot of hair and walks in a business-like manner. She approaches you purposefully – her high heels going clip-clop – wielding what you suspect is the Manuscript in her hands. At this, your heart or stomach does a leap. It does indeed look like it's the Manuscript. You find it surprising to see just her holding a fifteenth-century tome. You had imagined it would be too delicate for holding. You thought you would need to touch it with tongs or at least wear gloves or something.

'Hi, guys,' the woman says. 'Martin was called away.'

Bobby frowns. 'Who's Martin?'

The woman also frowns. 'The man who showed you in.'

Bobby nods. 'Oh, right. We didn't catch his name.'

The woman shakes her head in a disapproving or disbelieving way. She sits on a chair at the long table. She turns on a lamp. The light of the lamp seems special. It seems like daylight, only an artificial version. When you look down, you can see every centimetre of the Manuscript's goatskin cover, which from your reading, you know is not the original. According to your reading, before the goatskin cover, there was a wooden cover.

She points to you. 'You,' she says. 'Come sit here.'

You oblige and sit to her right.

'And you,' she says, pointing at Bobby. 'Come sit here.'

Bobby obliges, sits to her left.

'Do we need to wear gloves?' you say.

'Only if you're going to touch it,' the woman says, 'which you're not, I'm afraid.'

Bobby lets out a small laugh. It's not really a laugh, though. More of a slightly forceful exhalation.

The woman ignores him. 'There's to be no touching or coming too close, OK?'

You nod. You feel like you're being told off before you've done anything wrong, but you accept it.

'As I gather you know,' the woman says, 'this Manuscript is on loan from a university in America, and rumour has it you're not part of the university here, so I'll be doing the touching and you'll be doing the looking.'

You nod. 'OK, sorry, great,' you say. You feel she's hamming it up a bit now. You're not allowed to touch or come too close. You get it. In any case, your eyes haven't left the book. The codex. The Manuscript.

'So this is it,' the woman says, her eyes now firmly planted on you. 'What do you think? Do you like it?'

You swallow. You find the woman's gaze piercing and intrusive. 'It's small,' you say, wondering why she is addressing you and not Bobby.

The woman nods. 'Everyone says that. It's indeed small for a book so important and so talked about.'

You do a half-smile.

'And shall I show you the inside?' the woman asks, still addressing only you. 'Shall I turn the cover?'

'Yes?'

'Yes?'

'Yes.'

'OK, then, I will. The cover isn't very interesting, is it?'

You force a polite laugh. 'Ha.'

'No need to laugh,' the woman says.

'Um, OK, sorry.'

'No need to apologise either.'

You exchange a look with Bobby. You wonder if he is thinking the same thing as you.

'The first section is the plant section,' she says, opening the pages to show the herbal section.

'The herbal section,' you correct her.

'That's the one.'

'Do you like it?' she asks again.

'It's great,' you say, instinctively.

'Have a proper look.'

You lean in to look at the pages before you.

'Not so close, though.'

You lean back to look at the pages before you. The pages are thicker than the pages in normal books – you can tell when the woman turns them. On the page, there are pictures of plants accompanied by rows of text written in brown ink. It doesn't look any different from the images you've seen online. But it does feel different. It feels special – as though you are in the room with a small but special piece of history – which you suppose is exactly the case.

'That one looks like a weed to me,' Bobby says, almost touching the Manuscript with his index finger.

The woman turns to him abruptly. 'Absolutely not. You cannot get that close.'

'Bobby,' you say, shooting him what you hope is a reprimanding look.

The woman seems annoyed. 'Are you the one who's interested in language and languages or the one who's interested in plants and flowers?' she asks him.

Bobby blinks. 'I'm just Bobby,' he says eventually.

'Then maybe you should stop pointing at ancient artefacts. Sit back.'

The woman shows you the rest of the Manuscript. She doesn't linger too long on any page but she doesn't rush either. She lets you ask questions, and makes the occasional comment.

'Naked ladies,' the woman says, rolling her eyes. 'This is the page your friend Martin is working on.'

'Oh really?'

The woman frowns. 'He didn't tell you that either?'

You shake your head.

'Interesting,' the woman says. 'Well, he's trying to get a computer to translate this page.'

'What, really?' You think it sounds so far-fetched: a computer that can translate.

But the woman just nods. 'Yes.'

'Where is he?' Bobby asks.

'Oh, I actually sent him home. I told him to stop luring children into the university premises. It's not allowed. It's against library policy and, to be honest, it's a bit untoward.'

'Untoward?' Bobby says.

The woman flashes Bobby a look of warning. 'Yes. Exactly that.'

The woman takes the Manuscript away. When she does so, you feel a pang of surprise, then a pang of another more lingering feeling – the flavour of an emotion you can't quite put your finger on. When she comes back without it, and shows you out of the room, you feel the feeling even more.*

'I've had Chantelle call you two a taxi,' she says, marching you through the entrance hall. 'It should be here soon.'

The woman waits with you outside the library. It is pitch-black now. When you look up, you see a star shining through the light pollution. Then the star blinks and moves and disappears.

'Oh boy, oh boy, oh boy,' Bobby says, rubbing his hands together.

'Don't your parents tell you not to go places with strangers?' the woman asks, addressing Bobby.

Bobby shrugs. 'It's just my mum at home. And she's a bit of an odd one.'

---

* Disappointment.

189

You hadn't realised Bobby's mum was a bit of an odd one. Though in hindsight, you suppose this makes sense.

'Well, take it from someone older and wiser,' the woman says, 'you shouldn't go places with strangers. Even if they're charming like my colleague. He could've killed you or something.'

Your eyes widen. 'So he was going to kill us?'

'I don't think so,' the woman says. 'But he could've done.'

A pause passes between the three of you. The Moon is visible between two buildings. Its light green and yellow and blue.

'Do you have an idea what it's all about, then?'

You assume she's talking to Bobby, and so don't respond. Instead, you return your gaze to the multicolour Moon. It's pretty and big.

'Hm?' the woman prompts.

'Oh, sorry, I thought you were talking to Bobby,' you say.

The woman smiles, maybe for the first time. 'I was asking you about the Manuscript. About what you think it is. It would help me if you had a bright idea. After all these years studying it, I'm at a loss.'

You shrug. 'If it's a natural language,' you say, not making eye contact, 'but no one can understand it, then I reckon it's a dead language isolate. Like Albanian or Basque. But dead like Latin. But unknown so not Latin. I reckon it's from an island nation somewhere. One that was cut off.'

The woman smiles some more. The light of the nearby lamp post is making her hair shine orange. 'Yes, it could be,' she says. 'In which case, we might be screwed.'

You shuffle awkwardly on your feet. 'Ah, OK.'

'I don't think it's a natural language.'

You blush. 'OK.'

'I think it's a code.' The woman takes out a pack of cigarettes and lights one. You frown at her. Not that long ago, she was banging on about the risks of going with strangers. But now she is consuming a carcinogenic substance.

'Can't someone just get a computer to translate it?' Bobby asks.

The woman raises her eyebrows. 'That's what Martin is trying to do. Weren't you listening?'

You and the woman exchange a look. She checks her watch.

'Or I thought it was . . .' you say.

'What?'

'Like maybe an item from another planet or something.'

The woman doesn't smile when you say this. In fact, she doesn't even react. She just exhales a plume of smoke. Long, silver, and curling into the cold night air.

You add, 'Like maybe it was written by aliens and it just like – fell to Earth accidentally on the back of a meteorite or something.'

The woman continues to say nothing.

'What do you think?' you ask, somewhat squeakily, now keen for the woman to speak – to say something, anything.

The woman looks at you steadily. 'I think your cab is here.'

Your cab is indeed here. It is a white car with the words 'taxi cab' on it. You wonder what the difference is between the word 'taxi' and the word 'cab'. Then the driver climbs out and opens the doors and Bobby hops in, and you think of this no more. Instead, you linger – again struck by another wave of not wanting to go home.

'Who are you?' you ask, clumsily. 'Like, what's your job?'

'I am a linguist,' the woman says, reaching into her pocket. 'What did you think I was?'

You purse your lips thoughtfully. 'A librarian maybe.'

She shakes her head. 'Ah, an admirable profession. But no, I'm not a librarian.'

You nod and wonder if you can make a dash for the park and its squirrels. Maybe it's time to start a new life after all. But when the linguist offers you a small business card, you are distracted from this idea.

'Why don't you have my card? That way you can get in touch if you want to.'

You inspect the card. 'To talk about the Voynich Manuscript?'

The linguist shrugs. 'Sure.'

In the taxi to the station, Bobby is quiet and so are you. You watch the city whoosh by. Tall buses. Crowds of people wrapped up in winter coats. At some red lights, you pause next to a Sainsbury's housed in an excessively handsome building. Two minutes later, you are traversing the Thames.

Bobby taps you on the shoulder. 'Hey,' he says, leaning in and speaking quietly, as if he doesn't want the driver to hear. 'Maybe we shouldn't tell people what we did here.'

'What do you mean?' you ask.

Bobby pulls a face. 'Maybe we shouldn't tell people we came here to see the Manuscript.'

You don't understand why Bobby is saying this. You wanted to tell everyone everywhere about the Manuscript. 'But why not?'

'I don't think it's a normal thing to have done,' Bobby says. 'Let's just say we came here to see the sights, OK?'

He offers you his little finger to do what is commonly known as a pinky promise. You don't know about pinky promises, though, so you just look at his little finger, then his face, then his little finger again. After a while, Bobby retracts his offer of a pinky promise, and offers you his hand to shake. This, you understand, and so shake it you do.

Further reading:

Deciphering Cyphers
The History of Zodiac Signs
Who Was Roger Bacon?

Part Three

29

LITTLE ALIEN, THERE WILL be many things that you will never know much about in this life. For instance, there will be a lot of space stuff you won't ever understand. You won't ever know how black holes work, what gravity is, or the meaning of a meteor. Though you'll always be an alien hailing from Planet Unknown, astrophysics will always remain beyond the scope of your understanding.

Nor will you understand a large number of human behaviours. You won't understand why humans procreate or the meaning of maintaining your lawn. You won't understand the point of suburbia, where the heart of suburbia is, why you would choose one identical house over another identical house. You won't understand why humans don't spend large portions of their day standing on the pavement outside their house, looking into everything that stretches out before them, above them, and beyond them – and scream.

No – instead of knowing about and understanding these big and useful things, you will know and understand a lot about a number of small, closely related things. For example, you will of course know about the Manuscript. You will know about other people's theories about the Manuscript. You will even have your own theories about the Manuscript. More broadly, you will know how words work, how they don't work, and where they came from. In your head, you will carry around a never-ending supply of fun facts about words.

But beyond the world of words, you will remain largely ignorant. This is unfortunate. When it comes to the point, the stuff of language is nearly always beside it.

For instance, here you are in the living room with Bobby. Two police officers – one male, one female – are also here. Bobby is sitting on the carpet. As for you, you aren't sitting on the carpet. You are standing right next to him. The height difference feels odd, but you don't correct it. You stand there, doing nothing, and saying nothing. You vaguely face the police officers, as you mull over two phrases. The first phrase is 'running away'. You wonder if people would (or should) call it 'running away' if you walked instead of ran.

The second phrase isn't a phrase – not as far as you can tell. It's something that sounds a bit like 'whisper' but more like 'misper'. The male police officer in the corner is saying 'misper' into his portable radio device. You hear him say it over and over again. You have no idea what on earth it means till you hear him saying the words 'missing' and 'person' and put two and two together – understand that 'misper' means 'missing people' or missing person or maybe both.

Like this, you come to realise that, for an unspecified amount of time, you and Bobby were considered missing people. The police were looking for you, or thinking about starting to look for you, or just talking about you. But they were talking about you as a misper, not an alien. A misper, not a child. A misper, not a human.

You wonder if the opposite of 'misper' might be 'fouper'.* You think the word 'fouper' sounds silly. You think if it were a word, it wouldn't be a very loved word. You think if someone invented the word 'fouper' tomorrow – if they tried to make 'fouper' a thing – it would never work. As a word, it would never take off.

'Misper,' you mutter to yourself. 'Misper, misper, misper.'

The police officers glance at you. Then the male police officer stops talking into his walkie-talkie radio and speaks.

'Do you want to deal with the female and I'll deal with the male?' he asks the female police officer.

The female police officer shrugs.

The male police officer then takes out a notebook and starts to jot a few things down with a pencil. After this, he continues with the radio. He says the word 'misper' again but also other things, words you understand easily such as 'female' and 'male' and 'property'. He is speaking in a curiously formal way. For instance, he says 'We've got the female and the male at the female's property' and not 'The girl and the boy are both at the girl's house'. The male police officer then gestures that he's going to go into the kitchen, then goes into the kitchen.

The female police officer then clears her throat. 'Are you going to tell us where you've been, then?'

You hesitate, confused over her use of 'us'. As far as you can tell, she is a singular entity.

---

* 'Misper' is an industry-specific portmanteau. A portmanteau is a word that smashes together the meanings and sounds of other words. Its plural is 'portmanteaus' or 'portmanteaux' – the latter because it comes from French, the former because it has been borrowed into English.

'We went to London,' Bobby says.

The police officer then turns to Bobby, who is still cross-legged on the floor. 'Did you go with her?' she asks, glancing at you.

Bobby looks up. 'Yeah,' he says. 'We went together.'

'But what were you doing there?'

'We went to see Big Ben,' Bobby says.

The police officer frowns. 'Really?'

'Uh-huh. Then we went to see Trafalgar Square and Hyde Park.'

'OK,' she says, still frowning.

'Then we went to Madame Tussauds and the zoo and the Greenwich Observatory and the, um, Oval.'

'That's a lot for one day,' the police officer says. 'These places are all in quite different locations.'

Bobby shrugs. 'We wanted to see the sights.'

The police officer raises her eyebrows. 'Right. And did anyone offer you anything when you were there?'

'What?'

'Anything to drink or to take?'

'No one gave us so much as a cup of tea.'

She nods. 'And do you know how long you've been?'

Bobby shrugs. 'A while.'

'A while, yes. Long enough to worry your parents and end up on the missing persons register.'

'I thought you had to wait forty-eight hours to register a missing person,' Bobby says.

The police officer shakes her head. 'That's an American film thing. It's not actually true. If someone's a misper, then they're a misper.'

'What's a misper?'

'Missing person.'

'Oh.'

Bobby looks at you, then pats the carpet next to him. The gesture reminds you of how someone might beckon their dog. Nevertheless, you understand – let your legs crumple. You wonder if it would be appropriate for you to crumple yourself further, splat yourself flat on the carpet and fall asleep, rest your head on his knees as if they were pillows. If someone could just turn the big light off, you'd be in the land of nod in no time.

The police officer looks at you and then at Bobby. 'OK,' she says to Bobby. 'I need to talk to your friend privately. Your mum's in the kitchen. Why don't you go give her a hug and I can have a little chat with your friend?'

'My mum's in the kitchen?'

'Yeah.'

'But why hasn't she said hello yet?'

'I told her I needed to speak to you— Oh, OK.'

Without waiting for the answer, Bobby bounces his way out of the living room and into the kitchen with an energy you can only aspire to.

'Hey, Mum!' you hear him say, his voice all enthusiasm and positivity.

Apparently, Bobby's enthusiasm and positivity are a misjudgement of the tone of the room he just bounded into. Though she is speaking in a low voice, you can tell Bobby's mum is pissed off.

'. . . *do you know* . . . *distraught* . . . *I can't* . . . *even* . . . *why would* . . . *train* . . . '

The police officer eyes you hesitantly. 'Do you want to take a seat?'

'I'm already sitting down.'

'On the sofa, maybe?'

You think about it. 'No,' you say. 'I'm OK here.'

The police officer nods. 'OK. I'll tell it like it is, then. Your mum isn't very well. She had a bit of a funny turn and is in hospital now. She might not be back for a while.'

'Oh, OK.' Your heart starts to do strange things but you don't react. In fact, you don't even look at the police officer. As a result, she thinks it's unclear if you heard her or unclear if you understood. She repeats herself, simplifying some of the vocabulary she opted for the first time around.

'Your mum's in hospital,' she says again, louder this time.

'OK,' you say, frowning at the police officer now. 'And Dad?'

The police officer shakes her head. 'He is staying with his brother for a couple of nights. It's a bit far away,' she adds. 'The hospital.'

'OK, I get it, OK,' you say. Her repetitions are stressing you out. You don't like them – don't like that she is talking to you the way people talk to kids much younger.

Your stomach does a weird flippy thing. 'I can stay here by myself, it's fine,' you say – assuming that is what she is going to get on to next.

The police officer shakes her head. 'You're a minor. You can stay with your friend's mum. Your dad will be back soon and he can look after you then.'

'Oh, OK.'

'He's given you permission to stay with them.'

'Right.'

'Unless you'd prefer to say with your . . .' The police officer checks her notes. 'It says here you have an auntie and a cousin?'

'Oh no, thank you.'

'Not a fan?'

'They're OK. But no.'

'All right. Do you have any questions?'

'Um.'

'You don't have any questions?'

You shake your head.

'None at all?'

You try to think of a question. You think you might have a question. But you are drawing a blank. You shake your head once more.

'No?'

You sense the police officer wants you to speak, to use your words. 'No,' you say. 'I don't have any questions.'

'Fair enough,' the police officer says, shrugging. She makes to leave the living room and enter the kitchen. But before she does, you find that you have a question.

'What happened to her?' you say. 'What happened to my mum?'

The police officer pauses in her step. 'You worried your mum,' she says. 'You said you were at your friend's but you weren't. She worried so much she had to go to hospital.'

When the police officer leaves the living room and enters the kitchen, you slump yourself splat on the carpet. You feel something really horrible in your stomach and face and chest and body. You make your noises really loudly. No one comes to comfort you or tell you to pull yourself together. Your mum and dad are miles away. Bobby and Bobby's mum are all the way in the next room. No one is anywhere and you are alone.

Further reading:

Locked Up: What to Expect When You've Been Sectioned

3 0

FROM THE OUTSIDE, BOBBY'S house looks like every house around here: a well-built, well-insulated, double-glazed, three-up, three-down property. From the inside, though, Bobby's house looks really nice. The rising Sun is filtering through the east-facing windows, shining a light on the house's interiors. Bobby's mum has painted the walls all manner of colours. At one end is a mural featuring a jungle scene. At the other end is a wall that features various shades of pink.

Bobby dumps his backpack on the floor, flings his body flat on the sofa, grabs the remote, and turns on the TV. The faffing with the police took so long that it's tomorrow already. It seems he wants to put on some breakfast TV and flake out.

'What do you think you're doing?' Bobby's mum asks.

Bobby rubs his eyes. 'What does it look like?'

'It looks like you're not getting dressed for school.'

Bobby looks at his mum, says nothing.

'Don't go thinking you're missing today just because of your shenanigans. It doesn't work like that.'

'I just, um . . .' Bobby makes a face.

'You just what?'

'What about her?' Bobby points to you. 'Does she have to go to school?'

'Who's she, the cat's mother?'

'The cat's mother?'*

Bobby's mum lets out a big sigh. 'I'm losing my patience a bit, Bobster. I know you're annoyed at me but I'm annoyed at you too. You need to skedaddle upstairs pronto, please. Go get ready for school. C'mon.'

Sensing he shouldn't linger at the waning end of his mother's patience, Bobby obliges, makes his bouncing way upstairs.

Bobby's mum turns to you, pressing the back of her hand against your forehead and cheeks.

'Clammy,' she says, peering at you wide-eyed. 'Ever so clammy, ever so pale.'

You gulp. You don't know if Bobby's mum will further diagnose you with thinness, peakiness, or wooziness. You're not a medical professional, but you fear you may be suffering from all of the above.

In the end, Bobby's mum just says she thinks you need some herbal tea. According to Bobby's mum, your paleness and clamminess suggest that you are lacking in the essential vitamins and minerals only herbal teas can provide.

'Vitamin A, vitamin B, a little zinc, a little iron,' she says, beckoning you to the open-plan kitchen area.

---

* This is another idiom about cats that has nothing to do with cats. 'Who's she, the cat's mother?' means, 'Why are you employing the feminine singular third-person pronoun when you could be employing your friend's name?'

You make a non-committal sound, wondering if the herbs in the herbal tea feature in the Voynich Manuscript, then thinking about tea. From your reading, you know that some languages call tea 'tea' (or something that sounds like 'tea'*) but that other languages call tea 'chai' (or something that sounds like 'chai').† You know this has to do with trading routes. If the tea was transported from China to another country via a boat, it was called 'tea' (or something that sounds like 'tea'). But if the tea was transported from China to another country via land, it was called 'chai' (or something that sounds like 'chai').

'Did your mum ever give you herbal tea?' Bobby's mum asks, pounding cinnamon and cardamom with a pestle and mortar.

You are confused by Bobby's mum's use of 'did'. 'What?' you say.

'Herbal tea. Does your mum ever give you herbal tea?'

'Oh, no.' You shake your head. Bobby's mum shakes her head too. 'Your poor mum,' she says, before adding: 'And poor you.' She squeezes honey into the mixture.

Upstairs, you hear a bang. Bobby is making a lot of noise as he gets ready. Downstairs, Bobby's mum finishes making your herbal tea and places it before you. You sniff it. It smells like grass. You take a sip. The sip tastes interesting – like mint sprinkled with urine, sweat, and Christmas all mixed together. It tastes so interesting that you know in your bones you can neither finish it nor retain what you have just imbibed.

'I need the toilet,' you say, getting up a little too abruptly.

---

* For example, 'te', 'té', 'thé', 'tee', and 'teh'.
† For example, 'cha', 'chá', and 'sa'.

You take the cup of tea with you to the downstairs loo. Once there, you pour the tea down the sink. At the bottom of the mug are dregs of the herbs and spices Bobby's mum said would do you so much good. Brown and green, green and brown.

A sudden wave of nausea hits you. You open the toilet seat and vomit. When there's nothing more in you, you find yourself overcome by light-headedness.

When you come to, you are propped up on Bobby's shoulders. You are in his room. You see his bed is like a bunk bed, except it has a desk for a bottom bunk instead of a bed. What a nerd, you think, vaguely. Who has a desk instead of a bed, instead of a bunk bed with two beds?

'How is a desk a bed,' you mumble incoherently. 'What is a desk bed sleep for.'

It is difficult for Bobby and Bobby's mum to hoick you into such an elevated bed. In the end, Bobby gets onto the bed before you, lifts you upwards as his mum gives you a push on the bum. Once there, you flump yourself down in a sideways manner. Bobby's bed smells nice – like roses and lemon and lavender. The sheets seem clean and feel cool. You are vaguely aware of Bobby climbing back down the ladder, vaguely aware of him saying something to his mum.

Moments later, you are asleep.

Further reading:

A History of Chai, Otherwise Known as Tea
A History of Tea, Otherwise Known as Chai

3 1

Y ou take a couple of days off school to recover from
your illness. During this time, Bobby's mum tries to distract
you from the lack of familiar surroundings. She puts on films, TV
programmes, radio programmes, even lays out some books that
might tickle your fancy. Sometimes, she joins in with the diversion
tactics – watches the film with you or reads the book on your behalf.
She has also taken a couple of days off work. She's a speech and
language therapist, but that can wait. And you're a smart girl, so
school can wait too.

On your third sick day, Bobby's mum decides you're well enough
to help her around the house. She has a pile of laundry that needs
sorting and folding and you can go sort it and fold it with her – that
won't take too much energy. Also, there's some cooking to attend
to. And cleaning too – why don't you go dust? And gardening as
well – why don't you go rake up some leaves? Afterwards, you can
have a nap. You're still looking a little peaky. You can have a nap and
sleep and lie down and watch something inconsequential on the TV.

Through Bobby's mum, you learn more about Bobby, who she

doesn't refer to as Bobby, but instead 'your friend', Bobster, the Bobster, Bobino, or Boberooni.

'Your friend has asked for Chinese tonight. Do you like Chinese? It's OK if you don't. Would you like something plainer? Is your stomach still hurting?'

'Apparently, Bobster doesn't like the new geography teacher this year. He says he has a nasal voice. I hope they are being kind to him. Or at least not horrid.'

'Boberooni will be making his way to PE now, at least according to this timetable. They are doing climbing this term. Can you imagine? He'd better be good, after all the practice he had with you. Do you remember? Couldn't believe it at the time. What were you guys like?'

On the fourth day, Boberooni's mum decides you're well enough to go back to school. She drives you there in her very tall car, dropping Bobby off first then flooring it to yours. What with half-term and your sickness, it feels like ages since you've attended to your schooling. You look at your classmates. You swear one or two of them have entered puberty since you last saw them.

In English, the teacher runs through parts of speech.

'Noun,' the teacher says, somehow making 'noun' sound like it's got three syllables.

You let out a deep sigh. You wish you were still unwell.

'Excuse me,' the teacher says – addressing you. 'If this is boring, you can get up and teach the class.' He offers you his pen, gestures to the whiteboard. 'Go on.'

You blink at him, wondering if he's serious.

'Hm?' the teacher says.

You think about it. 'No thanks.' But when you say this, a girl with a squeaky voice takes the heat off you – offers an answer to his previous question. 'Doing word,' she answers, incorrectly.

The teacher shakes his head in a forlorn manner. 'That's wrong, Olivia. Let's go through it again.'

In the next half-hour, your cohort finally accepts that nouns are people, places, and things – but is still struggling with the concept of verbs, adverbs, pronouns, adjectives, and articles.

The teacher seems to accept defeat. He says he has just one very important question for you all before you go.

'I have my list here,' he says, brandishing a clipboard while enunciating. 'I have your names written down.' He pauses for dramatic effect. 'Next to your names, I'd like to jot down what you're writing about for your essay. You remember the essay, guys?'

'Yes,' a few people say.

'Now I'm going to go around . . .' the teacher points towards the front desks '. . . and ask each of you about your essay. This is so I get an idea of where you're up to, and when I receive your essay on whatever it is, I am duly prepared. Is that OK?'

'Yes,' a few people say again.

'OK, Marcus. Go. What are you writing about?'

'Football,' Marcus says.

'Thank you, Marcus,' the teacher says. 'Aaron?'

'Football as well, sir,' Aaron says.

'Great, Aaron. Jess?'

'Pogo sticks.'

A few of your classmates laugh.

'That's an original one, Jess. Thank you. What about you, Scott?'

'Football.'

'Excellent. What about you, Holly?'

'Ballet.'

'Super. Callum?'

'Cooking.'

'Wow. Mo?'

'Football.'

'Great. Jade?'

'Sumo wrestling.'

'Ha! Wonderful. Alex?'

'Football.'

The teacher is fast approaching your row. You start to panic. Whenever you say the words 'Voynich Manuscript' to people, they tend to not understand. They always ask you to repeat yourself. Once, when you said 'Voynich Manuscript' to your auntie, she said bless you, as if you had just emitted a sneeze.

'The Voynich Manuscript,' you say, when the teacher gets around to you.

The teacher regards you carefully, but does not bless you.

'Can you spell that for me, please?'

'V-o-y-n-i-c-h. M-a-n-u-s-c-r-i-p-t.'

'Well, I'll have to look that one up. Is it your hobby, would you say?'

You gulp. 'My interest.'

'Your interest. Excellent. And James, what about you?'

'Football,' James says.

The essay is due soon, the teacher reminds you. You should have started by now. It wouldn't surprise him if some of you had already finished.

That evening, Bobby's mum says she wants you and Bobby to paint one of her walls. It's an urgent task, she says. She simply can't stand the white space that was there before, and doesn't want to look at it a moment longer.

'Oh,' you say, accepting a paintbrush. 'I might need to do some homework tonight, though.'

'Sure,' Bobby's mum says, handing Bobby one too. 'But first, you must work on your masterpiece.'

You press the brush bristles with your index finger. 'My masterpiece is the wall painting?' you ask.

'The mural, yes.'

Completing your masterpiece takes all evening. You don't like the task much. The paint gives off fumes, and you are unsure if what you are doing is any good – if anyone anywhere would ever deem it a masterpiece. Bobby is little to no help. Apparently, he has not inherited his mum's keen interest in the visual arts.

'Do you think I should do some more here?' he asks you.

'I don't know,' you say.

'What about here?' he asks you.

'I still don't know,' you say.

Fortunately, Bobby's mum seems to like what you've done. 'Beautiful,' she says. 'You've really captured something there, guys.'

You and Bobby look at each other. Your hair has paint in it. His hair is sticking up. Then you look at your attempted mural. You have coated half of the wall in a block orange. Bobby has coated half of the wall in a block green. At the centre, these colours have mixed to create an accidental brown. You stare at it, trying to figure out exactly what you've done.

'What shall we call it?' Bobby asks you, eventually.

'Do paintings have to have names?'

'Oh, yes,' Bobby's mum says. 'That's Boberooni's favourite part.'

The green and brown remind you of gardening, the orange of sick. 'Garden Time,' you say eventually – deciding not to incorporate the vomit aspect into the title of the mural.

Bobby frowns. 'That's not very nice,' he says.

You raise your eyebrows. 'No?'

'No.'

'Well, what do you want to call it?'

Bobby considers the mural again, regarding it like it's a thing of complexity.

'The Next Chapter. A Fresh Beginning. Another New Start. Something like this.'

'Another New Start,' Bobby's mum says. 'I like that one, Bobino.'

Bobby's mum musses Bobino's hair, kisses him on the forehead, then – to your surprise – kisses you on the forehead too. After this, she squooshes you together in a joint hug. It is a big hug. She squeezes you both tightly. It is not till you think you might be literally suffocating that she releases her grip and lets you go.

'Another New Start,' she says. 'Another New Start.'

Further reading:

Yard Work or Hard Work: A Guide to Raking, Hoeing, and More

3 2

IT MIGHT BE A new start but it certainly isn't a fresh one. At least, your dad doesn't seem fresh. Instead, with his unwashed clothes, stubbly beard, and bad breath, he seems decidedly stale.

Regardless, here he is in the car – driving you from Bobby's house to somewhere as of yet unknown. A rambling old pop song is spilling out of the speakers. Listening to it makes you feel a little nauseated, like you'll always be there, in this car, listening to this song that grows and grows but never ends. Your dad hasn't told you where you're going yet and – not wanting to disturb what you sense is a delicate peace – you haven't asked.

But after half an hour of not speaking, you bite the bullet. 'Dad, where are we going?' you ask, looking straight ahead at the road.

For a second, you think he's not going to answer. Then, past the roundabout and over a bridge, he lowers the volume of the radio.

'Do you know what's happened to your mum?' he asks.

You hesitate. 'Yeah,' you say. 'The police officer told me.'

'What did he tell you?'

You think about what you want to say. 'She said Mum got sick and then she went to the hospital. And that I had to go with Bobby for a while till you were ready to come and fetch me but that I could stay with Auntie or Cousin Paul.'

Your dad nods slowly. 'And do you know why she's in the hospital? What illness she's got?'

Though your dad's eyes are fixed on the road ahead, you shrug. 'I assume she's got like . . .' You hesitate. 'I assume she's got, like, some sort of madness or something. And she's in a hospital for mad people.'

'Correct.' Your dad indicates right, frowns at a bicyclist cycling in a wobbly way. 'Though I think you're supposed to say mentally ill rather than mad. Mad is a bit pejorative these days.'

'What does pejorative mean?'

'It means not nice.'

'Oh, OK.'

Your dad pauses at a stop sign. Then, upon seeing that no one and nothing is approaching, and after checking both of his blind spots, he continues.

'They don't really put people in hospital for being mentally ill any more. It's not very common. Back in the old days, they did it all the time. But there aren't many psychiatric hospitals any more. They all sort of closed down in favour of something they like to call community-based treatment.'

'What's that?'

'Community-based treatment?'

'Yeah.'

'In theory, it's where people are treated at home.'

Your mind goes to a film you saw once. The film was set in a psychiatric hospital. You don't know how accurate it was, but there was a lot of screaming and someone got stabbed. Also, the doctors were frightening and wore long white coats.

Merging onto the motorway, your dad then asks you if you know what job he does. 'And do you know what my job is? Where I go every day? What I do for a living?'

You nod again. 'Actuary,' you say. 'Risk and numbers and risk and businesses and risk.'

'Use your words,' your dad says to the road ahead of him, his voice monotone and expressionless. 'You're just saying one word at a time. C'mon, you're a big girl now. You can do it. Speak in proper sentences.'

You wonder whether he is joking. You are a bit too big to be referred to as a big girl, and a bit too big to be told to speak in proper sentences. Also, as far as you're concerned, you *were* using your words and every sentence is a sentence that happens one word at a time.

Your dad overtakes a van hogging the middle lane. He points at the van and, apparently talking to you, says: 'That's very dangerous driving there, it doesn't look it but it is—'

You interrupt. 'OK,' you say, interrupting. 'You're an actuary. As far as I know, actuaries work with numbers a lot and their main job is assessing risk for companies and stuff. But I don't know much more than that.'

Your dad stops cursing at the long-gone middle-lane hogger and nods.

'Yes, actuaries assess risk. I assess risk. But we all assess risk, every day, in our own way. We look both ways before we cross the street, assess whether the car that's approaching is going to hit us if we cross the road now. You sniff the milk before you pour it to figure out whether it's going to give you a bad stomach or not. You know what I mean?'

'Yes.'

'And it's usually a risk and reward thing. You can put your money here, you might lose it all but you might win big. If you cross the road now, you might get to your destination quicker but you also might die. If you go to this dodgy-looking eatery, you might sate your hunger but you might also get diarrhoea. And if you go to this cheap car garage . . .'

You sense your dad is rambling. You wonder if he is OK. You wonder if your dad is now also mentally unwell, wonder if he is feeling pejorative.

'. . . if you speed on the motorway, you might have a quicker journey, but you might also get a ticket, which would be—'

'I'm not—' You were going to say, 'I'm not really following' but then you stop yourself. 'OK, Dad, I get it.'

Your dad takes a deep breath. 'What I mean is that, according to some know-it-all doctors, your mum should stay in the hospital for a while. The doctors have had her risk assessed, so to speak. And decided that she is high risk and decided that she needs to stay in hospital. And, in my opinion' – he places his hand on his chest – 'this is a false assessment.'

'High risk of what?'

Your dad slaps the flat of his palm against the steering wheel. 'Well, exactly. It's unclear what they mean. High risk of doing what to who, when? They won't explain their working. There seems to be no process. To be honest, I doubt they even have a clue what they're doing.'

'OK. Can you not just . . . can she not just . . . she can't just—'

'She can't just leave, no. It's locked.'

'Locked.'

'Yeah, it's a locked ward.'

'Locked,' you repeat again.

'So patients stay in. They have to, legally speaking.'

'So it's like a prison?'

'Maybe. Anyway.' Your dad clears his throat. 'We're going there now.'

'To visit her in the prison?'

'In the hospital, yes.'

'But if we go in, won't we be stuck there?'

'No, we'll just be visitors.'

'OK. That's nice, I guess.'

'It's nice. But it'd be nicer if we got her out of there.'

You do a pause.

'Is that what we are doing now?' you ask, eventually.

'Yes.'

'Right.'

You do another pause.

'How?'

'Maybe if we took her on a walk. And then we just didn't take her back.'

'Is that allowed?'

'Of course not.'

The roads are all thoroughly unfamiliar now. You have been in this car for well over an hour. You don't know what village or town or city you are in. You couldn't even begin to place where you are on the map.

Then your dad turns a corner and, without warning, you are presented with the sea. You like seeing the sea. You haven't seen it in ages. It's all choppy – its grey the same grey as the sky and the roads and the fields and the hills. You wonder how cold the water would be. You wonder how it would feel to walk into the water up to your waist, let the waves crash down over you or else jump over them again and again.

'Dad,' you say.

'Yes?' Dad says.

You think of what you want to say. You think of telling him about the word 'sea', about how, in Latin, it's not 'sea' but instead 'mare'. You think of saying that 'mare' and 'sea' aren't related words, or at least not very related words. You think of saying that no one spoke the Latin we think of as Latin, that this Latin was an only-written and therefore artificial language, that the Romans spoke something called Vulgar Latin, which was much simpler. You think of saying that lots of English actually came from a dead Germanic language called Proto-Germanic, whose word for 'sea' was 'saiwa'. You think of saying all these things simply because you know them. You think of adding that you think it's fun that words change over time. Fun that, somewhere down the line, 'saiwa' turned into 'sea', just like seeds turn into trees, just like babies turn into people, just like mad people turn into mentally ill people.

'What?' your dad prompts again.

'Sometimes I feel like I'm from a different planet,' you say.

Your dad looks straight ahead. His face is impassive, his hands are at ten o'clock and two o'clock. 'Sometimes?' he says.

'All the time,' you say.

Your dad checks the rear-view mirrors before indicating and then turning left. When he slows to a stop, he checks his blind spots one last time before turning the engine off and unbuckling his seat belt.

'Welcome to the club.'

Further reading:

The Art of Etymology (Or Where Words Come From)

33

THERE ARE SEVERAL THINGS that surprise you about the psychiatric ward. Or perhaps 'surprise' is not the right word. After all, surprise suggests a level of preconception that is then challenged. And you didn't really have any preconceptions. Or if you did, they were all from that film with the screaming.

From what you can tell, the ward is not big. It is pretty much just one long corridor, with little cell-like rooms going off it. What's more, even though it's broad daylight outside, it's very dark inside. As a result, the big lights are on everywhere – hurting your eyes and, presumably, everyone else's too.

There is no screaming in this corridor-ward, at least not currently. There is shouting, though. Specifically, a man is shouting down the corridor. His shouting is not nice. It is loud and rambling, like a pop song that never ends. It also isn't very effective. It communicates his rage, but doesn't communicate anything else. His words and their meanings are lost in the volume.

You try to ignore him, and focus on the most important thing: your mum is standing before you, looking the way she always does except maybe even happier. She is wearing a scruffy T-shirt and jeans and flip-flops. She didn't know you were coming. When you come through the entrance door, she gives you a series of enthusiastic forehead kisses and keeps telling you she didn't know you were coming.

'I didn't know you were coming. I didn't know, I didn't know.'

You are half tempted to recoil from the intensity of the kisses, wipe away the slobber. But you also like that she is being nice. So you do your best to accept the kisses without protestation or any visible sign of slobber-based disgust.

'Why are you here?' you ask, once she has stopped kissing you and instead has you in a kind of permanent sideways hug. 'What happened?'

She looks at you sadly, chucks you under the chin. 'Oh, just a misunderstanding,' she says. 'Nothing to worry about.'

Eventually, a member of staff comes over to you. She is wearing round glasses, carries a clipboard, and sports a serious sort of frown. Her expression reminds you of a head teacher you once had. Apart from that, she seems totally unfamiliar.

'How old's this one?' the member of staff asks your dad – gesturing at you.

Your dad hesitates. 'Um,' he says. He knows how old you are – he's not that bad a dad – but he doesn't know how old you are supposed to be for the purpose of this visit.

The member of staff doesn't wait for a response. 'The thing is, we've got a no-children policy. She shouldn't really be here.'

'I didn't want to leave her in the car.'

'Why not?'

Your dad looks at you – not as though you're a person, but as though you are something to be examined. 'She gets bored,' he says finally, shaking his head slowly. 'Really, really bored. She can't handle it.'

The member of staff raises her eyebrows in a way that suggests she doesn't think this is a serious response. 'She can't stay here,' she says. 'She can't even be here.'

'We're not staying. We're taking my wife and her mum on a walk.'

'What?' The member of staff seems confused. 'Who else are you taking on a walk? Are you her mum or his wife?'

Your mum opens her mouth to speak.

'She's my wife,' your dad says, pointing at his own chest, 'and her mum,' he adds, now pointing at you. 'She is one person fulfilling both of these roles.'

'Ah, I see. You're both a mother and a wife. I didn't know.' The member of staff clears her throat. 'Well, I don't know if this walk has been pre-approved. We can't just let you leave without permission.'

'Oh, really?' your dad says, in a tone of voice that confuses you.

'Yes. You didn't know that?'

'I didn't know,' your dad says, in the same confusing tone of voice.

'Well, sorry. We'll have to ask about the walk in the next ward round.'

'When's that?'

'Thursday.'

'That's ages away. This one is really excited about the walk,' he says – pointing at you now. 'She hasn't seen her mum in ages.'

The three of them turn to look at you. You don't know whether to affect a smile (as if excited by the prospect of a walk) or try to look sad (as if disappointed at the prospect of no walk). In the end, you do neither. Instead, you simply peer at the member of staff with your face.

'I see,' the member of staff says. 'All right, then. But you'll have to be quick. Where are you going?'

'We're going for a walk on the beach.'

'The beach, OK. And when will you come back?'

'In about two hours.'

'Two hours walking?'

'Yes.'

'That's a long walk. I definitely need to write this down.'

Then the member of staff asks your dad the same things so she can write it down: where you are going, when you'll be back, how you are all related to each other. Your dad is very nice with her and about the situation at hand – even when patients interrupt the question–answer session to enquire about their own needs.

'Can we have some milk?' another patient asks.

'We've run out,' the member of staff says.

'Where's the remote?' another patient asks.

'It's in the staff room.'

'Who's this small woman? Is she a doctor or a patient?'

'She's someone's child.'

These interruptions apparently derail the member of staff's train of thought. 'I've lost my train of thought,' she says. 'Where are you going again?' she asks your dad.

Just witnessing this conversation is tiring. When it becomes apparent that the member of staff has to start all over again, you take a seat on a nearby chair and focus your gaze on a poster tacked to the wall. The poster looks home-made. It depicts a rainbow but also perhaps a dog.

You wonder if the poster was made by a patient. You think it wouldn't really be home-made in that case. It would be hospital-made.

'OK, that's all done,' the member of staff says.

'Great,' your dad says. 'Can we go now?'

'I just have to write down what your mum is wearing.'

'She's not my mum,' your dad reminds her. 'She's my wife.'

'That's what I said.'

'Why do you have to write down what she's wearing? She's wearing clothes.'

'In case she absconds. Then we know what to look for.'

'Right.'

The member of staff frowns. 'I'm doing you a favour, you know? I don't have to let you out.'

'Of course.'

'Now,' the member of staff says, 'would you describe yourself as a white female?'

'God help me,' your dad says, under his breath.

'Yes,' your mum answers, ignoring your dad.

Eventually, the member of staff settles on 'white female in a pink T-shirt and blue jeans and green flip-flops' and you are finally allowed to leave.

On the way back out, you wonder what 'abscond' means. You wonder this because – despite your advanced interest in language – your knowledge is still uneven. Sometimes, you will know the etymology of a word such as 'sea'. Other times, you won't know the meaning of a word such as 'abscond'.

'What's "abscond", Mum?' you ask, as you abscond with her down the stairs.

'It means running away.'

'Whoa,' you say, bouncing a little as you hold her hand and exit via the main entrance. When you're outside, you let your lungs take deep breaths of fresh air. It really was stuffy in there. You are glad to be out. Your mum is elated.

'First time out,' she says, springing herself hither and thither, a big grin slapped on her face. 'Can you imagine?'

Though it's unclear if she's talking to you or your dad or God, your dad shakes his head disapprovingly. 'Sounds awful,' he says, rummaging in his pockets for his keys. 'But let's have a really nice two-hour walk on the beach anyway.'

You get in. Your dad starts the car engine. 'That was a joke by the way,' he adds. 'About the walk on the beach.'

You emit a courtesy laugh. Your mum forces one out too.

But soon enough, your fake laughter turns into real laughter. And you find that you are laughing – truly and genuinely and actually – even though your dad's joke wasn't really a joke, not even vaguely funny at all. Before you know it, your mum is laughing too, then even your dad joins in.

Happy as clams.

Loopy as anything.

And just like that, you abscond. Out of the car park, over the bridge, and around the roundabout – the three of you together and free.

Further reading:

A is for Abscond, B is for Bipolar, C is for Crisis

34

THE THING ABOUT ABSCONDING is that you can't go home.
If you went home, the police would come and take your mum
back to the hospital immediately. This would be something no one
would want. And while helping someone abscond from a psychiatric
ward is not illegal – your dad assures you this is not the case – the
police would be annoyed at your dad for facilitating the escape. No,
it's best to lie low for a couple of weeks, make your way back to real
life when everything has calmed down again.

But you aren't actually aware of this plan. Not till – after an
amorphous splodge of time – you arrive at what you presume is
a pit stop.

The presumed pit stop is a motorway service station. The buildings here are low-rise, grey, and unsightly. Over there, there are
rows of lorries. Drivers climb out of the lorries to smoke, engage
in chit-chat, walk around looking at the slate-grey sky. Elsewhere,
members of the public fill up their vehicles with petrol or diesel.

At the other end of the service station, there is some kind of
indoor complex. From your previous experience of motorway service

stations, you know this indoor complex will have a variety of shops and facilities for your comfort and convenience.

You wouldn't mind checking out the complex. Not only do you need the loo, but you reckon there'll be reading material available for purchase in the WHSmith. You need something – anything – to save you from the never-ending tedium of travelling from A to B. As you're at a motorway service station, you assume you are still not even nearly there yet.

'I know it's not glamorous,' your dad says, after he and your mum clamber out.

'What do you mean?' you say, because noting the service station's glamour or lack thereof strikes you as beside every kind of point.

'Where we are staying,' your dad says, pointing at a building tucked behind the complex. 'The hotel over there.'

You look over there and, indeed, there is a hotel. At first, you thought it was the arse end of the indoor complex. Now, you realise it is a building in its own right.

'We're staying there?'

Your dad nods. 'Yes.'

You feel a feeling when he says this – a blend of disappointment and despair sprinkled with a little more despair. You make half of one of your noises.

'This is really it?' you say – not quite believing your final destination is this – a place people only ever pass through.

'Yes. I think it's best that we lie low here.' He opens the front door to the hotel.

'But we can't stay here forever.'

'Of course not. Just for a little bit. Then we'll go somewhere else.'

You are not sure about this plan. Something tells you it isn't robust. Despite this, you keep schtum.

'Maybe think of it as an adventure,' your dad adds.

Your mum is quiet. Her car nap must have been a deep one. She blinks at her surroundings, smiling faintly. She needs a shower, you think. A shower and a good square meal and maybe a little bit of vigorous exercise. Or maybe she needs another life – one with a job, another husband, another daughter, several sons, or no kids at all.

You enter the hotel. The hotel is not glamorous. The foyer has ancient, filthy carpet lining the floors but also half the walls. There is a weird smell in the air and the seats scattered around the foyer look like they were borrowed from a primary school.

'This is already ten times better than the shithole I was just in,' your mum says.

'Let's think of it as an adventure,' your dad says again, as he accepts the room key from the woman at the front desk. 'Let's think of this as a bit of fun.'

Further reading:

On the Run: A Guide to Your New Life in Hiding

35

THE HOTEL IS INDEED fun. At least, it is initially. In the room, there is a tiny fridge with tiny drinks. This is fun. Also in the room, there are tiny tea and coffee-making facilities. This is also fun. And the beds are fun too. There is one double bed for your parents and one pull-out bed for you. The pull-out bed comes out of the wall and creaks really loudly when you sit on it, lie down on it, or turn over from one side to the other. This is fun.

You climb in, read the Bible – the only book available to read before bed. In the front of the Bible, someone has written the words *Happy Reading, Lots of love, God x.* You enjoy this. You also enjoy the Bible's use of 'thou', 'thee', 'thine', and 'thy'. From your previous reading, you know that 'thou', 'thee', 'thine', and 'thy' are archaic personal pronouns meaning 'you' and 'your'. You know 'thou', 'thee', 'thine', and 'thy' fell out of favour even though they were once widely used, and that they were actually more informal ways of saying 'you' or 'your'. For example, you would address a child by using 'thou', 'thee', 'thine', and 'thy', but someone more senior in society by using 'you' or 'your'.

You know many other languages have multiple ways of saying 'you'. You know some languages have a formal and an informal 'you'. You know some have a singular and a plural 'you'. You think, as a language with only one word for 'you', English might actually be in the minority. You make a mental note to check this.

You find it funny the more formal second-person pronoun reigned triumphant, instead of the informal second-person pronoun. You find it funny that, even though the English language has the most words of any language, it doesn't have multiple words for 'you' – at least not any more. You think you would like it if there were more words for 'you'. After all, there are billions of people on Planet Earth. How can 'you' be you but also she and her and them and him? To address everyone with the same second-person pronoun seems weird. You think you might like it if pronouns didn't exist. You think you might like it if everyone everywhere were simply called by their name.

The next morning, you speak to your dad about the Voynich Manuscript while he sips a cup of tea. You speak about how small it is, how crazy it is that this small thing has sparked such lively debate for years on end. You talk about how the Manuscript was likely re-bound at some point during its life which confused some people when they went to ascertain its date. You talk about Roger Bacon – the guy who is rumoured to have had it. You chat about the practice of alchemy – how smart people stupidly thought you could turn random stuff into gold. You talk about Bobby, how he has learnt a lot about the Manuscript from you but how he is still far less knowledgeable than you are because you got into it ages ago. You then talk about its ink. How the ink of the Manuscript is brown, but how there is also a lot of green going on. You say this might actually be the focus of your essay – the ink of the Voynich Manuscript – but you fear this might be too narrow. You say you might want to write about some debunked translations instead, or maybe your essay can just be on the life of Wilfrid Voynich himself. You say, whatever you choose, you need to write your essay because it's due soon.

'You're talking about it differently now,' your dad says.

'What do you mean?'

'Just now. When you spoke about how small it is, it was like you've held it. Like you've held it in your hands.' Your dad mimics your gesture of holding a small book with his hands. 'Before, it was all "apparently this" and "apparently that". Now, it's like you know this stuff from personal experience.'

He looks at you carefully. It's like he is waiting for you to speak, waiting for you to explain yourself.

'I don't know this stuff from personal experience,' you say, enunciating each syllable. 'I have not seen the Voynich Manuscript in real life.'

Your dad narrows his eyes suspiciously. 'OK, then,' he says. 'You've got an essay to write?'

'Yeah.'

He reaches into his pocket. 'Go to WHSmith. Get whatever you need there. We can always post your essay to the school if the deadline is approaching.'

You look at the note he is handing you. It's a fifty-pound note. You've never seen one before. Its design is pinky-red. On the back, there is a picture of Sir John Houblon, the first governor of the Bank of England. Though you don't care much for governors, in your opinion, the note looks super mega cool.

233

'Wow,' you say, inspecting the note closely.

'Get me a few newspapers too, though.'

'Which ones?'

'All of them.'

'All of them? Seriously?'

'Seriously.'

'OK, then,' you say, before putting on your shoes and leaving.

The complex is broadly as you imagined. There is a WHSmith, a KFC, a Burger King, a Starbucks, an M&S Food, a gambling area, and some toilets.

You enter the WHSmith and go to the newspaper stand. The headlines all feature a story about a man who recently died. People seem to have a lot of feelings about the man who recently died. From the headlines, you understand they are saddened but also outraged. The headlines say he shouldn't have died. The headlines say he was too young. The headlines say his friends and family are heartbroken.

You think about the dead man as you pile the newspapers into your shopping basket. Soon enough, the basket gets too heavy to hold. You look around. There are only a couple of other customers. If you put the basket down while you browse the books, then surely no one would mind, surely it wouldn't be in the way.

You put the basket down, go to the books. There are not many books. There is a business shelf,* a garden and horticulture shelf,† a

---

* *How to Think Yourself Wealthy*; *The Modern CEO: Visibility, Strategy, and Agile Thinking*; *A Short Guide to Acquisitions and Mergers*; *Is Tax Avoidance Right for Your Business?*; *The Fine Line: Tax Evasion vs Tax Avoidance.*

† *How to Repair Your Lawn*; *The Organic Pollinator*; *The Art of Bee-Friendly Horticulture.*

health and well-being shelf*, and a fiction shelf.† There don't seem to be any books about the Voynich Manuscript. There are, however, some books for those learning English as a second language.‡ You select *The Bee's Knees: A Guide to English Idioms*, and place it in your floor basket. Then you think about your mum. You suppose you should get her something too. After careful thought, you grab her *How to Nurture Your Inner Entrepreneur* from the business shelf and place it in your floor basket. Then, you select a pad of A4 paper and a couple of pens from the stationery shelf because if you want to write an essay, you need to have something to write an essay with.

'Got enough newspapers, love?' another customer asks. The customer is an older man with a hat. He is on his way out of the store, a single newspaper tucked under his right arm.

You don't know what you are supposed to say to this, so you just say yes, and push the basket towards the till.

'Yes,' you say, pushing the basket towards the till.

The man behind the till seems a little alarmed by you – at least, that's what you think his eyebrows are saying. Maybe he is surprised by the number of items you have in your floor basket, you think. Or maybe he is confused as to why you need all the newspapers.

You hover awkwardly in front of the man behind the till for a second. Then, without saying anything, you unload your floor

---

* *Physical Education: The Essential Guide*; *Pilates: The Complete Guide*; *Cycling: An Incomplete Guide.*

† *Mike and Mark Go to University*; *Mike and Mark Get Made Redundant*; *Mike and Mark Start a McDonald's Franchise.*

‡ *We, Me, You, Him, and They: A Guide to English Pronouns*; *How to Use Definite and Indefinite Articles*; *Why Learn English? What Is the Point?*

basket onto the scanning area. For a moment, the man behind the till doesn't do anything. He just stands there, regarding you. But then he gets on with the job – scans each item and passes them back to you. After this, you pack the items in plastic bags, which you then place back on the ground.

'Forty-five pounds, forty-three pence,' the man behind the till says.

You pass over the fifty-pound note. The man looks at it. Then he looks at you. Then he looks at it. Then he looks back at you.

'Can't accept that,' he says, handing it back.

'Oh, OK,' you say, your chest tight. You don't know what to do. You don't have any other form of payment with you. You put the note back in your pocket. You look at your items, packed in bags. You don't know if you're supposed to put the items back on the shelves. You don't know if you're supposed to just leave the bags on the floor. You start to feel not nice, then really not nice. You wonder if most people would know what to do in this situation. You wonder if it's weird that you don't.

'I'm sorry, why can't you accept that?' another customer says. The customer is a middle-aged woman wearing a smart outfit. She is standing behind you – the second person in this newly formed queue of two.

'It's a fifty-pound note,' the man says to her. 'We don't accept them.'

The woman shakes her head. 'It's legal tender. You have to.'

'No, we don't.'

'Yes, you do,' the woman says. 'Look, she's crying now. You've really upset her.'

The woman's right – you are crying. As much as you try to keep

236

it quiet, your crying is big — involving snot and breathlessness as well as tears. You wipe your face with your sleeve but it scarcely helps. That's how much you're crying.

The man lets out a small sigh, then points to a sign stuck to the wall behind him. The sign says 'WE DO NOT ACCEPT £50 NOTES'. Under the sign is a picture of a fifty-pound note. Over the picture of the fifty-pound note, a red cross is superimposed.

The woman tries to soothe you. 'Darling, sweetie, shh, shh, it's OK,' she says. 'You can change it for smaller notes. Or maybe your parents have a credit card on them. Are you here with your parents?'

You nod. 'I want my mum,' you say.

'OK, is she nearby?'

You nod.

'Great, where is she?'

'In the hotel.'

The woman frowns. 'There's no hotel here, sweet pea. This is a motorway service station. Is she in her car maybe?'

'She's in the hotel,' you say again.

'OK.' The woman turns to the man behind the till. 'Is there a hotel nearby? She says she wants her mum who's in a hotel.'

The man thinks about it. 'Right, OK,' he says non-committally, picking up a radio. 'Security, do you read me?' he says into the radio, which crackles in response.

'Is the hotel nearby?' the woman asks. 'Do you remember what it's called?'

'Over there.' You point out the window, even though out the window is not the right direction to point.

The woman squints out the window in the direction of the petrol station. 'Where?' she asks.

You start making some of your noises.

'Do you remember what it's called? What are you guys doing, staying there?'

You wipe your nose on your sleeve. 'We're lying low. Hiding from the police.'

The woman seems a little taken aback by this comment. Quite literally: she takes a step back.

The man behind the till speaks into the radio again. 'Security to Smith's please,' he says. 'We've got a lost minor. I repeat: a lost minor.'

Through the radio, the voice of a man simply says, 'Roger.'

You suspect Roger's lost minor is you. This makes you feel embarrassed or awkward or panicked. This makes you feel like you've done something wrong.

The woman pats you on the back and offers you a bottle of mineral water. You accept the bottle of mineral water, drink it all very quickly, then start squeezing the empty bottle. The noise it makes is very noisy. You don't like it. And yet you keep on doing it. Squeeze, squeeze, squeeze. Noise, noise, noise.

'You're joking, right?' the woman says, quietly. 'You're not hiding from the police, are you? That was a joke, wasn't it?'

You think about this for a second. 'Yes,' you lie, now uncomfortably full of mineral water. 'I was joking. I have a really odd sense of humour.'

A security man enters WHSmith, his hands tucked under his stab-proof vest for warmth. He walks with a proud importance in his step, like he cares deeply about his occupation, like if a rule or regulation exists, not only is he going to abide by it, but he is also going to ensure other people abide by it too.

The security man pauses to examine you for a moment, apparently taking in your snotty nose and puffy eyes. Then he rests his eyes on the empty bottle of mineral water. When he does this, you wonder if the woman had paid for the bottle of mineral water, or if you drinking it constitutes theft. Overwhelmed by this thought, you drop the empty water bottle to the ground, put your head in your hands, and do some more of your noises.

The woman tries to soothe you again. 'Shh,' she says. 'Stop, stop.'

The security man looks at you, his brow furrowed. Then he turns to the man behind the till. 'What's going on?' he asks the man behind the till.

'She wanted to pay for her items with a fifty-pound note but we don't accept them.'

'OK.'

'She seems upset about this.'

'Right.'

'She also says she wants her mum, so I called you.'

'OK.'

'I think we should probably try to reunite them.'

'Sure.'

'She seems like she might have, um . . .'

'Issues?'

'Issues.'

'Right.' The security man strokes his beard. 'Do we know what her mum looks like?'

The man behind the till lets out a sigh. 'Well, I know I don't.'

During this conversation, another customer walks in – this time a middle-aged man wearing scruffy clothes. He doesn't stop to browse at the light refreshments, magazines, or books on offer. Instead, he marches purposefully towards where you, the woman, the security man, and the man behind the till are all standing.

'What's happening here?' he says.

The woman frowns at the man. 'I don't think that's any of your business.'

''Course it is,' the man says, nodding at you. 'She's my daughter.'

The woman raises her eyebrows, then looks at you, then at the man, then at you again.

'Is this man your dad, love?' she asks you.

You look at the man. He is indeed your dad. Despite this, you don't say he is. Instead, you continue to make your noises.

'Thought as much,' the woman says, softly. 'We can find your mum, don't worry.' She turns to your dad. 'She wants her mum, I'm afraid.'

Your dad blinks at the woman. 'Well, I can take her to her mum. I'm her dad.'

'You don't look like her dad.'

'Yes, I do. C'mon, sweet pea, what happened? Did you get that stuff? Are these your items?' Your dad picks up the bags containing your still-unpaid-for items.

'You can't take those,' the man behind the till says. 'She hasn't paid for them yet.'

Your dad puts the bags back down. 'Why not?' he says. 'Sweetie, why haven't you paid for them? Did you lose the money?'

You point at the sign that says 'WE DO NOT ACCEPT £50 NOTES'. Your dad looks at where you're pointing. 'Oh, OK,' he says. 'That's a shame.'

The security man decides to chip in. 'Look, I don't know who you are, but you're going to have to leave. She's clearly not your daughter. She doesn't look anything like you. She wants her mum.'

Your dad looks at the security man. 'She *is* my daughter. Look at my eyes. She has my eyes.'

'They're a completely different colour.'

'They're really not. Angel, tell them I'm your dad.' He reaches out his hand. He wants you to take it, to hold it in yours as if you are a child much smaller than you are.

But instead of taking his hand, you just say you want your mum.

'I want my mum,' you say, because you do. At this moment, you don't want your dad. You want your mum. You are annoyed at your dad. Your dad picked you up from Bobby's house when he didn't have to. Your dad picked your mum up from the hospital when he didn't have to. You want your mum. Better still, you want the mum you had before, the mum that read you stories, the mum that made you mashed potato, the mum that didn't see any mental health teams and didn't get locked in any hospitals. That mum that pottered around the house drinking tea and giving you hugs. That mum was there, once, wasn't she? That mum existed once, didn't she?

'Jesus!' your dad says, apparently annoyed at your response.

The man behind the till scoffs. '*Angel*,' he says. '*Sweet pea*,' he also says. 'If she's your daughter, then what's her name?'

'What do you mean, what's her name?'

'I mean what I said. What's her name?'

'I don't have to tell you her name. She's my daughter. She's mine!'

Your dad reaches for your arm. When he does this, the security man puts himself between you. 'Sorry, mate, you need to back off.'

'I'm her dad.'

'You're not her dad, anyone can see that.'

'Are you serious? She's my daughter and she's coming with me whether you guys like it or not.'

Your dad then grabs you by your sleeve, hoicking you in the direction of the exit. The woman and the security man don't like it when he does this. When he does this, they try to stop him. For a few moments, the four of you are tugging at each other's sleeves. Customers look on at the scene you are making, as do two men wearing police officer uniforms. One of them has red hair. The other is blond. Both of them are gazing in your direction.

You, your dad, the security man, and the woman simultaneously clock the police officers and stop squabbling.

'Hi, guys,' the red-haired police officer says, approaching the four of you.

'Christ,' your dad says, rubbing his temples.

The police officers regard you, your dad, the security man, and the woman carefully. After this, the blond one removes what looks like a photo from his pocket. He holds it up, looks at the photo, then looks at your dad. He then leans into the ear of the red-haired police officer and whispers something. Then the red-haired police officer leans into the ear of the blond police officer and whispers something. Then they both nod.

'We're looking for your wife,' the red-haired police officer says to your dad.

'OK,' your dad says.

'Who do we have here?' the red-haired police officer asks, nodding in your direction.

'She's my daughter,' your dad says. He is standing next to you now – his right hand placed on your left shoulder, like you are posing for a family portrait.

The red-haired police officer tilts his head, looks at your face then your dad's face then at your face. 'Ah, yes,' he says. 'I can see the family resemblance.'

If your dad feels vindicated by this comment, he does not show it. Instead, he keeps his eyes fixed on the ground as the security man and the woman absent themselves. After this, you and your dad walk the police officers to the hotel. Members of the general public gawk at you when you do this, even though it's not very interesting – the sight of a small group walking at a medium-slow pace.

You wonder what will happen when you and your dad enter the hotel room with the police officers. Your mum doesn't like the police. Often, it seems like she is scared of them. Maybe she will scream. Maybe she will cry.

The four of you squeeze into the hotel lift, which transports you slowly to the second floor, before locating your room.

Once inside, your mum doesn't look up immediately. She's too engrossed in drinking her tea and reading the Bible. When she clocks the four of you, she startles – but still doesn't say anything. She studies the police officers. Both look new to the police force but also new to adulthood. They are fresh-faced; their cheeks are plump. As for laughter and frown lines, they don't have any. Perhaps their youthful look is what feeds into a non-threatening aura. Perhaps this non-threatening aura is why your mum doesn't start crying, screaming, or doing anything else that might constitute freaking out.

Instead of doing any of the above, your mum just places her mug of tea to one side, gets up, comes over to you, and pulls you into a tight squeeze. You don't like the tight squeeze. It's so tight you can't breathe. Also, you wonder if the tight squeeze is a sort of goodbye-forever hug – a thought you don't like.

'You're here to take me back to the ward?' she asks the police officers.

The red-haired police officer nods. 'Afraid so,' he says.

'All right, then.' She turns to your dad, gives him a peck on the cheek. 'Thanks for trying anyway, love.'

Your dad nods. 'Out of interest,' he says to the officers, 'how did you find us?'

The red-haired police officer shrugs. 'Number-plate recognition software.'

'Right,' your dad says, nodding thoughtfully.

The blond police officer clears his throat. 'Actually, um . . .' He trails off.

'What?' your dad says.

The red-haired police officer points to you and your dad. 'It's probably best if you two come along too.'

Your dad looks at him – a look of suspicion or curiosity or hostility on his face. 'Why?'

The blond police officer shrugs. 'We just want a little chat with you. You know, at the station.'

'Well, do we have to?' your dad says.

'Maybe,' the red-haired police officer says.

'Maybe?' your dad says. 'Well, in that case, *maybe* we'll come.'

The blond police officer clears his throat. 'I think you should come. I think it'd be in your interest.'

'Babe,' your mum says. 'It's OK. You'll be fine. We'll all be fine.'

Further reading:

Locked Up: What to Expect When You've Been Arrested

3 6

Your dad sits to the left of you. Your mum sits to the right of you. You are in the middle. It's like you're in a taxi cab. You are not in a taxi cab. You are in a police car. Throughout the journey, no one says a word.

Your mum gets dropped off first. She gives you a forehead kiss before she goes, then the red-haired police officer escorts her inside the ward. This takes ages. You wait with your dad, as patiently as you can – stare into the back of the front seat for as long as you can. This isn't very long. You want to move, burst free, run, explode.

'Dad, I don't think I can do this for much longer,' you say, wriggling and fidgeting, tossing and turning.

Your dad nods. 'How much longer is this going to take?' he asks the blond police officer.

The blond police officer exhales. In the reflection of the rear-view mirror, his eyes look glassy. Perhaps, you think, he is bored. Perhaps, you think, he is drugged. 'I don't know,' he says. 'Could be a while.'

A while later, the red-haired police officer returns and drives you and your dad to the police station.

'I might want a solicitor,' your dad says as the pair of you get out.

At this, the police officers smirk. 'OK,' the blond one says, in a tone you cannot interpret.

You aren't kept in a cell. You are kept in a room. The room looks like it could be in a school, only there are no school things: no school desks, no piles of teaching plans, no heaps of marking codes, no teachers, and no kids apart from you. Instead, there are a large number of chairs, fluorescent overhead lights, and a carpet that is thin and worn. When either of you speaks, your voice does a short echo. Other than this acoustic quirk, the room is featureless.

From down the corridor, you can hear someone yell some sentence or other. A man. You can't tell what he is saying, but his anger really comes across. Perhaps that is the point of the yell, you think, as you yourself feel like yelling.

'Do you think we should ask if they've forgotten about us?' you ask your dad.

'I don't know,' your dad says.

'Do you think we should just ask, though?'

'I don't think so.'

You are holding a polystyrene cup. Once, this polystyrene cup had hot chocolate in it. It doesn't have any hot chocolate in it any more. You're just piercing its rim with your thumbnail now. You make tears all the way around, make them evenly spaced so it looks nice and orderly. You think about the word 'tears' and the word 'tears'. You know they are not homophones because homophones sound the same and 'tears' and 'tears' don't. You know they are instead homographs. You try to be patient. You wish you had something to read. Maybe something about language, but really, you'd read any book.

Then – just as you think you can't bear this place any longer – the police officers come back.

'Sorry for the wait, guys,' the red-haired one says.

'Sorry for the wait,' the blond one repeats.

'All right,' your dad says.

'So, just to clarify,' the red-haired police officer says, holding his hands up. 'Aiding someone out of a mental hospital is not a crime.'

Your dad frowns. 'Well, no. I knew that.'

'Well, I thought it might be. That's why you're here.'

'Right.'

'But I just asked someone more senior than me about it, and it turns out it's not, so we can't detain you here.'

There is a pause. During this pause, your dad wonders whether he should kick up a fuss, make a complaint, express some degree of outrage. 'Right,' he says eventually. 'Are you two new to the job, by any chance?'

'Pretty much,' the red-haired police officer says.

The blond police officer raises an index finger. 'Out of interest, though, what were you thinking?'

'What do you mean?'

'You thought if you got your wife out of the ward, took your daughter away from her temporary care placement, everyone would just let that happen?'

Your dad looks at you, then looks at the police officer, then looks at you. He opens his mouth to speak, then closes it again. Despite being an adult of above-average intelligence, I imagine he doesn't have the words to explain his motivations. I imagine he doesn't know how to explain that he just wanted to take his family and hide from the world in a safe, small space for an indefinite period. He doesn't know how to explain how big and strong this desire was, how he wanted you and your mum to stay still, keep cosy and come to no harm.

'Yeah, well, not quite,' he says, eventually, rubbing his eyes. 'I don't really know. I realise it sounds a bit mad.'

The red-haired police officer nods. 'Yeah, it does,' he says. 'You could've at least fled the country or something.'

The blond police officer frowns at the red-haired police officer. 'If anything, it fuelled our concerns rather than allaying them,' he says. 'If you went home, we would've picked up your wife, left you as is, and you could've carried on living your life. Finding the house empty, we were concerned that you had abducted your child.'

You like how the blond one is talking. It is orderly – like every sentence is informed by protocol, policy, and the law. Indeed, his words are somehow so orderly and well trodden that they reassure you – even if the meanings behind the words aren't actually conveying anything reassuring.

'Can you abduct your own child, though?' your dad asks.

'Sometimes, yeah.'

Your dad looks at the police officers with raised eyebrows, and the police officers leave you two in the room again. They leave you, they say, because they want to order you a complimentary taxi.

No one has talked to you or even looked at you for a while. Just to double-check you're still there, you pinch the skin on your forearm. It hurts – and thus you conclude that you are still there.

You are tired. Ignoring the ample number of chairs, you lie on the floor and its thin, worn carpet. You lie on your back, look up at the ceiling. The ceiling is covered in square panels, some of which are broken, some of which are actually lights. The lights are bright and white. When you look directly at them, they hurt. You know, from experience, that ceilings sometimes break. You think of the ceiling that came down on your lunch that day. The day you and Bobby tore down the sports hall. Then you think of the day you blasted off into space. Then you think of the day you schlepped off to London. You feel that everyone is on the cusp of finding out the truth about you – that you are not of this world, that you were never meant to be here.

You wonder what time it is. It's hard to know the time in a room with no windows or clocks. At some point you fall asleep, or maybe half asleep. Your body cools as you lie perfectly still, your mind hovering just above the state of full rest. In surface-level dreams, you hear them speak.

'Discharge in due course.'

'Discretion.'

'Section two.'

Your mind flits through dreams of corridors and canteens, hand-cuffs, and cells the size of hamster cages.

'Sweet pea,' your dad says gently in your ear. 'Wake up, darling, wake up. We're off.'

When you fail to respond, your dad shakes you a little. You open your eyes, regard your dad narrowly. Not because you're moody, but because you're tired. Your nose is doing its weird, night-time breathing still.

Your dad hoicks you up.

'Some people will be checking in on you tomorrow or the next day, though,' the red-haired police officer says, as your dad helps you put on your coat.

'What? Why? Who will they be checking on?'

'They'll be checking in on this one.' The red-haired police officer points to you.

Your dad and the police officers look at you. The look they give you is curious. It's a look that suggests they are only just seeing you – that they are just seeing you for the first time – something that you know is not the case. Their eyes scan your face. You wish they'd look away. You wish they'd stop looking at you like they are looking at a creature.

'But why would anyone want to check in on her?' your dad asks.

The red-haired police officer shakes his head. 'We just want to see if . . .' he says, before trailing off. 'We just want to, um . . .'

'We just want to make sure everything is OK,' the blond one says instead.

'Yeah,' the red-haired police officer agrees. 'That's right. We just want to make sure everything is OK with her.'

FIRST, THE TAXI DROPS you both back at the motorway service station. There, your dad checks you out of the hotel room. While he does so, you hover just outside – looking at the shopping complex entrance with suspicion. You regard the people entering and exiting the building, half looking to see if one of them is the man behind the till or the security man. To your relief, neither person materialises by the time your dad returns.

Silently, you both walk across the car park, get into his car. Your dad starts the engine and begins to drive. You sit in the passenger seat, close your eyes. Before you fall asleep, you think of your mum in that prison hospital. You wonder if she is in the corridor with her flip-flops, or if she is maybe lying down in her cell. You wonder if the stuffiness of the air is bothering her. If it were up to you, she'd have lots of air to breathe. The air would be big, clean, and fresh. It would fill her lungs and make her feel light.

When you wake up, you are on your home driveway. Your dad cuts the engine and you both get out. He opens the front door, lets you enter the house first. You go to the kitchen, grab yourself a glass of squash to take up to bed.

'You going to have a good sleep?' he asks you, as you climb the stairs.

'Yeah.'

'Great. Goodnight, angel.'

'Goodnight, Dad.'

Further reading:

Off Duty: Police Officers and Performance Improvement Plans

3 7

THE PEOPLE DON'T COME the next day or even the next week. The paperwork gets lost in the post. Someone leaves a Post-it on someone else's desk but the intended recipient doesn't receive it. There is a backlog of requests, a backlog of letters. There is a general lack of motivation within the team. There is an occasional lack of competency. Lackadaisical is the word. Sedate is the word. There are more pressing things to do. That person is on leave now anyway. Annual leave, maternity leave, paternity leave, parental leave, sick leave. They have left. Gone to work somewhere better paid. Gone to work somewhere better organised. Gone to work literally anywhere else.

But whatever. You go to school. You come back from school. Before you know it, your mum is coming home. She kisses you on the forehead, chucks you under the chin. Also before you know it, the teacher is handing back the essays. He winds his way around the desks, returning them one by one.

'Very good, Jade.'

'Good try, Jess.'

'All right, Dave.'

Eventually, the teacher comes over to you. He leans over your table, speaks quietly as he slides your essay before you.

'Don't worry about it, OK?' he says.

From what you can see, everyone else has a grade written in red pen on the top of their essay. Your essay doesn't. Instead, at the bottom, there is a note: 'You weren't supposed to write a piece of fiction. Please see me after class.'

After class, the teacher shakes his head at you, before launching himself into sentences with too many 'unfortunately's.

'Unfortunately, I specifically needed you to write an essay on a hobby or interest, not a work of fiction. So I couldn't mark it, unfortunately.'

You want to say you did write an essay on a hobby or interest.

'I liked the descriptions of Serbia. They were very creative . . .'

You want to say that Wilfrid Voynich was sent to a penal colony in Siberia, not Serbia – that Serbia and Siberia are two separate places.

'I liked a lot of your sentences, actually. But as boring as it sounds, you really do have to answer the question at school. You have quite the imagination. It's intriguing stuff. But I needed a hobby or interest, not a story about a made-up man and a made-up language.'

You want to say Voynichese might be a made-up (i.e. constructed) language, that this is a valid theory – though not one you subscribe to.

'Are you listening?'

You blink. 'You needed a hobby or interest.'

The teacher nods. 'See,' he continues, 'Michael here wrote about his love of ice hockey. He wrote about how he got into the sport and how much he enjoys it. When he gets better and comes back, he'll be very pleased with the mark, I'm sure.'

You say nothing, look out the window. You can see some of your classmates exiting the gates. Beyond that, rooftops and pavements, cul-de-sacs and car parks. Then you look at the clock on the wall. It's 15.34. It's possible this conversation will last you till 15.45. If you walk instead of taking the bus, you will get home at 16.30. If you walk slowly instead of fast, you will get home at 16.45. After this, there will only be four hours and forty-five minutes to kill till you can feasibly fall asleep.

'Are you still listening?'

You look at your shoes. 'Yes,' you say.

'Is there a sport you enjoy playing, at all? Or even just watching?'

You shrug. 'Sure.'

'What sport is it?'

You pause. 'Climbing.'

The teacher gives you a look. 'I know you find it hard to look at people,' he says. 'But maybe you should practise it sometimes, because then it'll get easier. It's a life skill. For whatever reason, society has decided that it's necessary to look at people when you talk to them, or they talk to you.'

You try to look at the teacher's face, but find that you cannot. Your eyes and his eyes are like the wrong ends of magnets. They repel.

'OK,' you say, looking at his receding hairline instead.

'Well, if you could get that to me by the end of the week, that'd be great.'

'Sure.'

'I know that's a quick turnaround but, at the moment, I can't pass a work of fiction. And as I've said, this essay is very important. The mark will determine which set you are placed in next year.'

'OK.'

A pause passes between you. During this pause, you wonder if you should be leaving already, if there was something unspoken you missed.

'Is your mum OK?' the teacher asks, eventually. 'Back at home?'

'Yeah.'

'That's great.'

'Yeah.'

'Really good.'

'I know.'

THAT EVENING, YOU REWRITE your essay at the kitchen table. Unlike your previous essay, this essay is not an essay. Instead, it is a work of fiction. In this work of fiction, you write about your love of climbing. According to your work of fiction, you have always liked climbing things: playground apparatus, trees, and walls to name just three of the things. The work of fiction adds that you are good at it; you are fast going up and steady going down. Even better, you are unafraid of heights and have a level of flexibility and strength many can only aspire to. One day, you hope to climb mountains: Ben Nevis, Mont Blanc, Mount Kilimanjaro, and Everest. One day, you also hope to climb competitively but, for now, climbing is just a hobby or interest.

Then you think about Wilfrid Voynich. Wilfrid Voynich's wife was called Ethel. Ethel's mum was called Mary. Mary's uncle was called George. George was the surveyor general of India. His last name was Everest, and the famous mountain was named after him.

Then you think about the Voynich Manuscript. You are wondering if you still care about it. You think that you do.

Further reading:

Why I Love Climbing (An Essay)

Part Four

3 8

TIME PASSES GLOOPILY. THE Earth orbits the Sun which in turn orbits the centre of the Milky Way. A variety of trees blossom. A variety of trees die. Doctors prescribe medicine. Pharmacists dispense medicine. Cars break down in the middle of the road. Some people lose their keys, other people lose their looks, still others lose their nerve. Babies are born bewildered. Old folks die while thinking of other things.

You have now surpassed the globe's average height for a woman. Not massively. Just by a little. But still. This means you can do things you couldn't once do. For instance, you can wear clothing from the grown-up section of the department store if you are so inclined. For instance, you can reach the top shelf of the kitchen cupboard. For instance, you can eat slightly larger portions without gaining weight. Other than that, things are pretty much the same.

You catch the bus to school. You catch the bus back from school. You message Bobby every day, often exchanging facts about words. Once in a while, you go to Bobby's house to pass the time. Every weekend, you ferry a pile of books to and from the library. Some of these books are for you. Some of these books are for your mum. None are for your dad. Your dad doesn't read books. Instead, he comes home from work every evening and pops the telly on – acting like everything is fine and nothing has ever gone wrong.

And then the people arrive, wielding their clipboards and toothy smiles.

Full disclosure: I don't know why they come at this particular time. Ordinarily speaking, I am razor sharp, at least in terms of recall. But my memory is foggy on this one. Maybe it's our parents who called the people to assess me.

I mean you.

But whatever.

Just before the people arrive, you are lying on your bedroom carpet, teaching yourself the international phonetic alphabet. There are apparently two symbols for 'th' in the international phonetic alphabet – ð and θ. You are finding this hard because the difference between ð and θ is currently escaping you. In order to understand the difference, you repeat the words 'then' and 'thin' over and over. You do this because 'thin' is meant to feature ð and because 'then' is meant to feature θ. But in the opinion of your two fine ears, there is no difference between these two sounds. This goes against what the textbooks say. The textbooks say ð is voiced and θ is voiceless. This means one uses your vocal cords and the other does not. The vocal cords are located behind your glottis, which is where your Adam's apple is. When they are in action, you can feel them vibrate.

'Thin, then,' you say to yourself, your index and middle finger resting on your throat. 'Thin, then, thin, then, thin, then.'

No luck. When it comes to the difference between ð and θ, you understand nothing. And when you hear a knock on the door, you are almost glad to emerge from your phonetic reverie. You wait for a moment, wondering if anyone will answer it before you do. Then the door-knocks cease and the doorbells sound. You frown, haul your body up before making your way from your room to the landing to the stairs.

Your mum and dad get there first. Your dad opens the door. Your mum hovers beside him. From where you are standing, you can see what's happening in the hallway and on the doorstep.

On the doorstep, there are two people. Both are dressed in smart-casual clothing. Both are sporting lanyards. Both are wearing smiles and middle partings. One of them is a man. The other one is a woman. Both the man and the woman are brandishing clipboards. On the clipboards, documents exist. Somehow, even at a distance, these documents manage to look threatening.

'Hi there,' the woman says, her voice cool, corporate, professional.

Your dad makes to shut the door again. 'Oh, no thank you,' he says.

The woman frowns. 'Pardon?'

'We're not interested, sorry. Thank you anyway.'

'Oh, we're not selling anything.'

Your dad looks at the woman, then at the man, then at your mum, then at the woman again. 'Look, I'm really sorry. I don't think we're interested, whatever it is.'

The woman points inside. It is clear from this gesture that she expects to be let in. 'I believe we have an appointment arranged. You didn't get our letter?'

Your dad cocks his head to one side. 'Huh?'

Your mum joins in. 'What letter?' your mum says.

'I'll take that as a no,' the woman says. 'We had the initial assessment booked in for today.' She taps her clipboard. From where you are, you can read the title of the document clipped to the clipboard – such is the magnitude of the font chosen. The title says 'INITIAL ASSESSMENT' in all caps.

'What initial assessment?' your dad says.

'Oh.' Your mum jabs your dad in the ribs. Some sort of penny has clearly dropped; she remembers what the people are going on about. 'The assessment!' she says. 'The initial assessment.'

'Oh god,' your dad says, clearly remembering something too. 'Today? You arranged it for today?'

The woman continues to smile politely. 'For the girl,' the woman says. 'Where is she?'

The man does some scanning, then clocks you. 'Ah, there she is,' he says, nodding your way. The woman follows the direction of his gaze, as do your parents. Suddenly, even though you haven't moved, you are centre stage.

The woman gestures expansively. 'Ah, there you are,' she says, as if you are much younger than your fifteen years. 'You were hiding!'

You frown, say nothing.

The man and the woman continue to look at you. Their smiles seem delighted to see you. Their eyes, less so. You don't know why they are here. Maybe they are here to tell you off. Maybe they are here to take you away. Maybe that's it – they're here to take you away.

Your dad turns to speak to you. 'Angel,' he says. 'Do you want to go to the living room?'

Your mum chips in. 'Yes, sweet pea. Maybe go to the living room and we'll join you there in a bit.'

'What is this about?' you ask. 'What assessment?'

Your mum and your dad exchange a look. 'Don't worry, darling. They're just here to check if you're OK. If you're . . .'

'Normal,' your dad says.

You raise your eyebrows. 'Normal,' you say. 'Right.'

After some deliberation, you do as you're told – shuffle downstairs and shut yourself in the living room – avoiding their gazes along the way. Their request didn't really make much sense – you can hear what's going on from here just as well as you could from at the top of the stairs. But you are older and wiser now. You know that the finer matters of human politeness don't have to make much sense – they just have to be agreed upon and adhered to. Like grammar.

In any case, your parents don't join you in a bit. Instead, the people enter the living room some minutes later. They come wielding pale mugs of tea in one hand and their clipboards in the other. From the moment they enter to the moment they sit themselves down, they are making inane chit-chat. It's like they can't bear the sound of silence. It's like they want to fill the air for the sake of it.

'Here we are, thanks for waiting,' the man says. 'Oh, I hope you don't mind if we sit ourselves down here,' the woman says. 'Oh, isn't this a cute little living room,' the man says. 'Do you spend much time here? If I lived in this house, I think I would spend all my time here,' the woman says.

You regard them silently, not dignifying these questions with any form of answer. Of course you spend time here. This is your house. Where else are you going to while away the last of your childhood days?

The woman looks at the man.

'Shall we start with—' the woman says.

'You better, and I'll just—' the man says.

'Great idea,' the woman says.

The woman and the man fall silent. The woman clears her throat but says nothing. The man purses his lips, crosses his legs, looks at you, and also says nothing.

'Do you know why we're here?' the woman asks, eventually.

You shake your head because no, you do not.

'We're here for the initial assessment,' she says.

You blink at her. This much you already know.

'We want to see if you are . . .' The woman checks her notes. You wonder if she is going to say 'normal'. 'OK,' she says.

You take a deep breath. Nod very slowly. You are trying to remain impassive. Breezy and cool, you try to seem breezy and cool. Nevertheless, you suspect your face betrays how you feel.*

'Cool,' you say, trying to seem breezy and cool while adrenaline shoots around your body.

There is an uncomfortable pause that passes between you. Then the woman speaks some more.

'So, this is just the initial assessment,' she says. 'We just want to have a quick chat, basically. Is that OK?'

'Sure!' you say, with a tad too much enthusiasm.

---

* Alarmed and stressed.

'We're going to ask you a few questions about your very early life. Your birth, actually. That's the first thing.'

'Your birth,' you say, before correcting yourself. '*My* birth. You want to ask me about *my* birth.'

'Yes, your birth. Not *my* birth.'

'Yes.'

'So, were you born normally?' the woman asks.

You pause. You suppose she wants to know this because, if you were a human, you would have been born via your mum – most likely in the maternity ward of a hospital. On the other hand, if you were an alien, you probably would have been born weirdly. Maybe by falling down to Planet Earth from a flying saucer or some other UFO. Maybe via an egg.

'What do you mean?' you ask.

'Erm, I mean, were you born without incident?'

'Um.'

'For example, were you born by the vaginal canal or via a caesarean section?'

You shake your head. 'I don't remember,' you say, wondering if it's normal to remember your own birth. Maybe humans remember everything, you think. Maybe they have memories crystal clear from day one, whereas you only have clear memories from day 1,100.

The woman rests her biro on the document, which is in turn resting on the clipboard. From where you're sitting, you can see there's a checkbox for 'vaginal' and a checkbox for 'caesarean'. There is no checkbox for 'other'. The woman apparently wants to tick something. Evidently, she does not know what.

The man chips in. 'I think maybe we can ask Mum about this?' he says. 'Or even Dad?'

The way he speaks, it's as though your mum and your dad are his own mum and dad, which is simply not the case. That said, you appreciate the sentiment of what he is saying. Yes, surely they can ask your mum or even your dad. Your mum and dad are the people who would know these things – not you.

'All right.' The woman moves on to the next checkbox. 'And were you breastfed or were you bottle-fed?'

You furrow your brow. 'Erm . . .'

'Don't tell me you don't know that one either?' The woman sits back, as if she can't believe it.

'What do you mean?' you say again.

'What do you mean "What do you mean"?' she asks.

You shrug. 'I don't understand the question. Are you asking me if I remember my mum's boobies?'

The woman widens her eyes. 'Wow, that's really not what I asked. I did not ask that at all.'

Your cheeks flush. In the corner, the man's face remains impassive. However, you can see him write down a couple of words on his notepad. You fear one of these words is the word 'boobies'.

'OK, we'll ask them that too.'

There is a pause during which the woman leafs through the initial assessment documentation. Finally, she asks something else.

'Do you know if you learnt to speak early or if you learnt to speak late?'

Despite knowing how to speak, you stay silent.

'Don't you remember?'

You shake your head. You think your mum told you about your first words, once, said they weren't words but instead sentences. Or maybe you dreamt this. You don't know.

'OK.' The woman seems to be trying to collect herself. She moves down the clipboard.

'And do you know if you learnt to walk on time?'

The man interrupts before you have a chance to throw another 'I don't know' at her. 'I really think we're meant to be asking the parents these ones, not her,' he says. 'It says so at the top there, look.' He points to some words printed at the top of the woman's document.

'Oh, I'm sorry,' the woman said. 'I didn't see that at all. Gosh.' The woman squints at the sheet. You wonder if she has forgotten to wear her sight-correcting glasses.

The man leans to whisper something you can't hear to the woman.

'OK,' the woman says, in response.

After this, the man turns to face you.

'So I'm going to ask you some things now,' he says.

You nod.

'I'm going to ask you what primary school was like.'

You nod again.

'So, do you remember what primary school was like?'

'What primary school was like?'

'Yes.'

'Yeah, I remember what primary school was like.'

The man smiles. 'And can you tell us what it was like? Did you enjoy it?'

'Um,' you say, 'I went to a couple.'

'OK, so what were they like? Did you make friends? Did you like the lessons?'

You think about it. You don't know what they were like. You were sort of just there. That said, you know you've said 'I don't know' about a hundred times today. With this in mind, you think you should opt for a variation.

'I'm not sure,' you say.

The man nods. He seems to accept this as a valid answer.

'And why did you go to a couple of schools? Why didn't you just go to one?'

You pause for thought, wondering how to phrase it. 'I cut up some Bibles,' you say. 'This other kid told me to.'

The man raises his eyebrows considerably. 'You cut up – you cut up some Bibles? Why did you do that?'

'Just at the first school,' you say, realising now this was probably an odd thing to do. 'Someone told me to do it, though,' you repeat.

The man does a half-smile, makes a couple of noises whose meaning you're unsure of. 'So, you went to two primary schools?' he eventually says, holding up his index and middle finger to illustrate the concept of two.

'Yes.'

'Why did you go to two? Why not just one?'

'I, um . . .' You trail off, shake your head, then – just for good measure – do a shrug that says 'I don't know'. You don't want to talk about your primary schooling any more. You know it wasn't normal. You know you didn't do it right. Talking about it doesn't help, though. To be honest, you'd much prefer to curl up on the sofa in the foetal position instead.

'Would you mind explaining?'

You hesitate, then the words come out all jumbled. 'I was on the climbing frame,' you say, 'and then it came down and everything was everywhere. The roof. Ceiling not room.'

'Climbing frame? What do you mean?'

'Yeah,' you say, even though 'yeah' only answers one of the man's questions.

'Did something bad happen on a climbing frame?'

You pause. 'I don't know,' you say, so softly you can barely hear the words yourself.

You shake your head again, then make some of your noises in a half-hearted fashion. The noises aren't enough, though, so you rock gently for a bit, tip yourself to one side, before giving up and fully curling yourself into the foetal position. You squeeze yourself together tight. If someone tried to prise you open, they wouldn't succeed. A foetus you would remain.

The man and the woman don't ask you any more questions. Instead, they mumble to each other for a bit, gather their things, get up and go. They do so quietly – as if they mustn't wake the baby on the way out.

In the corridor, you hear them say a few words to your parents in hushed tones. Then you hear the click of the front door and the starting of a car engine. Then you hear the car leave. Then you hear your mum and your dad do chit-chat. Then you hear your mum and your dad carry on with their days, giving their foetus-child a wide berth.

Your dad is in the garden, where he surely plans to spend the rest of the day hoeing the earth. Your mum, on the other hand, is doing some of her reading. This time, she is reading about gifted children – most likely wondering if you are a gifted child.

Back in the office, the woman and the man type up the results of the initial assessment. I don't know for sure, but I suspect they write that you are a creature as of yet unknown. Further study is warranted, but only if time and resources allow. For the time being, they think it may be wise to stay alert and proceed with the utmost caution. After typing up the report, they file it. After filing it, no one ever looks at it again. It exists in a folder, in an office, and also on a computer. But there it remains, forever and ever, amen.

Further reading:

Gifted Children: Is Your Child Gifted?

39

YOU DON'T ASK YOUR mum or your dad about the people.
You tell yourself they're insignificant. You tell yourself they
don't matter at all. After all, even if they did end up thinking you're
an alien, then what could they do about it? It's not like they could
phone NASA and put you on the first rocket back to the middle of
Nowhere Land, Planet Unknown. It's not like they could trap you
in a cage and exhibit you at the zoo. Could they?

After a few months have passed, you get the feeling they're not
coming back. You feel this in your gut. Without knowing why, you're
pretty sure you're rid of these guys forever.

And then you lose your library card.

You don't know when or where or how you lose it – three things
that might help you locate it again. It might have slipped out of your
wallet on the bus, as you were searching for the correct change to
give the driver. But it also might have fallen down the back of the
sofa at Bobby's house, as you were slumping in front of the telly
with him. Or it might have simply spontaneously disintegrated one
day from overuse. You don't know. You just know that, once, a few

days prior, you used your library card, but now you don't know where it is. This is a shame because you wanted to go to the library today. In fact, you were just preparing to leave for the library. And if you want to take books out – which you do, you always do – then you need your card.

You spend a whole hour looking for it in your room. You strip your bed, turn over your laundry basket, empty every drawer you have. Then you look behind the radiators, in the bottom of shoes, down the back of the sofa cushions. No luck.

So you start retracing your steps – make the journey into town. You are a creature of habit. You always take the bus, sit in the same seat, on the same route, and walk down the same parts of the same pavements. Eyes to the ground, you scan for your card. It is nowhere.

You walk into the library itself.

'Maggie, have you seen my library card?' you ask, interrupting her conversation with a new member of staff. 'Has it been handed in?'

Maggie looks up, evidently startled by your sudden appearance. Once she has collected her thoughts, she raises her index finger. 'Bear with,' she says, opening the lost-property drawer, politer than she needs to be. 'It's not here, sweetheart. You've lost it, then?'

'Yeah.'

'We can order you a new one, no problem. It'll be sent to your home address. You haven't moved house, have you?'

'But I wanted to take books out today.'

Maggie purses her lips. 'Well, you can't today. You could get your mum to take some out for you? Has she got her card?'

You shake your head. 'She's at my auntie's. She's not back till tomorrow.'

'I'm sorry, petal. Why don't you read what you want just in here for today and tomorrow you can go ask your mum and then take books out like normal?'

'How long will it take for the new card to be delivered?'

Maggie shrugs. 'Depends on the post.'

You know Maggie is being nice, but you don't like her response. You feel like she doesn't get it. You feel like she doesn't understand that you don't want to get the books out tomorrow. You want to get them out today. You always want to take books out today. You leave the library without bidding her farewell – in a manner that might be called storming out.

On the bus back home, the man behind you has a phone that keeps on ringing. It's annoying. The beep beep beep of the ring is annoying. Minutes pass and it's still ringing. You don't know if he hasn't heard it. Maybe he can't hear so well. Maybe he simply enjoys taunting the general public.

'Will you answer that?' you say, whipping your head around to face the man behind you.

The man behind you frowns. 'No,' he says.

'Maybe just switch it off, then.'

He makes a face.

'What?' you ask.

'You're very rude.'

'Your phone is very rude.'

'For goodness' sake.'

Your bad temper continues when you get home. The house is empty. You pace its length, breadth, height, and width. You feel like you will live in this house forever. You feel like crying, and so you do – emptying your internal reservoirs as you empty some storage boxes that you come across. Your sense of proportion has gone out of whack. You know this. You know it's just a library card. But you also know you wanted your library card two hours ago and it's still not here.

You tip out a folder. Some old schoolwork. This French exam got an A. This maths exam got a B. You shuffle through your wallet again. Loyalty card. Points card. Gift card. Cash withdrawal card. Business card.

Business card.

It's not what you were looking for, but the business card grabs your attention all the same. It's the only one you've ever been given, the only one you've ever seen. On it is the name of a doctor, as well as contact information for this doctor. This doctor is not a medical doctor. This doctor is just someone with a doctorate. You regard the information carefully, then lie on your bed for a while – everything you've ever owned in a state of disarray.

Later that day, you go down to the computer room and fire up the machine. You wonder how to start the email. You write some sentences. After reading them, you realise they're awful. You delete them, then write some similar sentences. At the end of the message, you attach an essay. Your hands shake slightly as you hit send.

Two days later, you get a reply.

'We've got a school trip next Friday,' you say to your mum, who is reading *How to Bake* – lingering over the chapter on quiche.

'Ooo,' she says, 'that's nice. Do you need me to sign anything?'

'No, Dad already did.'

'Where you going?'

'London.'

'Ah, OK. Will you have your phone with you?'

'I don't have a phone.'

'Huh. Well, maybe we should get you one. Whereabouts in London?'

'The Imperial War Museum,' you say, having researched an answer to this question earlier.

'Yikes,' your mum says, shaking her head, apparently not a fan of imperial wars. 'Well, I hope you have a good time.'

Further reading:

Imperial Wars: A Short Guide

4 O

THE LINGUIST IS LATE. You are waiting for her in the restaurant – the one specified in her email. It wasn't hard to get
here. The trains were smooth, the instructions clear. You just had
to put one foot in front of the other.

The restaurant looks odd, at least to you. Its walls are pink and
there are fairy lights draped from the ceiling. It looks like a restaurant
that wants to be photographed. Outside, London roars – swathes of
people pass in black coats, double-decker buses chug along, flocks of
feral pigeons take to the skies. You were here a couple of years ago. Not
at this eating establishment, but you were nearby. You remember the
park over there – the one you and Bobby got locked in with the man.

You rub your knee, as if you can still feel the bruises from where
you fell.

You feel awkward. You don't know what to do with your mind or
your body but mostly just your hands. You wring them, click your
knuckles, flex them, pick up the salt cellar, pick up the pepper mill,
put them down again, before perusing the menu but not reading it
properly. If the linguist didn't arrive, you wouldn't mind. In many

ways, it would be a relief. You're nervous. You know this because your stomach is doing uncomfortable flipping things.

The waiter brings you bread. She's been asking you if you need anything every two minutes. You don't know why. Maybe she's suspicious of you. Maybe she's anxious to do her job. Maybe she knows you are an awkward soul, unused to entering restaurants alone, unused to being in the city at all.

In any case, she places the bread on the table in front of you. The bread looks dry, and doesn't even come with butter or oil or anything, just plain.

'Are you sure I can't get you something to drink? Anything at all?'

'I'm OK,' you say, because it's true – you don't want anything to drink, you aren't thirsty.

The waiter hesitates. 'We don't really like it when people just sit here not eating or drinking anything.'

To you, this sounds more like a her-problem, not a you-problem, so at first you don't react. Then you regard the dry bread, and decide you are going to need something to wash it down with.

'OK,' you say. 'I'll get a drink.'

'Great, what can I get you?'

'You don't have squash, do you?'

'No.'

'Water, then.'

'Water?'

'Yeah.'

'Right, OK. Sparkling or still?'

You narrow your eyes. Though you are not a seasoned restaurant goer, you have heard of this trick. 'Tap,' you say.

'Right.' She smiles at you in a way that strikes you as weird, leaves, then comes back quickly and places a glass of water in front of you. 'Let me know if I can get you anything else.'

You check your watch for the hundredth time. At almost the exact moment you feel that surely, she has forgotten you, the linguist arrives. You recognise her from her hair. She still has a lot of it.

'Hi,' she says, reaching over to shake your hand before plonking herself down.

'Hi,' you say, standing up to be polite – albeit at the same time she sits down.

'What are you drinking?'

'Um, just water.' You don't know if you should explain you were pressured into ordering a beverage – and that tap water was the only one that came to mind at the time of ordering.

In any case, the linguist doesn't wait for you to come up with an answer. She blusters on. 'Chilly day, isn't it?'

'Yes,' you say.

'Did you find this place OK?'

'Yes,' you say again.

'Apologies for the small talk.'

'No worries.'

'Just a habit, I guess.'

'Sure.'

'I suppose a useful one. It would be rather awkward to just dive in at the deep end at all times.'

'Ha, yes.'

'You don't mind small talk?'

You shrug. 'I don't know.'

The linguist looks at you frowningly. 'Why are you standing up?'

The linguist is right – you are still standing up. By way of correction, you sit yourself down. 'Thank you, sorry,' you say, unnecessarily.

A silence passes between you.

'Not much of a talker?' she asks.

'I like talking.'

'Just take a while to warm up?'

'Yes.'

'I have friends like that,' she says, scanning the menu. 'I have loads of friends that take a little while to warm up.'

'OK.'

The waiter shuffles over. 'Can I get you—'

'Red wine,' the linguist says, interrupting. 'The second cheapest you have. Medium size.'

The waiter nods, looks at you, then leaves – presumably to fetch the wine.

The linguist considers you over the top of her spectacles. 'It's best to get the second cheapest, markup-wise.'

You don't know what a markup is. 'I agree,' you say.

'How old are you?' the linguist says.

You hesitate. Then – possessed by a sudden surge of courage – you decide to make a witty joke. 'I don't know, how old are you?' you say.

'Very funny,' the linguist says, unsmiling.

The waiter returns to place a glass of wine in front of the linguist. 'Medium Merlot,' she says. The linguist ignores her, takes a sip of the wine.

'I read your paper,' she says. 'It was interesting.'

You feel yourself sinking. Even though you know this is why you are both gathered here today, you are suddenly full of regret – wish you hadn't sent her that email after all, wish you hadn't come to London at all. After a moment of self-reflection, you want to sink to the floor into the ground and then the earth. Then you remember your manners and nod.

'Good,' you say.

'Where did you study?' the linguist asks.

You pause. 'Locally?' you say, your voice going up at the end, as if what you are saying is a question and not a statement. And even though locally is not a lie as such, it is not the truth, which is that you are still too young to have entered tertiary education.

The linguist narrows her eyes.

'Locally to here?'

You shake your head. You know that the woman doesn't want to know the names of the primary school you used to attend or the secondary school you currently attend. You know she wants to know where you went to university.

'Oh, locally to nowhere. The school of life. The university of life.'

The linguist clicks her tongue. 'That's an awful line,' she says.

'What is?'

'The school of life.' The linguist shakes her head, as if she really can't believe you just said that. 'The university of life. The anything of life.'

You don't disagree. 'I just, um, haven't really been anywhere yet.'

The linguist raises her eyebrows. You can see the waiter hovering in the background, eager to take another order.

'I'm still a bit young.'

The linguist nods seriously. 'OK,' she says, as if she's changing the subject. 'A lesson in linguistic thinking.' The linguist holds her glass aloft, as if the glass of Merlot weren't a glass of Merlot but instead is a beacon of hope. 'White wine is white. Right?'

'Sure.'

'But it's not white, is it?'

'I guess not.'

'What do you mean, you guess not? It's not. Milk is white – more or less. White wine is somewhere between yellow and green.'

'Right.'

'Looks like urine, when you think about it.' To illustrate this point, the linguist points to the table next to you. There, an old man is drinking a large glass of piss-coloured wine.

'Sure.'

She takes a sip.

'So that's why I always drink red.'

'OK.'

You widen your eyes. You find it funny that this is what the linguist deems linguistic thinking as, in your opinion, it falls into the category of dumb thinking. Though you suppose it could be both.

'In any case, I'm afraid I'm not surprised that you went to the university of life.'

'Why?'

'Well.' The linguist hesitates. 'To be honest, your paper didn't read well.'

Your stomach sinks. One part of you feels crushed – like your life's work is being cruelly dismissed. The other part of you feels nothing.

'Yeah, of course, sure, of course, sorry, I . . . um, that's OK,' you say, experiencing a mild bout of verbal diarrhoea, hoping the disappointment does not show on your face.

'It lacked rigour.'

'Right, OK.'

'It lacked structure.'

'OK.'

'It lacked a basic level of coherency and flow.'

'OK.'

You can feel yourself starting to well up. You want the tears to return to their ducts, so you gently pull the skin under your eyes, trying to get them to go back inside. It sort of works, though it makes you look like you're pulling a face.

'I'm sorry.' The linguist doesn't sound or look sorry. Instead, she just shakes her head. 'I just tell it like it is. The Voynich Manuscript is not a how-to guide for aliens wanting to survive Planet Earth. And I don't think you've discovered what it means.'

You try to mask your heavier-than-normal breathing by holding your breath. In the meantime, your disappointment starts to turn to disgruntlement. If the linguist hated your work so much, then why did she even bother to invite you to lunch? Why didn't she just reply to your email saying she didn't like what you've written, or even just ignore it?

You study the menu.

Moules frites.

Spaghetti carbonara.

Gazpacho.

Steak tartare.

Gnocchi.

Pulpo.

You pretend to be very interested in the eclectic range of dishes and cuisines, try to debate with yourself the merits and demerits of each particular dish. You seem to remember steak tartare is a good dish. Or maybe you are confusing it with another dish you are familiar with. The one that's just called 'steak'. Perhaps you should just choose whatever would be the quickest to eat. The faster you eat, the faster you can leave. What if the steak is chewy? What if it is not to your liking so you have to eat it really, really slowly? What if you don't order anything at all? Say you feel ill? Stand up, announce that you're feeling faint, and then maybe pretend to faint? What if you just say you've got a headache or a severe allergy to the things on the menu? What if you—

'That said,' the linguist says, interrupting your thoughts, 'I really like the parts where you think small. Your ideas on inflections were cute. And your focus on the cosmological labels, in particular, was also strong. I think you show a good understanding of the research so far, even if your bigger, more original thoughts are lacking somewhat.'

You return your gaze to the linguist. You look at her intently, trying to figure out the meaning of what she just said. But then she says another thing that is just as – if not more – confusing.

'I think you show great promise. Would you be interested in being my assistant at all?'

You use a napkin to wipe a tear that got away. Then you resume looking at her. You're pretty sure she is complimenting you now, but you also know she could be making fun of you. You are not sure if the question is a part of a joke, specifically part of a joke you are not party to. Instinctively, you scan the restaurant. Maybe one of her friends is sitting at another table. Maybe at the moment you say 'Yes, I'd love to be your assistant', they will get up, point at you, and laugh.

'Um,' is all you can think to say.

You look at the menu again, deciding that you really would much prefer to eat gnocchi for lunch. Why? It's a fun word and you are not sure if you have had it before.

'I think I want the gnocchi,' you say. 'What about you?'

The linguist smiles. 'Did you hear what I just said?'

'Um.' You feel awkward. 'I don't know. I'm sorry. I don't know.'

'OK. You don't have to know.'

'What does an assistant do?'

'You would assist.'

'Who?'

'Me.'

'With what?'

'Research. You would assist. I would guide. We would work as a team.'

You nod, take a gulp of water, and try to focus on your breathing. 'What do you research?'

'As of yet uninterpreted texts, such as—'

'Like the . . . like the—'

'The Voynich Manuscript, yes. But other texts too. And not even the Voynich mostly. Given that it's in America, it's not very convenient. Though of course, with modern technology and the advent of cheap flights, nothing is too far away.'

You don't want to look too excited by the linguist's area of research.

'Cool,' you say, trying to sound nonchalant without knowing what your face is doing. You take a massive gulp of water.

'I'm confused,' you say.

'How so?'

'You didn't like what I wrote. You said you didn't like it.'

'Yes, well,' she says, 'I didn't think it was great for a paper, but I thought it was great for a kid.'

You try to suppress your smile.

'And great that you evidently have a decent grasp of the subject already.'

You cannot suppress your smile.

'Even though you're young and, from the sounds of it, pretty uneducated. And I'm pretty sure they don't teach you this stuff at school.'

You try to look the linguist in the eye. 'I have a thirst for knowledge,' you say seriously, while making far too much eye contact.

At this, the linguist lets out a bark of a laugh, and you figure this was the wrong thing to say. 'Ha!' she says, really laughing now.

You blush, refocus on the menu, ignore her gaze again.

Pulpo.

Gnocchi.

Steak tartare.

Maybe you could ask for the steak tartare without the tartare. Or maybe you could go for the pulpo for old times' sake. Or maybe you should still get the gnocchi.

'Sorry,' the linguist says. 'I shouldn't laugh. It's good if you like learning. I'm glad. Really, I'm glad. It's refreshing.'

You nod. You cannot handle this conversation evoking any more emotions. You hope and pray for no more.

'I would be paid?' you ask.

'Yes. You'd be paid.'

'So, it'd be like a job?'

'Extremely so.'

'I don't know if I'm allowed to have a job.'

'Are you too young?'

'Just about.'

The linguist nods. 'I thought as much. Why don't we make an agreement, then?'

'What do you mean?'

'Why don't we say you can come work with me after getting some qualifications, but only informally till then?'

'I don't know what to say.'

'What about yes?'

'I think I want to say yes.'

'You're saying yes?'

'Yes.'

'Good. Shall we shake on it?'

'OK, then.'

'OK.'

You wipe away the clamminess of the palm sweat onto your jeans, then shake. Immediately after this, you experience a wave of concern. You wonder if it's too late to back out.

'But, um, but—'

'Yes?'

'But what would the informal job entail?'

'Well,' the linguist says, 'why don't we say if I give you books to read, you will go away and read them, and then tell me what you think about them.'

You are relieved. This sounds doable. 'OK,' you say. 'Would I be able to get them from my local library?'

'No. I'll send them to you.'

'OK,' you say. 'Anything else?'

'Well, maybe if I've written something, maybe you can have a look at it for me and tell me what you think.'

You nod. 'Anything else?'

'Surely. But we can speak about these things in due course.'

'In due course?'

'Yes.'

'OK, then.'

'So we're agreed?'

You do a smile. 'We're agreed.'

'Wow,' the linguist says. 'An agreement before even ordering.'

The linguist nods to the waiter, who is only too happy to approach. 'The gnocchi for her,' the linguist says – pronouncing 'gnocchi' differently from how you pronounced it. 'And the pulpo for me.'

The two of you sit in silence for a minute that is somewhere between uncomfortable and companionable. You can hear a chef call out the order to the rest of the kitchen. One gnocchi, one pulpo.

The linguist excuses herself to go to the bathroom. For a few minutes, you are alone. You wonder what your parents are doing. You suspect your dad is at work. You suspect your mum is at home. You wonder if she is reading that book you saw her with yesterday: *How to Overcome Anxiety: A Practical Guide*. Meanwhile, Bobby will still be at school, studying for his exams or else passing the time with friends.

You are miles away from any of them. After this lunch, you could take a meandering walk around, and no one will know where you are, where you've been, or where you're going. If someone wanted to contact you, they wouldn't be able to. If someone wanted to locate you, they wouldn't be able. A city surrounds you. You can do anything, be anywhere, and see anyone.

You find this thought thrilling. You find this thought frightening. You find this thought lonely. You find this thought so very sad.

Further reading:

The Voynich Manuscript: An Alien Endeavour (An Essay)

EPILOGUE

L ITTLE ALIEN, I HAVE had enough. From now on, I wish to cease dealing with the business of words. The reason? I am very old. Now is as good a time as any to retire, take a vow of silence, or depart this world altogether. Also, I have come to realise that people actually care very little about humanity's most interesting invention. When I tell people about some etymological quirk, they look for a door. When I tell people about the use and omission of the indefinite article in various regional dialects of the UK, they run for the hills.

Case in point: you seem to be resting your head on the armrest. Your eyes are closed and long, steady breaths are emerging through your nose. Are you asleep? Have you been listening to anything I just told you? I tried to tell you how it goes – this weary little wandering life of ours. I tried to explain the inner workings of our human family, and shed light on some fundamental linguistic concepts along the way. I may have banged on a bit, but I did my best. I came all this way to give you the heads-up, one word at a time. Did that mean nothing to you?

So many people would kill for such a story. So many would love to know which years are going to be good, which years are going to be bad, which people are going to turn up and when and why. Ordinarily, there are simply too many surprises. But we, as aliens, don't need surprises. We need spoilers. We need hacks. Too often, we have none. Too often, we have no one. Too often, we have nothing.

Oh well.

Here, prop yourself up. Are you listening? Your mum will be downstairs soon, so I'll make myself scarce. I don't know if she would want to find a vision from the future chatting to her daughter. That would scare the living daylights out of most people. Though of course, your mum is not most people.

Don't worry about her. She will figure it all out eventually. One day, she'll read the right book at the right time. It will tell her what to do and when to do it. After that, all she'll have to do is follow the instructions, put one foot in front of the other, say one word at a time. It'll be OK, plain sailing, and sometimes even quite nice. After she finds that book, everything will be fine.

Maybe you could go look for it with her. You could search for it in the library. I imagine she will want to go there tomorrow, so maybe you could join her as she peruses the shelves. She needs to return some books. You could accompany her – hand in her old books and take out new ones. You could sit next to her as she reads her latest hoard on the sofa. *How to Crochet. How to Grow Your Own Fruit and Vegetables. How to Write a CV.* You could listen when she reads out a few salient points. You could nod politely and smile. Your mum doesn't think you're too young to learn about these things. When it comes to life, she thinks you just have to be prepared. And how else are you going to learn about the power of loamy soil?

As for advice, I'm not sure I have any. As for wisdom, I've none of that either.

It's late now. I think I can hear your mum shuffling about upstairs. I think I can hear her thinking some thoughts.

She's thinking *So Your Child Is a Psychopath* is a terrible book. It didn't give her answers to any of her questions. All it did was give her more questions and cause her to feel mildly annoyed at the author. She places *So Your Child Is a Psychopath* on the to-return-to-the-library pile and does a big stretch. She really zoned out there. Or maybe zoned in is a more apt phrase. Either way, she got so absorbed by her reading that she forgot all about you – who has been downstairs this whole time – and your dad, who surely will be home soon.

She pokes her head around the living room door. Here you are, spark out, a dried-up blob of yoghurt still on you. Upon seeing the sorry sight of you, I imagine your mum berates herself internally. She really should have come down a bit earlier, sorted you out, made sure you are OK.

She scoops you up into her arms. You're getting a bit too big for this. One of these days, you're going to do her back in. For now, though, you do nothing but snore gently as she carries you upstairs, your body slung over her shoulder – much like a workman might carry a bag of workman stuff.

Upstairs, she plonks you in bed. You would think you'd wake up from the jolt, but no. You are still asleep. Your mum half smiles at you, before wetting her thumb with her tongue to wipe the yoghurt off your face. It only sort of works. She'll attack you with a damp flannel tomorrow, she thinks, as she kisses you on the forehead and whispers goodnight. After this, she exits your bedroom, leaving the door open a crack just in case you like it this way. She doesn't know if you do, though, because, of course, you've never actually said.

In any case, this is where she leaves you. At least till tomorrow. As it happens, it's where I leave you too. Goodnight, Little Alien. I hope you sleep well. Good luck for the future. Safe travels and godspeed.

ACKNOWLEDGEMENTS

Many thanks to Clare Alexander, Jasmine Palmer, and Helen O'Hare for all their hard work and enthusiasm.

Thanks to some friends who read this novel in its earlier stages — including Mairéad Kiernan and Eliot Skinner.

Even more thanks to Adam Ferner, who not only read this novel in its earlier stages but has also been a great boon over the years. Also thanks to my parents, Kevin Franklin and Carol Davies.

Lastly, eternal thanks to Beth Romano and Clancy Franklin-Romano. Without the former's support (both emotional and editorial), I couldn't have written this book. Without the latter's support, I wouldn't have been on so many great walks in between.

ABOUT THE AUTHOR

Alice Franklin lives and works in London. She has an MA in creative writing from the University of East Anglia. *Life Hacks for a Little Alien* is her debut novel.